Never Now

LINDSAY DEE

LZD Publishing

I dedicate this book to Isabelle.
Thank you for letting me tell your story.

Table of Contents

Some say fear and love is all there is.

If we strip everything raw, they would be there — in the bones.
A constant negotiation between heart and mind,
they battle and stir, and prick us from within.

But how much love are we willing to trade for the comfort of
our fears? We trade connection for fear of rejection, conceal
our truth for fear of judgment; push our desires down deep
only to live every day in fear that the truth will destroy us.

If we shed our old skin, who will we become?
What if we lose our tribe?

Are we destined to live forever in our cages of fear?
Or will we listen to our brave heart when it whispers,
"What would love do?"

Prologue

1646 -1665, London

Chilly air nipped the back of King Charles' neck as he took his final steps up the creaking scaffold.

"Off with his head!" someone sneered from the crowd that was an otherwise silent sea of snarls and pity.

Corpses of those who chose their loyalty to the crown lay rotting in the streets as Oliver Cromwell's army of rebellious Roundheads stood shoulder to shoulder and watched their final prisoner cross the stage.

With England's Royal family hiding in exile, six years of civil war and centuries of imperial rule were about to meet their end with the single swipe of a steel blade. The dishevelled King's last sight would be the treasonous eyes of his subjects; those who once begged just to touch his flesh, standing silently waiting for his blood.

Surrendering to his evanescent legacy, the King closed his eyes and knelt before the block. The wood, still soaked with the blood of his loyal comrades, was wet against his cheek as he idly drew his last breath.

An engorged looming shadow slowly came to life, lifting a forged steel blade well above its head.

High in the air, the razor-edged sword stalled only for moment before cleaving down — instantly severing England from sovereignty's grip for the first time in history.

The King's blood spattered across the cheeks of his traitorous soldiers who smirked with devilish pride. Moans of dread scattered through the crowd while silent crosses were drawn from chin and shoulder.

Subjects of the newly established Common Wealth left the square with a dreary sense of hope that day — however the years that followed were anything but revolutionary.

With England's fate now resting in the democratic hands of parliament, Oliver Cromwell was named Lord Protector of the Realm, but without a God appointed bloodline to determine a true leader, governments were established and dissolved many times over. Tensions only worsened upon Cromwell's death when even his own regime fell into near chaos.

Left sinking in a sea of political anarchy, the people of England ultimately demanded the return of their trusted anchor of sovereignty, and in 1660, the true heir to the crown sailed back up the Thames to restore the monarchy as King Charles II.

Memories of mutiny faded quickly in the newly luxurious and sexualized London. Hedonistic desires above all else, the merry monarch ruled peacefully for nearly half a decade before disputes with Dutch merchant ships destroyed his long-awaited jubilance.

When tensions on the high seas began to threaten England's status as a leading European trading power, the King finally stepped in and declared war against The Netherlands.

Unwilling to lose his first war as King, the monarch tasked his trusted friend, Lord Arlington, with fortifying his Royal Navy. Armed with a King's purse and an unrelenting determination, Arlington managed to secure over three hundred new additions in merchant ships alone.

Captains and their eager crews were sent to the naval dockyard in Gillingham for training and refitting before joining the rest of the royal fleet already engaged in battle on the North Sea.

Though a sailor's time in this quiet coastal town would be brief, the ripples of their presence were about to alter the lives of the virtuous yet rebellious daughters of some of the most powerful men in England — many of whom were just beginning their final summer of innocence in the affluent seaside town of Gillingham.

Chapter 1

LADY ISABELLE

Her beauty was magnetic, whether to know her or not.

Many people thought they knew her. Ogled like a bird in a cage, the daughter of the King's favourite nobleman maintained the facade of a perfectly poised young woman as she passed by buzzing whispers and shifting eyes.

In her nineteen years, she had already mastered the art of placation. Her answers were short and calculated. Her words met every expectation then she would gracefully slip away with her truth still hidden inside, left untainted by the judgments of this world.

Her father's apartments at Whitehall Palace constantly brimmed with ears and eyes. If they weren't those paid to serve or teach, or clothe or bathe her, it was the endless slew of thirsty courtiers who ached just to be seen at her side.

Her potent beauty was always alluring but her father's new raise had created an exhausting level of attention she was already growing tired of. Most young women would give their voices just to live in the palace but Isabelle's bones were screaming "We don't belong here!"

They ached to be back in the solitude of her family's coastal estate in Gillingham where she grew up — a place where the only buzzing came from the bees bumbling in her grandmother's blossoms.

However, having grown into a beautiful young woman, Isabelle's father now demanded her womanly presence at court where he could show her off like a gleaming trophy to some of the most powerful men in England, yet barely speak a word to her otherwise.

She was bait — and everyone was biting. Her father quickly found himself with a line of prestigious men willing to give him just about anything he wanted for permission to wed the stunning daughter of the King's new favourite.

Isabelle had met most of these men when she arrived at court years ago, it seems they had all been suckling at the King's tit nearly as long as her father, but now she was being introduced to them as a young woman, a possible wife — a bearer of sons.

These men stared at her in a way that made her stomach writhe but Isabelle kept her breath even and her chin straight while her soul screamed silently within.

She would never quiver. These drab aristocrats weren't worth her fury; like colourless paintings hung on palace walls, each one lacked the substance she would have expected from such pride of place.

Her only salvation lay in the warm summer months when it was more fashionable not to be seen at court; when the wealthiest men in England would send their kin to the countryside while they travelled abroad in an attempt to return with the most envied stories come autumn.

They lowered the heavy chain barricade and allowed the Barrington back into the impervious naval dockyard she had departed from at first light that June morning.

Once the Barrington retook her place along the main dock, soldiers rushed from the ship, heading straight towards the Tudor-styled storefronts of Gillingham's picturesque marketplace in search of a hot meal, some cold ale, and a warm cheek.

Although Jon knew this war was necessary, and signed freely alongside his mates, he still hoped it would be swift, just a few months as Arlington promised. But a heaviness lurked in his stomach as he watched the blundering soldiers swiping at each other. Arlington told him the sailors would be the real heroes of this war by steering their ships to victory, and Jon was beginning to think that might actually be true.

He looked back to Thomas. "They're training us in arms 'cause half these men are going to end up dead. We're the replacements in the rigging."

A shrieking blast from the Boatswain's pipe pierced Jon's gripping honesty, effectively ending another long day of training.

The exhausted soldiers sighed with relief but the crew of the Barrington returned their weapons and sprung to their posts.

"Make sail!" Captain hollered to his crew.

"Aye Captain!" Jon and Thomas shouted as they climbed aloft to free the sails.

Gulls jeered overhead as the Barrington opened up and caught the wind. Slicing through the white-capped waves, her crew held a steady course straight for the Thames estuary, but when the square-rigged ship entered the harbour, they didn't steer her up the infamous Thames as one may expect. Instead, they pushed her south, skilfully manoeuvring around islands in the southern bay before entering the mouth of the humble River Medway.

After a short sail up river, a nod from Clarkson signalled the guards standing ready at their riverside posts.

"Back at it!" an officer commanded from Clarkson's side. "You're a soldier with the Royal Navy now boy. You best get used to living on the sea!"

The young recruit nodded then stumbled back to his sparring partner.

While the land-locked soldiers struggled to find their balance on the waves, the hired merchant sailors found themselves right at home on the thrashing sea, however, the weapons they now possessed were causing a much bigger issue—

"Christ! You nearly shot me!" Jon sheathed his sword then felt around his head for any trace of blood before glaring back at his best mate whose firearm had a ribbon of grey smoke rising from the tip.

Thomas smirked. "Well move your thick head out the way next time!" His hands were swift in the rigging but that was his first shot with a firearm. "How are we to shoot straight in swells like this anyhow?" he hollered.

Jon stomped towards his friend. "That's why I told you to choose a sword!" he said, swatting Tom's gun to the side.

Shaking a clump of windblown red hair from his brow, Thomas peered down the barrel of his foreign weapon. "We signed as sailors. Why are they makin' us learn this shite?"

Jon glanced around their faithful ship while the clanging of clumsy swords rattled through the air. These men looked like children play fighting without any suspicion they would ever actually get hurt.

For the past two years, the only feet aboard these planks belonged to the same twelve men who lived, breathed and bled for this ship — but a persuasive meeting with Lord Arlington a few weeks ago had changed all their lives rather quickly.

Chapter 2

SAILORS AND SOLDIERS

The North Sea showed no mercy to England's newest naval recruits. Perhaps brilliant soldiers on land, they looked like newborn fawns stumbling around the ship in these incessant swells. Now humbled by the weight of their own swords, nearly every swipe tossed them off balance, sending them tumbling to the deck of the three-masted Barrington.

A bead of nervous sweat ran down Vice Admiral Clarkson's face as he observed his newest batch of trainees from the forecastle; leftover soldiers, merchant men, crew from this ship — none of whom were remotely ready for the war they were about to face.

Clarkson filled his lungs and boomed his frustration across the deck. "How do you men expect to beat the Dutch aboard their ships when you can barely stand upon your own?" The words spit from his lips as the putrid smell of vomit filled his nose.

He glanced down to spot one of the youngest recruits getting sick over the railing. The poor lad was still wiping his face when he realized he had an audience.

"Apologies Admiral. This is my first day aboard a ship."

Eagerly anticipating her permissible escape, Isabelle had counted down every sleep since Christmas morning. When she laid her long golden hair against her pillow last night — only one number remained.

Looking down to the courtyard from her bedroom window, a smile slowly slid to Isabelle's cheeks.

Palace hands were loading the last of her perfectly packed trunks onto a wagon while her new coachman readied the silver carriage that would carry her over the Thames and back into the quiet wilds she had been craving all winter.

Soon, she would be free.

It would only be for the summer but she would be free from the prying eyes of the palace, free from her father treating her like some purebred show dog, and most importantly, free from the swirling rumours of her impending betrothal.

Drawing a deep breath, Isabelle pushed her feelings of dread down to burrow with inadequacy, abandonment and guilt, then pulled her shoulders back and raised her chin.

"Lady Isabelle," a servant called from the doorway, "your carriage awaits."

Chapter 3

GENTLE WAVES

"Evening, Miss."

A passing soldier tipped his hat to a plump young woman leaning against one of the stone flower planters along the main dock. But Elizabeth Mayfield paid him no attention and kept her eyes locked on the ship in front of her. She had spent her afternoon catching up with old friends in the square but had impatiently been awaiting this moment all day — nothing would break her focus now.

"Maybe he's working on the other side of the ship today, Beth," Victoria whined impatiently from the bench between the flower planters.

"He knows I'm always here at this time of day. He'll come to look for me. True love requires patience," Elizabeth sweetly answered back without any dissuasion at all.

Victoria squiggled her petite porcelain face as she rose. "Love? You've known of this man no more than a week — you've never even spoken a word to him. What could you possibly know of love?" Her tight blonde ringlets slipped from her shoulders as she laughed. "Careful Beth, if your mother heard you speak of love for a vagrant shipmate, she'd call you back to London immediately," she quipped, crossing her arms as she continued to giggle.

But Elizabeth ignored the jabs and kept her eyes strong on that ship. Mere months ago, her only sense of stability was ripped from her life in a single breath. The wound of her father's sudden passing was still raw and the gentle waves she shared with this rotund redheaded sailor had become the only source of light in her currently dreary existence.

"You're wasting your time, Beth," Victoria said, wrapping an arm around her friend in hopes of heading back for their awaiting carriages.

"I'm not leaving until I wave to him!" Elizabeth shouted, pulling herself from Victoria's grasp. "Besides, your sister is still over there talking to those lads, and Izzy is still in Mr. Bouvier's shop. Leave me be!" She ran her hands down the front of her puffy royal-blue satin dress. "We're not all as lucky as you, to be marrying such an exotic Prince," she added spitefully, instantly regretting her words. She knew Victoria had never even met her soon-to-be husband and therefore, also knew nothing of love.

Victoria and her oldest sister Anne were the only remaining unwed daughters of Chatham's illustrious Davenport family. Their father was an obnoxiously wealthy shipping magnate whose boastful pride had left a sour taste in the King's mouth. Forced to seek his royal recognition elsewhere, Davenport's most recent business venture found him in the Near East, where a picture of his youngest daughter had strategically made its way into the hands of one of Calvaria's royal family members.

Enticed by her white hair, icy-blue eyes, and flawless porcelain skin, Victoria was admired as a rare beauty amongst the dark-haired women of the Calvarian Empire. One of the many princes saw her portrait and immediately professed his love. Calling her his 'fair angel,' he vowed to take her as his only wife.

Upon receiving an offer from the Calvarian crown that was impossible to refuse, Davenport promised to wed his youngest daughter to the love-struck Prince on her eighteenth birthday, which was now only a mere two months away.

Victoria plunked herself back down on the bench. She was about to be shipped to some far-off land and would likely never see anyone from England again. She certainly didn't want to spend her last summer in Gillingham quarrelling with dear friends over innocent gestures.

With Victoria settled, Beth turned her hopeful eyes back to the ship. "He'll come to see me...I just know it."

Chapter 4

LEAP OF FATE

"Reel faster!" Thomas yelled to Jon at the other end of the spar. "If I miss lookin' into those beautiful eyes, I'll wring yer neck!"

Still fervently reeling, Jon yelled back with a laugh. "I'll let you stare into *my* eyes all night if you miss her just this once!"

"I've stared at you too long as it is! Pull 'er in!"

Knackered from their long week of training, both men were losing steam as they worked to furl their last sail. A few more turns and they were free to enjoy their leisure.

"Done!" Jon shouted, springing up to discover Tom was nowhere to be found. With his line safely belayed — he had vanished.

Thomas moved quickly across the bow, slamming past his shipmates as he rushed to the wooden railing to search the dock below.

There she stood, in her royal-blue gown with black bows and white lace trimming. Her cinnamon locks, tightly curled, blew gently in the sea breeze. The moment he caught her eyes she lit up and began waving so vigorously she was nearly trembling.

Thomas had waved to her at the end of every day this week but still failed to muster enough confidence to walk the gangplank and speak with her. He was quite shy around women and often left in the shadow of the handsome, more charming lad he'd just left in his wake.

"Are you going to spend the rest of our time here just staring at her?" Jon pestered, catching his friend at the railing. "Go speak to her, ya wanker!" He smacked Tom's back in encouragement.

"She's a proper woman," he meekly replied. "This'll take time."

"Time is not something we're owed, mate." Jon tightly gripped his friend's shoulders. "Look at her cheeks, she's blushing...and look at that smile. You'd likely make her entire day if you went down there. Our duties are done, go talk to her!" He nudged Thomas again from behind, attempting to rouse any sense of gumption. "What if our ship is called to war tomorrow? You'd regret not getting off this fucking boat to see how soft she really is."

Thomas stared into the longing eyes on the dock as he contemplated Jon's words. "Aye...we really could be dead tomorrow," he said with a nervous laugh.

As though sensing his need for reassurance, Beth waved again.

"You know what...you're right." Thomas sprung up with a spritely confidence. "I'm going down there."

"There it is!" Jon said with another smack on his back.

Thomas was a whirl of nerves as he left his friend at the rail. He had spoken to wealthy women before but not without Jon's lead and never with one he fancied as much as this beauty waiting patiently on the dock below.

Floating as he disembarked, his legs had gone completely numb yet he still managed to walk straight up to her.

"Hello Miss. My name is Thomas," he announced with a deep bow. "You must be the most beautiful woman in this port." He had heard Jon use this line many times and hoped it may tickle her heart.

Completely smitten, Beth nearly collapsed in a fit of giggles, but on the bench next to them, Victoria simply rolled her eyes at the sailor's generic opening line and tried to feign disinterest in their conversation entirely.

Instead, she turned her attention towards her sister Anne who was standing in the shade of shop awning at the end of the square — surrounded by a gaggle of men. She wore a bouffant scarlet gown with a corset pulled so tight it looked as though her breasts may pop right out of her dress should she laugh just a little too hard.

Victoria found her sister's fashion sense slightly lewd for afternoon attire in the country but red had somehow managed to become Anne's signature colour because, as she claimed, 'men are drawn to it.' And perhaps she was right, as Anne was never more than an arm's length away from at least one man at any given moment.

Although Victoria and her friends had managed to maintain their innocence, the same could not be said of her oldest sister. Much to their father's dismay, Anne was never one for obedience. Ordering her to do something such as — maintaining one's virtue — only seemed to push her further in the opposite direction.

Anne cackled like a hen as she let the men drape themselves all over her, but Victoria knew all three of those men quite well and none of them were *that* funny.

Shaking her head, Victoria dropped her gaze to the wooden planks. All she wanted to do was walk back through the square, get in her carriage and be taken home where she could sulk about her foreign

15

future in peace, yet now she was waiting on everyone! And where is Izzy she wondered, looking up at Monsieur Bouvier's shop.

His art store was Isabelle's favourite stop in town. She could spend hours in there talking about paintings or artists from around the world but she knew her friends were waiting today and wasn't expected to take this long as it was.

In a huff, Victoria stood up to excuse herself and walk back through the square alone.

"Oh! And this is Victoria Davenport," Beth announced, finding her friend by her side. "Vic, I'd like you to meet Thomas. He's a sailor with this ship the...what was the name again?"

"The Barrington," Thomas answered with a proud smile as though he owned it himself.

"Lovely to meet you," Victoria replied, "but if you'll both excuse me, I'll be heading back for my coach."

"Just wait for us, Vic! Or go in there and see what in the world is taking is Izzy so long today."

Still perched on the Barrington's bow, Jon saw the young woman point to a store at the edge of the square just as the shop's wooden door opened.

In awe, Jon watched the most beautiful woman he'd ever seen come strolling into the sunlight. Strands of her long golden hair caught the breeze as she left the shop with a smile on her face that could've easily lit the darkest soul on fire.

The threads of her simple yet elegant pale-yellow silk dress glistened in the sun as she sashayed from the store gripping a paper-wrapped parcel so tightly to her chest it could have contained the soul of Christ himself.

But that smile — that innocently thieving smile gut him from navel to nose and left him breathless.

On the dock below, Isabelle breathed in that nostalgic sea air. The new art supplies she clutched to her chest were mere moments from being turned into a rolling coastline or a blazing sunset, but as she approached her patient friends on the dock, Isabelle noticed a red headed sailor standing amongst them. Was that the same sailor Beth was just telling her about? She couldn't believe they were standing there speaking face to face. Isabelle was certain Beth would've lapsed into a fit of giggles had any man spoken to her, let alone the one she'd been swooning over all week.

Though happy for her friend, the joy slowly faded from Isabelle's face as she wondered just how long she'd have to wait before enjoying her new treasures.

As Jon watched her angelic smile melt away, his body began to burn. Overwhelmed by an unbridled sense of urgency, he untied a rope from the railing, looked up to make sure it was still well-attached above, then wrapped it around his wrist and held on tight.

Glancing at the dock below, he judged the group to be a mere fifty feet away. He'd make it, he thought with a nod.

Jon backed up as far as he could, huffed a confident breath then bolted across the deck. Quickly running out of planks beneath his feet, he leapt onto the railing and propelled himself off the ship in a move he'd only just learned earlier that week.

Flailing through the air, he caught the attention of everyone at the river's edge, but his stunt didn't quite end as he'd planned. He flew right over the end of the dock and plunged down into a berm of dirt.

17

Springing up quickly, he wiped the dirt from his white cotton shirt as he looked back at his ship. That manoeuvre was designed to get a soldier aboard an opposing vessel so he could slice through the heart of his mortal enemies, but in this case, Jon simply hoped it had impressed a beautiful woman.

He looked back to the group who had ceased their conversation and were now staring at him in utter confusion. He'd startled all of them except Isabelle who had watched him fly gallantly off the ship — his eyes locked on her the entire time.

Jon's act of valour even managed to steal Anne's attention away from her three suitors. She quickly said her goodbyes and started towards the dashing seaman.

"You alright?" Thomas asked as Jon came walking towards them. He knew Jon was a bit impetuous but leaping off the ship like a flying pirate was definitely new to them both.

"Oh my word, that was bewildering!" Anne shouted as she quickened her pace in hopes of intercepting her new prospect.

But Jon kept his sights on his golden beauty as the sea air whipped her wispy locks around her face. Even with all the commotion, she stood unfazed and fixed upon his eyes.

Everyone around her was fussing over the sailor who'd just leapt from the ship, but Isabelle had never felt calmer in her entire life. She couldn't imagine being able to sketch a more handsome man. His hair was so short she could barely make out the colour, but his freshly shaven face revealed a square jawline and a small cleft in his chin.

As he got closer, Isabelle noticed his eyes were as blue as the sapphire sea. They reminded her of the deepest parts of the ocean she used to sail over as a child and they were quickly drawing her in like a receding tide.

"Is this man bothering you?" Jon asked her gently, gesturing to Thomas.

Protective over her new beau, Beth quickly interjected. "Oh, Thomas? No, not at all. He's been quite the gentleman," she replied, beaming a smile in Tom's direction.

Jon looked over at Elizabeth for the first time since he stepped on land. She was quite a full-figured woman who fit snugly in her puffy satin dress, but he also noticed her pretty smile and how her curls bounced upon her large breasts when she spoke with such excitement. Seeing Thomas standing next to her with his prideful grin made Jon's lips curl in amusement. "That pleases me to hear," he answered politely before turning back to Isabelle, who hadn't taken her eyes off him for a second. "But I mean you."

He whirled around her, ending with his back to the square, forcing her to turn away from the distraction of her friends and face him alone.

He looked straight into her amber eyes that shone like pots of honey in the afternoon sun. "Was this man bothering *you*?" he asked again.

"What makes you so concerned for my happiness?" Isabelle replied with no more than half a grin.

Jon took a step closer. "Have you ever looked at someone and felt the fate of your entire life shift in a single moment?"

Isabelle rarely paid a man a second glance, but somehow this dirty yet handsome sailor already had her full and complete attention. "I don't believe I have," she replied coldly, trying to seem unamused by his grand gesture.

"When you walked out of that shop, you had the most beautiful smile on your face, but then it faded, and I needed to know if there was anything I could do to bring it back."

His charming grin left Isabelle tingling.

"You're wasting your time talking to this one," Anne interjected. It had been one entire minute since she was last the centre of someone's attention and she was beginning to get restless. "Lady Isabelle is not permitted to converse with anyone outside of noble lineage," she added, inserting herself between them.

"A Lady?" Jon shifted to gaze upon Isabelle again.

"Well of course," Anne replied. "Don't you know who you're speaking to lad? Her father is the King's new favourite, Lord—"

"Anne!" Isabelle interrupted. "Not now, please."

Even though Isabelle had spent a fair amount of her life here in Gillingham, this was her first summer under her father's new title and she had already heard everyone in town remarking about it. The fact that she had come face to face with seemingly the only person in this town who didn't know who she, or her father was, was a rather refreshing reprieve she didn't want spoiled by name-dropping and frivolous titles.

"My name is Isabelle Bennett," she replied.

"And I'm Anne Davenport of Chatham, daughter of Ernest Rolland Davenport."

"Nice to meet you," Jon answered before turning back to Isabelle.

"And you are?" Anne asked, still trying to steal his attention.

He stared at Isabelle as though she was the one who'd asked. "My name is Jon," he said with a smile.

"Of...?" Anne continued to pry.

20

Jon looked to Thomas as though some answer might be found in his closest friend's eyes, but Thomas only shrugged, for neither of them had any titles, family, or land of their own.

Jon took a step back, spread his arms to the side and proclaimed loudly, "Of the Sea," before bowing forward to jest the pompousness of aristocracy.

Isabelle chuckled at the gesture causing him to look up with a smile.

Anne stepped in closer. "Well, Jon of the Sea, that was quite the entrance. Where did you learn a little trick like that?" She gently placed her hand on his shoulder as he stood back up.

"If you'll excuse me," Isabelle interrupted, "I must be getting on." She moved around the red draped obstacle and started towards the square. She had seen Anne work a man before — sometimes it was a quick catch, other times it required quite a bit of charming, either way, Isabelle had no interest in sticking around to see if Anne was about to snag her first sailor.

"I'll join you!" Victoria burst with excitement. She linked Isabelle's arm and they started back towards the busy square.

Jon leapt to catch up to the girls with Anne following closely at his heels, leaving Beth and Thomas alone to finish the conversation they'd started before being interrupted by a gallivanting sailor.

"Are you often down at the square?" Jon asked, reaching Isabelle's side.

She looked at him with a sideways grin but revealed nothing.

"I only ask because your friend has been at the dock every day this week, but I've only just seen you for the first time."

"Are you certain of that?" Isabelle asked with a slight raise in her brow.

His reply held a piercing sincerity. "I'm sure I would've remembered you."

Isabelle tried to ignore him as she did all the others, but he felt...different. Not ready to dismiss him just yet, she offered a gentle smile since that was all he truly wanted in the first place.

"May I ask what's in your parcel? You seemed quite pleased with it when you left that shop."

Wondering just how long he'd been watching her, Isabelle was hesitant to reply. "Colour pastels and a dip pen from France. First of their kind here in England."

"Ah, you're an artist?"

"Anyone who creates something may be considered an artist I suppose."

"Izzy's writing a story as well," Victoria added proudly, causing Isabelle to look over and exchange a friendly smile. "It's a love story," she added with a grin.

"A woman writing a story? Haven't heard that before."

"It's just something to pass the time this summer. Vic will likely be the only one to ever read it."

"What's it about?"

"The rebellion!" Victoria shouted with excitement. "The girl's father is a parliamentarian and she's in love with a royalist who is being driven out of England by vicious mobs...but he can't seem to leave his beloved behind," she added sweetly. The idea of two people falling in love was a fantasy Victoria knew she would be robbed of forever. Being able to take Isabelle's story of true love with her to Calvaria was something she would cherish for the rest of her life — she only hoped

Isabelle would fulfill her promise to finish it before she was shipped off at the end of the summer.

Jon glanced to Isabelle. "Do they live happily ever after?"

"We'll see," she answered with a coy smile, "the story has only just begun."

Victoria spotted her coach near the large stone fountain. "Ah, brilliant." She broke away and started straight for it. "See you at church tomorrow, Iz!" she yelled over her shoulder as she entered the white carriage.

"Is your coach here as well?" Jon asked as they approached the fountain.

"No," Anne interrupted as she stomped by them in a huff, clearly upset about being overshadowed yet again by Isabelle's beauty. "Lady Isabelle prefers to walk," she scoffed.

Before Anne's foot hit the carriage step, she turned back to her friend and bowed deeply. "Good afternoon, *Lady Isabelle*," she said flippantly as she curtsied — a gesture that was unnecessary and obviously meant to mock Isabelle's new status.

"Good evening, Anne," she replied, already growing tired of the teasing. Isabelle noted the snarky grin cinched in Anne's cheek as she took her coachman's hand and stepped into the carriage.

"You walk home alone? Don't noblewomen prefer to be carried on the backs of their servants?" Jon asked with a chuckle.

"Not all of us," Isabelle answered curtly. Was everyone out to ridicule her today, she wondered. "Besides, carriages only serve to rush people from one place to another. In the country, I prefer to stop along the coast to write or draw, and I despise the feeling of someone waiting on me."

"A noblewoman who doesn't want servants waiting on her? Haven't heard that before either." Jon expected a beautiful woman dressed in such expensive silks to be tended constantly yet here she was, all alone in the square, speaking with him.

"If you'll excuse me, I really must get on. It was nice to meet you, Jon of the Sea," she said facetiously before turning towards the small pedestrian gate.

Not willing to let her disappear into the countryside just yet, Jon caught up to her again. "May I walk with you?"

A laugh of confusion fled her lips. "Whatever for?"

"I suppose I could ask anyone here in Gillingham but I'd prefer to hear it from you."

"Hear what from me?"

Jon answered with an honest smile. "Who you are."

His genuine interest caught Isabelle's attention. Most men knew exactly who she was before they were ever introduced, but to this sailor she was simply another girl in the square whom he wished to speak with a bit more.

"I don't mean to sound audacious but ladies of noble lineage are truly not permitted to be escorted home by random vagrants," she replied sarcastically, letting him know she was not above teasing him as well.

"There are only a few estates up that road but if anyone does happen upon us, I give you full permission to say I've captured you," he added in jest.

"Captured?" Isabelle laughed. "Are you not fond of your head Jon? Holding a noblewoman against her will could see it quickly removed."

With a smile, he stepped closer and looked into her eyes as though her soul was already spilling her deepest secrets. "I just want to talk with you a little more. If it costs me my head, something tells me it'll be worth it."

His sultry grin fed the curiosity swirling in Isabelle's belly. She had received many gifts from men bidding on her hand but none had ever been bold enough to offer his own head.

After a short hesitation and a deep breath, Isabelle slowly began to nod. "Alright then, but it is quite a long way down the road, Jon. I hope those sea legs remember how to walk on land." She flashed him a coy smile then turned to leave through the arched gate.

There it was again. That smile.

It turned her into his enchantress and Jon knew right then — he would follow her anywhere.

Chapter 5

TREADING EARTH

Stepping onto the quiet dirt road, Jon found the wind blowing through the back of the dockyard unusually humid for June. He watched the gusts play in Isabelle's hair, lifting her satiny locks as they came and left. Suddenly jealous of the passing breeze, he tried not to notice the late afternoon sun glistening off her silk threads as the elements conspired to hypnotize him with her beauty.

"Your dress is mesmerizing," he said, lightly shaking the trance from his head.

"Thank you." Isabelle ran her hand down the fitted bodice. "My father purchased the fabric but I designed it myself. I prefer simplicity out here. Petticoats and poofy gowns are much too cumbersome for the countryside…for anywhere really."

Isabelle kept her chin straight and her shoulders back while Jon sauntered next to her, swaying from side to side with a rugged elegance of his own.

"Have you spent many years on ships?" she asked, noticing his seafaring gait.

"Aye, Tom and I hopped our first ship seven years ago. Since then, I only find myself on land for cargo, ale, or beautiful women."

The smirk on his face left Isabelle wondering if his intentions may include more than just an escort home and she stopped them both in the street. "Perhaps I made a poor decision in accepting your invitation."

"Was it something I said?"

"No...well...yes I suppose," Isabelle replied honestly. "It is quite a long walk and I fear you may be wasting your precious time on land with me."

"Never." His eyes, steady and soft, held a masculine confidence Isabelle had never seen.

"I just...perhaps your affections would be better suited towards another woman who..." she chose her words carefully "...who is not so virtuous and perhaps in a better position to reciprocate your generous intentions."

"My only intentions are to know more about you and to see that you arrive home safely."

Isabelle searched his sea-blue eyes for any signs of deceit before offering a hesitant reply. "Alright then," she conceded before starting down the road again, "but are you certain your captain won't wonder where you are?"

"Oh, not at all. Tom will tell him I'm with a beautiful woman, and he'll understand."

Feeling slightly less important than she did just moments ago, Isabelle raised her chin before responding. "I see...chasing unattainable women is a cherished past time for you and your crew?"

Jon glanced to the ground with a toothy grin. "Most women are more easily attainable than you might think."

Isabelle's nose wrinkled at the vulgar thought of a woman giving herself so freely to a man she'd likely never see again — no matter how charming he may be.

"May I hold your parcel for you?" he asked.

"Oh, no thank you. I'd prefer to keep it if you don't mind."

"You don't trust me?"

"I trust no one," she replied coldly.

"Yet you walk alone down a deserted road looking as innocent as you do?"

"There is no one who means me any harm down this road, I assure you."

"Well, I feel much better knowing you have a safe escort home today."

"I'm quite able to take care of myself, thank you."

A sarcastic laughed left him. "My apologies. Of course you are."

"I am! I nearly dismembered a man twice your size last year."

"Ah yes, England's first living giant, I'm sure," he said with another patronizing chuckle.

Isabelle held her poise as she peered at him. He was certainly not an acceptable suitor, and she would likely never see him again, but that swirling in her belly was urging her to tell him the truth.

"He wasn't a giant," she started slowly, "just some drunken fool who happened to find me alone in our stables in London. I had just returned from my evening ride when he crept out from one of the stalls. I'll never forget that look in his eye when he reached down to rub his crotch," she said in utter disgust.

"Were you scared?"

"Not for one moment. It was that look in his eye…it was as though he thought he owned me. But then, something fierce came over me. The only thought in my head was — not today. I grabbed a knife from the workbench and held it out in front of me. I told him to leave or I'd gut him!"

Jon hung on her every word. Captivated now by more than just her beauty, she was also brave and tenacious.

"He laughed then charged right at me! But when he wrapped his hands around my neck, he left his most vulnerable bits unattended," Isabelle's eyes shifted to the sailor at her side, "so I thrust the knife right into his groin."

Jon's jaw dropped open and he quickly covered his own vulnerable bits.

"He fell to the floor," Isabelle added proudly. "I told him to leave or I'd finish him off. I meant every word and he knew it. My father's men tracked him to the city but they never found him, and I haven't left home without a blade since."

"A blade?" Jon asked with a raise of his brow. "Doesn't seem like a sword would match your beautiful dress," he teased while looking for this illusive weapon, wondering if her entire story was indeed false.

"It doesn't have to." Isabelle turned to face him.

Still holding her package, and much to Jon's pleasure, she bent forward to lift the hem of her skirt, revealing a fair-sized dagger strapped to her slender calf.

She wasn't lying.

Jon chuckled nervously. "I'll remember to stay in your good graces."

"Both evil and lust live in the heart of every man," she added. "A woman's small hands alone will not save her should either one conquer his sanity."

"I've spent years living amongst crews of drunken men. You're smart to carry that blade," he said as they continued down the road. "I however am not much of a fighter...I'm more partial to making love."

Isabelle didn't flinch at his enticing grin. "I see. Your crew is down at the dockyard training for the love-making war, is that it?"

Her wit made him laugh. "Our ship was commissioned by Lord Arlington for her speed and agility. We're a crew of seamen, not soldiers. Arlington came looking for us when he heard we turned hauls faster than East India Trading. He made us an offer we couldn't refuse, and here we are."

"Just like that?" Isabelle asked sternly. "He offered you a king's salary in exchange for your life and that was good enough?"

"Our crew did alright without the King's purse. We've split every haul equally for the past two years. We didn't come here just for the money and I certainly don't intend to lose my life in this war."

"A sailor who doesn't like fighting and has no interest in a King's salary. I'm confused on why you're here at all?"

Her tone held more offense than Jon expected. "Dutch fleets have blocked our ships for nearly a full year. They're staking claim to the entire Eastern Passage — they've taken shots at English vessels! If England loses this war, we'd best hope the New World is as prosperous as they say, for that's the only direction we'll be allowed to sail."

"I see," Isabelle replied in an effort to placate him.

"But I don't expect our ship to be called any time soon. Arlington knows our value. He's got us training men from new ships as they arrive. We take 'em out to sea and show 'em how a real crew turns a ship."

Isabelle found his naivety endearing however, being the daughter of a military royalist, she knew all too well that some men didn't always make it to the other side of a battlefield. "Your ship will get called one day, Jon," she gently reminded him.

"And I welcome it! We've been fighting off the Dutch for months now. This time our ship will be filled with cannons, and firearms, and soldiers!"

Isabelle watched him grow fiercer with every word. "I will never understand why men venture into this world solely to destroy each other."

Jon took a breath to calm himself. "Some fight to protect their families or their pride, others for retaliation...but this war...it's greed. That too lives in the hearts of all men," he gestured to Isabelle's skirt, "and women."

His accusation stopped her in the street. "My dress? What are you implying?"

Jon kept walking as he answered. "You wouldn't have your fancy silks or exotic perfumes if brave English men hadn't fought off those Dutch filibusters."

Isabelle took a deep breath and held it. She raised her hands to her hips but said nothing.

Noticing the silence, Jon turned around but couldn't read her face at all. Was she even breathing?

Her glaring stare was starting to make him uncomfortable so he decided to rouse her a bit. "If it weren't for those brave men willing to destroy each other, you could be standing here in a grain sack right now."

Isabelle didn't laugh as he'd hoped — but she did begin to march straight towards him. "You are bold to assume I'm the one demanding to wear silks!" she contended, stopping only to glare into his eyes before continuing to walk right past him. "I suppose it would shock you to learn of a noblewoman who prefers to wear cotton, or leather — one who rides astride a horse...and carries a dagger!" she yelled over her shoulder, growing frustrated by his accusation that she was in any way a cause for this war.

"I didn't mean to antagonize you, Lady Isabelle," he said, reaching her side again.

"Please don't call me that."

"Alright. Izzy was it?"

"That will do."

"I never meant to offend a woman of your beauty and stature," he offered, causing Isabelle to roll her eyes at his common compliments. "I quite enjoy the company of noblewomen above anyone else really, well...after my mates of course."

"And why is that?" Isabelle asked, stopping them both with her poignancy. "Would it be because we smell of exotic perfumes and wear mesmerising silk gowns?"

Jon's confident grin dropped from his face.

Isabelle threw both arms in the air. "And the circle goes 'round again!" she exclaimed before continuing her journey home.

"Well, yes," Jon turned to catch her again, "but it's more than just that. They're usually quite smart, well travelled...*very experienced.*" His salacious tone made Isabelle believe he was referring to more than just their conversation skills.

"They're much more amusing to spend time with than the usual port hags who wait for horny sailors to arrive."

"And what of you?" Isabelle asked sharply, having heard enough of his judgments of women. "You say you live on the sea yet you use words like antagonize and stature. If you've spent your life with crews of drunken sailors, how is it you're so well spoken and presume to know so much about noblewomen?"

Unfazed by her resentment, Jon chuckled. "My mother was a kitchen maid in a noble household when I was young. She took me with her when my father was away at sea. The Baroness only had daughters and took quite a liking to me. She treated me like one of her own and had me tag on to music and tutor lessons. I learned to read and write in both English and French.

"Tu parles Francais?" Isabelle asked to verify his honesty.

"Oui. Ne me testez pas s'il vous plaît." He knew she was testing him.

Satisfied with his response, Isabelle raised her eyebrow in surprise. "And where was this noble household?"

"Back home, on Jersey Isle."

"Ah, it all makes sense now. A boy surrounded by water must have been destined for a life at sea."

He laughed. "Aye, perhaps. My father was a sailor, his father too. He did short hauls when I was younger, but once his captain heard of the money in furs from the New Americas, I started to see much less of him."

Isabelle caught the sadness in his voice. "Are you close with your father?"

"I was, but one day his ship pulled out for the New World and, they just, never returned. An entire crew of men...vanished. Their families had no money for investigators." Jon's sullen gaze shifted to the rolling sea. "If it weren't for the trail of children they'd left behind, it would've been as though they'd never lived at all."

"Your father was a brave man," Isabelle offered. "I could never cross the ocean. I must be able to see the shoreline at all times or it sends me into a horrible panic."

"Really? I find the open water the most freeing place on earth. You can go absolutely anywhere."

"Yes well, it's not for me. I much prefer to keep my feet on solid ground." Not wanting to wake her sleeping demons, Isabelle quickly changed the subject. "Did you and your mother live alone after your father...disappeared?" she asked delicately.

"Aye, but not for long. She remarried the blacksmith in town. He'd had his eye on her for years. I swear he was just waiting for my father to disappear," he said, nearly snarling. "He had bulging eyes and was always red in the face." Jon's empty gaze was far in front of him. "He was not like my father at all. My mother was the most kind-hearted woman I've ever known. She deserved better than that growling toad."

Isabelle spied Jon's clenching jaw and wondered if her innocent deflection had unknowingly awoken his demons instead.

Appreciating his honesty, she decided to let him into her own world a little more. "You're lucky to have had such loving parents. My father only cares about what is best for the King, and my mother only cares about wine and jewels."

"You don't get on with your parents?"

"I barely know my parents," she sighed. "They pursue their own interests, and apparently, I am not one of them. I only sparked my father's attention when he realized my hand in marriage could be used to gain even more power for the King. Once he marries me off, I'm sure he will completely forget he even has a daughter."

"He doesn't sound very pleasant."

"Actually, he's very well respected at court. It seems he reserves all his spite for me." Isabelle dropped her gaze to the dirt road as it began to veer from the coast.

The thick forest forming at their sides left a new stillness in the air broken only by the sounds of rustling leaves above and the stories they candidly shared.

"I must say," Jon grinned, "I'm surprised there wasn't a line-up of men waiting to escort such an enticing woman home today."

"Suitors understand they must go through my father. None approach me without knowing whether they have my father's approval — and he never gives his approval."

"My apologies, I didn't know your companionship came with a set of rules." But Jon wasn't sorry. He was here with her, and anyone playing by her father's rules, was not.

"The men bidding on my hand are only looking to further their own interests. They are never enticed by who I really am," she added sheepishly. "But I suppose this is the cross I'm meant to bear."

"I know many barmaids who'd kill someone to have your troubles."

"I would trade for their freedom in a heartbeat," Isabelle replied. "They will quickly realize that being locked in a world of silk gowns and expectations will not leave their hearts fulfilled."

When Isabelle looked to Jon, he saw a tinge of sorrow eclipse her amber eyes.

"I will be wed to the wealthiest and most powerful man my father can align with just so I can bring sons into this world," she added. "My entire life will be no more valuable than some prized breeding sow."

Noticing Isabelle's efforts to contain herself, Jon stepped lightly. "But, if your father is already a favourite of the King with his own estates and fortunes, why—"

"Power," Isabelle answered bluntly. "The more men that stand together, the more destructive they can be. Take your own naval training. They have good reason not to send one ship into a battle alone," she stated, making her point very clear. "I am a mere pawn in the politics of men."

"Well…you could always sail into the horizon with me," Jon offered with a smile.

When Isabelle glanced at him, she could've sworn a tiny voice inside her heart whispered — *that's it.*

"I don't like the open water," she finally replied.

Holding her gaze, Jon said nothing, but his cheeky grin made it seem as though he too may have heard the faint whispers of her heart.

"Besides," Isabelle continued, "If I did want to disappear, I would do it on horseback. I'd ride until I reached a place where no one knew my name. A place where I could be anyone, choose a new life and simply…start again," she added hopelessly.

"Live like a gypsy woman? Moving from town to town telling fortunes for coin?" Jon laughed. "I understand you're a competent woman, and I mean this with the least offense, but you wouldn't last one night out here alone, whether you carry a dagger or not."

Undeterred, Isabelle's words came confidently. "When I was younger, Mr. Tilly, our groundsman here, he taught me quite a bit about living by what the land provides." She motioned to the dense forest next to them. "This is all my family's land. I've spent a fair amount of time in these woods. It's the only place where I can truly be alone."

"Your father doesn't mind his noble daughter running through the woods like some forest nymph?" he chuckled.

"My father rarely comes to Gillingham. As long as my lessons are completed and I attend the required events, he tends not to pry into my life here."

"Where does he stay?"

"Wherever the King is," she answered dryly. "He holds apartments at Whitehall and we have a home in London as well. This was my grandfather's estate where he grew up."

"Whitehall Palace? Not only a Lady but a courtier at that," he teased.

"It's not as exciting as you may think."

"You'd rather live in the forest with your grandparents?"

"Well, yes I suppose. However, my grandmother died just after I arrived, and my grandfather, two years after that. The Tillys and governesses raised me until the crown was restored and my parents returned to England. Since then, I've only been permitted to summer here."

An opening in the bramble caught Isabelle's attention. "Look there," she said playfully. "Beth made that trail when we were both children. She would find a way out of her house at night and turn up beneath my window, then we would spend hours running about in the night. So you see, I'm not the only forest nymph around here," she added with a grin.

"Does she still come see you at night?"

Isabelle shook her head. "Once we outgrew our governesses, we had no need to skulk around in the darkness. Besides, I prefer to spend my leisure alone now."

A twinge snagged Isabelle's stomach when she spotted her gates just ahead. Two towering stone columns held a row of iron spires, breaking the natural beauty of the forest with their verboten rigidity.

Wishing the walk home was just a little longer today, she sighed. "Well, it seems you have delivered me safely. This is my home."

Jon noticed a copper sign on one of the stone pillars had tarnished to an earthly teal. He walked up to read it aloud.

"Bluefields Manor."

Peering through the spires, he'd hoped to catch a glimpse of Isabelle's woodland sanctuary but the curving cobble laneway and enveloping forest blocked his view. He could only spy a modest carriage house with a shiny silver coach parked just outside.

Enamoured by Jon's curiosity, Isabelle joined him at the gate just as her new coachman, Mr. Graham, came strolling out of the carriage house.

Gasping at the sight of him, she quickly grabbed Jon and yanked him away.

Pinning him firmly against the stone pillar, she peaked around the side to find Mr. Graham sitting on his stool with his back to the gate, obediently polishing the underside of the carriage.

Jon felt Isabelle's entire body sigh in his arms. Her outburst had caught him completely off-guard but having this forbidden beauty pressed tightly against him was an unexpected, yet welcomed surprise.

He ducked down to meet her eyes. "And you made it seem as though you wouldn't return my affections," he said sarcastically.

Realizing her predicament, Isabelle glanced to the ground and pushed herself off him. "I'm so sorry," she backed into the forest to stay well out of sight, "but if that man were to see me with you, it wouldn't end well for either one of us."

Isabelle knew Mr. Graham reported everything back to her father whenever it suited his own best interests, and reports of her unacceptable escort home would certainly be highly rewarded information.

Jon flashed that charming grin again. "No need to apologize," he pushed off the pillar, "I didn't mind that at all."

"I don't create these standards but I do have to live by them." With her poise already broken, Isabelle shamefully dropped her gaze. She knew her life of restriction must sound ridiculous to a man who lived his based on the ever-changing wind.

But unbeknownst to Isabelle, Jon found himself captivated by her rare moments of vulnerability. He started walking towards her.

As she watched him approach, Isabelle felt herself wanting to sink into him again. The few heartbeats she'd spent within his arms had not nearly been enough.

With a deep breath, she summoned years of programmed decorum, straightened her posture and whirled past him. "Thank you for your accompaniment this afternoon, sailor," she started backing towards the gate, "and please don't speak a word about me to anyone, not even

Thomas. If I see you at the square, I will wave to you." She offered one last smile then turned away.

"A wave?" Jon yelled. "But I quite enjoy your conversation."

When he caught her at the pillar Isabelle spun around to stop him. "I'm sorry, but that is all I'm permitted to offer you, and even that would likely become the topic of conversation for many." Isabelle looked to the ground, which only drew Jon in further.

He playfully ducked his head beneath hers. "May I see you tomorrow?" he asked with a smile.

"Did you not listen to a word I've just said?" Isabelle gestured to the road they'd just travelled.

"I'm not asking for your hand in marriage. You're allowed friends, yeah? Beth and...Anne was it?"

Hesitating briefly, Isabelle slowly nodded.

"Are you permitted to see them tomorrow even though they're not bidding on your hand?"

"Their fathers are businessmen and shipping heirs. They don't—"

"Aye, and my father disappeared into the sea. Look, I'm not interested in who their father is, or who your father is. I'm not here for long...perhaps none of us are," he added softly. "I have a small boat that I use to find some solitude on my Sunday leave. Last weekend I explored an island just off the coast here and I didn't see another living soul all afternoon. I thought, since you seem to enjoy solitude as well, perhaps you'd like to join me? You could bring your new pastels or write another chapter of your story. I won't speak a word to you if that is what you wish."

When Isabelle didn't immediately turn him down, Jon persisted. "I believe I passed right along the back of your father's property here. There's a grassy pier back there, yeah? Atop a sandy dune?"

Knowing the coastline of her beloved Bluefields better than the walls of her own bedroom, Isabelle nodded.

"I'll offer this," Jon continued. "We finish our orders near mid day. I'll be by here a short time after that. If you decide you'd like to go on an adventure with me, come to the pier. If I see you there, I'll come in to collect you."

Jon's inviting grin made Isabelle contemplate riding off the edge of the earth with him and leaving all this noble nonsense behind, but she replied with a sly smile that went no further than her eyes. "I told you, I don't like boats."

"Did you?" he asked jovially. "I understood it as you didn't like the open water. Not being able to see the shoreline, was it?"

Impressed by his accuracy, Isabelle's brow raised just slightly.

"We'll follow the shoreline to the channel then cut across from there. You can see Gillingham's coast from the island. I promise to keep you safe."

Unsure of how to respond, Isabelle took a deep breath. A short while ago, her answer to this question would've been a firm and easy no thank you, but the walk home with this inviting sailor may have softened her cautious heart just a bit.

"Perhaps," she answered with a smile.

"I'll take it." Spreading his arms to the side, Jon backed away. "I wish you a wonderful evening, Miss Izzy."

With a courteous bow, he turned and started walking back to his ship. Isabelle waited to see if he'd look back at her, but he didn't. He passed beyond the trees and disappeared.

Chapter 6

BUTTERFLIES AND STONE

Startled by the sound of iron gates clanking shut, Mr. Graham swirled around on his stool to find the Lady of the manor strolling gracefully up the laneway. He promptly stood and removed his grey brimmed hat. "Good afternoon, Lady Isabelle. You've arrived earlier than expected."

Hired only weeks ago, the new coachman had already slithered so far up his master's backside, Isabelle could practically feel her father's eyes upon her all the way out here in Gillingham. "Good afternoon," she replied without stopping or offering another word.

Pleased to find his eyes lacking insinuation, Isabelle continued up the lane skipping lightly over resilient weeds that had grown through the cracks of broken cobbles. Her father's penchant for palace perfection hadn't quite trickled down to his nearly forgotten childhood home. Left in the hands of only two now elderly servants, the sprawling estate always seemed in a slight state of disrepair, but Isabelle didn't mind in the least.

She looked up the lane as she rounded the curve; each stone, shaped exactly as the next, lined up in perfect little rows.

The broken ones were different. They caught her eye with their signs of life and offered no apologies for their fragility.

With a smile, Isabelle playfully hopped over one more broken stone then looked upon her cherished country home.

Vines of English Ivy climbed all three stories of the century old, grey-stone manor, blanketing nearly every window peak and chimney in swathes of emerald leaves.

Tiny ivory butterflies flit through her grandmother's once perfectly manicured gardens that now grew beautifully wild. Fluffy peonies, pink hydrangeas, blue delphiniums and creamy roses welcomed Isabelle home in a symphony of colourful chaos.

The garden's sublime perfume slipped from Isabelle's lungs with a sigh while the sound of trickling water from the ornate stone fountain soothed any last bit of unrest in her bones.

Passing by the formal front entrance her father would have expected her to use, Isabelle chose to follow a pathway of flat brown stones around the backside of the manor.

After strolling through the vegetable gardens, Isabelle entered directly into the kitchen through a small servant's door that creaked as she pushed it open.

"Wanker!" A loud smack erupted from the corner of the room.

Caught off guard by the commotion, Isabelle let out a half-winded chuckle when she spied Bluefield's loyal housekeeper, Moira Tilly, standing on the counter swatting a housefly with her cloth.

Employed at Bluefields for over forty years, Moira was a boisterous old bitty who was quite well organized yet always seemed a bit frazzled. Now the oldest living residents of the estate, she and her husband took pride in the manor they kept but always understood their humble place here.

"Gotcha!" Moira stomped her foot in excitement after delivering the fly's fatal blow. "I swear it, love," the petite stout older woman huffed as she lumbered off the counter, "I welcome the warmth but these flies will snatch my wits."

Moira walked over to Isabelle with a beaming smile and her arms outstretched. Not able to have children of her own, she showered Isabelle with all the love the poor girl certainly never got from her real mother. She had waited patiently through three seasons for Isabelle's return yesterday, and hugging her tight was a novelty that had not yet worn thin.

Practically raised by the woman since she was a young girl, Isabelle welcomed Moira's embrace and felt grateful to be back in the only place she ever truly considered home.

"Did you get him, Milly?" Isabelle asked as she strolled over to Moira's workspace and pulled up a stool. Isabelle had coined Moira's pet name as a child when calling her 'Milly Tilly' one night had sent them both into whirl of giggles.

"I should've let that bugger live. He could've told his friends not to come 'round here," Milly replied with a wink before getting back to her task. "I'm still preparing some bits for your ride. Why is it you're not drawing down by the coast? Have the pastels not arrived?"

"No, they're here." Isabelle placed her parcel on the table. "I just thought I'd save them for the sunset."

The Tillys were the only people in Isabelle's life that ever showed her any real sense of love. She certainly didn't want to lie to her sweet

BUTTERFLIES AND STONE

housemaid but Isabelle had already decided the distraction of her charming escort would need to remain her little secret.

On the corner of the table, a white envelope caught Isabelle's attention, but it was the waxy palace seal that turned her stomach. "When did that arrive?" she asked without lifting her eyes.

"Just after you left. Leave it for tomorrow, Iz. Go enjoy your ride."

Expecting word of her betrothal any day now, Isabelle knew the letter from Whitehall would almost certainly contain her fate. She didn't need to read it, she already knew what said — 'Her life had been signed away to a dynastic political family, and she should spend the rest of her days meeting every order and expectation that will come along with the responsibility of becoming a politician's wife…'till death do you part.'

Not wanting to extend her torture into another day, Isabelle straightened her posture and reached for the envelope. "That would only ruin my peaceful Sunday."

She slipped the letter from its pristine sheath and skimmed it silently. Her palace poise suddenly eased — it was only her summer schedule. Needlepoint on Mondays, Latin on Tuesdays, art lessons in her grandfather's studio on Wednesdays, voice lessons on Thursdays, dance lessons in the Davenport's ballroom on Fridays, and brunch with her favourite French tutor, Perrine Rigal, on Saturdays. She must also attend church every Sunday, as well as tea twice a week with a different noblewoman of her father's choosing.

A list of required society events followed, including the Solstice Festival next weekend, and the re-launch of the HMS London in three weeks time — a ship that Isabelle and her family were quite familiar with yet dreaded to step foot upon.

48

Commanded by Captain John Lawson, the famed war ship had been a home-upon-the-sea to exiled Royalists during the rebellion. To this day Lawson was still loyal to the crown as an admiral leading the Royal Navy against the Dutch at this very moment.

With the London's refit finally complete, the King wished to show off his favourite warship before reuniting her with her allegiant captain. Advertised as a spectacle of reward for ones unrelenting loyalty to the crown, the King had arranged an afternoon voyage from Gillingham to London for three hundred of Admiral Lawson's closest friends and family, set to depart immediately after the ceremony.

"This says my father will speak in honour of the King at the re-launching ceremony. You don't suppose he will request me for the sail as well?"

"What does the letter say, dear?"

Isabelle read the last part again. "He only requests my attendance at the ceremony. It says his household will arrive early to prepare the manor."

"Sounds like they'll be stayin' that weekend." Milly looked up to catch Isabelle's reaction.

Though news of her parents' arrival at Bluefields was certainly not Isabelle's favourite thing to hear, the letter said nothing of her attendance aboard the London, nor any mention of her betrothal. "Well," Isabelle dropped the letter on the table, "they're not coming today." She snatched her parcel and started for the stairs. "I'll be at the cape."

"Here," Milly yelled as she tossed the finished packet to Isabelle, "take this with you, love."

Never one for grand entrances, grand staircases or any other form of grandeur, Isabelle chose the cramped creaky servant's staircase at the back of the kitchen for its quick access to the chambers upstairs.

After weaving through the service corridors, Isabelle popped into the hallway along the backside of the manor then strolled down the velvety red carpeting. Her grandfather's paintings adorned the wainscoting walls with landscapes of moonlit fields and portraits of their family's small lineage — none of whom were noble before her father's raise.

When she reached her chambers, Isabelle pushed the heavy door open to discover her bedroom had been cleaned immaculately. Her four-poster bed was made perfectly without so much as a wrinkle. The drapery had been tied back, every decorative pillow fluffed and placed with care, and the empty water glass and burnt candle at her bedside had been cleaned and replenished.

On the other side of the room, beneath a towering glass window, sat her grandfather's intricately carved writing desk. Isabelle sauntered over, placed her parcels on the hardwood desk then pushed the window open that overlooked the forest all the way to the sea.

A fresh breeze wafted through the room as Isabelle changed into her riding clothes. This task would've required at least two chambermaids at her palace apartments but here, Isabelle simply loosened the specially designed side-closures, slipped the dress off, draped it over the chaise then walked into her closet wearing nothing more than her lacy French under garments.

The setting sun called her through the windows as Isabelle let a white cotton dress cascade over her head and down her body. She then slid her arms into her leather riding-jacket and grabbed her satchel.

On her way out, she stopped at her desk to grab a few sheets of canvas, her new pastels, and Milly's snack.

Shoving everything into her bag, she made her way to the balcony doors where her thigh-high riding boots were still waiting patiently from the night before.

After sliding on the well-worn leather boots, she pushed both doors open to a welcomed blast of sea air that whipped right through her.

She filled her lungs with the salty breeze then stepped onto the balcony, brushing her fingers along the potted evergreens already plumped under the unusually warm spring. Reminiscing about the day Mr. Tilly planted them 'just for her' she was grateful to feel them beneath her fingertips again.

She spiralled down the stone staircase, crossed the formal dining terrace then bounced down the final stairs into the flower gardens beneath her window. She breezed past the roses Mr. Tilly also planted just for her, then ducked into the forest and followed a path leading straight to the riding stables.

The woods running throughout Bluefields were thick and densely wild but Isabelle knew every oak, every birch, every knot of every tree and felt safer here, hidden within the thick foliage of her familiar forest, than she ever did behind the walls of a heavily guarded palace.

As she passed the livestock barns, Isabelle peered through the trees and spotted Mr. Tilly still hard at work. Though not a man of many words, he was the most dedicated worker this estate had ever seen. As far back as Isabelle could remember, she would always find him with a tool in his hand. The only exception was dinnertime when Milly forbade him from bringing his work to her table.

Isabelle's grandfather had hired him when they were both young men but with the eldest Bennett now laying six-feet-under in the family plot up the hill, Mr. Tilly was still here turning the soil, tending the animals, and repairing his home.

"Hello, Mr. Tilly!" Isabelle shouted as she continued on her way.

Waving his blue cap in the air, the old man smiled. "Have a lovely ride, Miss. Izzy," he yelled before dutifully returning to his work.

When she finally arrived at the stables, Isabelle slid the door open to a waft of fresh hay and a greeting from her two favourite companions. The colt standing next to his mother let out welcoming whine.

"Well hello to you too, Gryphon." Stroking his muzzle, she glanced around to discover Mr. Tilly had already mucked their stalls and refilled their food and water. While Isabelle normally would have enjoyed tending her own horses, she ached to use her new pastels and was grateful for Mr. Tilly's insatiable work ethic today.

With Gryphon clearly keen for a ride, Isabelle tacked him quickly then mounted up with one leg on either side of the saddle. Hunkering into her seat upon the eager colt, she held the reins tight.

A soft tap to Gryphon's side was all it took to send them both flying through the open barn door.

Charging across the property, Isabelle ran him as far and as fast as the young colt could bear. Through the forest then over the open fields, they ran until there was no land left beneath their feet.

When they finally reached the edge of the earth, Isabelle dismounted in the serenity of her golden cape then spent the next few hours basking in solitude as the sun slowly slipped into the sea.

Chapter 7

DAY OF REST

Finding her relationship with God stronger in a forest than a pew, Isabelle had never been fond of religious congregation — or early mornings — but at the behest of her father, she had dressed for church in a bouffant lavender gown and was now battling the weight of her eyelids in the back of her gently lulling coach.

She had awoken this morning in a ball of tangled satin after spending the night stirring in her sheets. Her dreams had found her on the bow of a massive second-rate ship faced headstrong into the wind. Her footing was sturdy as the unyielding ship cut easily through the calm water below. With her eyes closed, Isabelle let the sun warm her face and felt as though she hadn't a care on this earth.

In that brief moment of surrender, the breeze blowing against her nape turned bone chillingly cold. She slowly opened her eyes to find ominous storm clouds, bloated with rolling thunder, swallowing her perfectly clear blue sky.

The sea, turning bitterly violent, shook Isabelle from her footing just as the clouds released their fury and started pelting her from above.

Stumbling around the deck, Isabelle searched for a safe place to weather the storm but the waves thrashing aboard kept knocking her to the planks.

She pulled herself up just as another towering crest thundered down upon her, this time sweeping her clean across the ship.

Caught in its foamy grip, she felt powerless.

The vengeful wave was about to haul her right over the railing when Isabelle felt something within her begin to burn.

The sea would not take her — not today.

She reached for the gunwale as it passed beneath her, slamming hard against the ship when she grabbed a hold.

But her hands were wet.

She was slipping.

Dangling over the raging sea, the last of the slick wood was about to slide from Isabelle's fingers when she looked to the blackened sky for strength. Beneath the cracks of lightning and pounding rain, Jon suddenly appeared on the ship. Standing calmly above her, it seemed not even the rain was touching him.

He reached over the railing. "I'll save you," he said with a smile.

Isabelle sprung awake instantly and hadn't been able to shake the thought of him ever since. Even here in her coach, she found herself consumed with thoughts of his peaceful eyes in that raging storm.

Shaking the dream from her head, Isabelle glanced through the window just as Mr. Graham pulled up to the church.

In an effort to avoid conversation today, Isabelle had timed her arrival perfectly. She snuck in just before the church doors closed, said a polite good morning to Father Bellows then sat down with perfect poise in the back pew, well out of sight from her friends in the first few rows that contained Gillingham's most ostentatious daughters.

Eternally bored by Father Bellow's monotonous droning, Isabelle's mind swirled with new narratives for her book, yet she still managed to sing every hymn and recite every prayer with perfection.

On the final "Amen," Isabelle quickly popped up and was the first person out the doors. She had made it halfway to her carriage when she heard a familiar voice call out.

"Izzy!" Beth shouted.

Isabelle squeezed her eyes shut in frustration. She cared for her friend dearly but was in absolutely no mood for a chat this morning.

"Why are you hurrying off?" Beth asked as she approached.

Isabelle took a long breath then turned around. "Good morning, Beth," she sweetly replied. "How was your visit with that sailor yesterday?" she asked, hoping to divert Beth's interests.

"Oh, Thomas? He's so sweet, Iz. We talked for quite awhile before his captain called them back to the ship however...it seemed Jon was nowhere to be found." Beth lifted her eyebrow, leaving Isabelle unsure if that was a statement or a question.

"Why are you looking at me like that?"

"I just thought perhaps you may know where he ran off to."

"I don't presume to know what that man does with his life." Though hoping to avoid lying to her oldest friend, Isabelle didn't want to provide any more gossip for the wagging tongues of Gillingham this summer. Beth had a well-intentioned heart but she was hardly a vault of secrets.

An unconvinced grin slowly crept to Beth's face. "Mmmhmm."

Choosing to ignore her friend's insinuating hum, Isabelle's eyes shifted to the sea of awaiting carriages.

"Will you be joining us for lunch?" Beth persisted. Gillingham's young and wealthy often met in the square after church as it was the only time they were all free from schedules and tutors.

"I'm afraid not." Isabelle kept her gaze on the carriages in hopes of avoiding Beth's look of despair.

"But Iz, this is your first Sunday back in Gillingham. Do you not want to see everyone? You'll miss everything," she whined.

"I'm sure you will tell me all about it when we see each other next."

Beth ribbed her gently. "William will be there."

Isabelle's shoulders dropped as she glanced to her friend. "All the more reason for me not to attend," she dishearteningly replied.

William Cunningham III was just a child during the rebellion that ended in the King's execution. Having been in great favour with Oliver Cromwell, William's wealthy politically connected father was hoping to regain some notoriety at court by marrying his son to the daughter of the King's new favourite.

With their contract close to being finalized, Isabelle had hoped to leave the Cunninghams in London this summer but coffee house gossip informed her yesterday that William had made his way to Gillingham and apparently spent his first countryside night in the arms of two different women — neither of whom were Isabelle.

"Gillingham was supposed to be my reprieve from all this betrothal nonsense," Isabelle haplessly replied. "Besides, I'd prefer to work on my story today."

Tilting her head, Beth's eyes silently pried for the truth.

"My father will likely sign the contract any day now, Beth. When I marry into the Cunningham family, I will be watched constantly again. I just...I wish to spend my last summer here in as much solitude as possible, and I certainly don't want to spend any more time with William Cunningham than I'm forced to by law," she added sternly.

While most young women were spellbound by the strappingly confident William III, Isabelle found his flavour slightly arrogant, noxious even, and was definitely not enthralled at the prospect of becoming his submissive wife. The thought of having to spend the remainder of her life listening to a self-professing, egotistical social-climber was enough to make her throw herself upon the tiny dagger concealed beneath her formal Sunday dress.

Completely understanding of Isabelle's plight, Beth offered a sweet smile. Both girls had been raised by paid help but ever since the death of Beth's father, the size of the Mayfield's household had shrunk quite a bit, and Beth had since been enjoying her bittersweet freedom as well.

"Besides," Isabelle continued, "I didn't sleep well last night. I'm truly not up for conversation today."

"Alright," Beth conceded.

"I'll visit in a few days. I just wish to get settled a bit," Isabelle added for reassurance before glancing back to the crowd of carriages. "Ah, there he is," she exclaimed after spotting her coachman. "Have a lovely time in town," she yelled over her shoulder as she gracefully hurried off. "Tell everyone I miss them!"

"Do you though?" Beth shouted as she watched Isabelle climb into her carriage and ride away.

Even though Isabelle had spent most of her morning daydreaming about her story, Jon's invitation for an afternoon at sea had also crossed her mind.

In a perfect world, she would certainly enjoy a short sail with a new friend, but Isabelle knew her place in this life was not meant to entertain such liberties — not with men unknown to her father, and certainly not with a vagrant sailor she found herself yearning for this morning.

With a deep breath, she closed her eyes and tried desperately to think of something else just as the carriage passed through Bluefields' gates.

Mr. Graham halted the horses at the front entrance then climbed down from his seat. He opened Isabelle's door and extended his arm to help her but she exited the coach without taking his hand.

"Thank you, I will be home the rest of the day. You may take your leave now," she stated as she stepped to the ground.

Mr. Graham bid her a lovely afternoon with a tip of his hat then steered his horses around the fountain back towards the carriage house where he was free to enjoy his own day of rest.

Isabelle entered the manor to find it brilliantly quiet. Now a young woman in her own right, she insisted the Tillys take a full day of leave and not tend to her or the house at all. They had decided to spend some time at a friend's home in town leaving Isabelle completely alone in the house for the first time ever.

The deafening stillness was a welcomed change from her father's apartments at Whitehall. Voices were ever present at the palace but here, the only sounds were the creaking beneath her footsteps as she made her way back up the tiny hidden staircase.

Isabelle pushed the chamber door open to find her room exactly as she'd left it — the bedding was still a tangled mess, the empty water glass and melted candle still sat at her bedside.

The sight of her things left untouched caused Isabelle's first genuine smile of the day. She fixed her covers, disposed of the melted candle then poured herself a glass of water from the crystal carafe, sipping it as she walked to her desk.

Before taking a seat, Isabelle pushed the window open to allow the fresh breeze to waft over her as she spent the next few hours filling pages upon pages with her new metal dip pen.

> *"If you give up your loyalty to the King, we can be together," Charlotte pleaded. "My father will find you a position in parliament...you will no longer have to fight." Holding tight to the collar of his red officer's coat, she knew this was the only way.*
>
> *Gareth tenderly wiped a tear from her cheek. "How did we find ourselves here?"*

Lost in her paradoxical world of rebel war and young love, Isabelle hadn't noticed the sun pass over her window sill. Only when she found herself stumped for a word did she pause to lay down her pen and lean back in her chair.

Twirling a lock of hair in her fingers, she glanced through the window to the distant waves. It was late afternoon by now and Jon would've likely been well beyond the peninsula.

Dazed by the endless rolling sea, Isabelle suddenly realized the thought of not joining him today left her feeling hollow, as though she'd been robbed of a memory never given the chance to exist.

She knew the rest of her life would be kept to a strict schedule under the watchful eyes of a household of servants but...not today. A smile slowly slid to her cheeks as she twirled the golden lock in her fingers.

No one was watching today.

Isabelle sprung up from her chair and rushed to her closet where she whirled around, exchanging her fancy church clothes for a white cotton dress and a long brown leather vest complete with coattails down the front and back. She latched the gold buttons and finished her outfit with white stockings, leather ankle boots, and the trusty blade she concealed beneath her skirt.

Knowing it would be windy on a sailboat, Isabelle pinned the crown of her hair into a quick bun and picked up her satchel. She walked back to her desk to grab the pastels and a few sheets of canvas; should Jon's charm wear off at some point, she could always excuse herself to draw by the sea.

On her way out, Isabelle stopped in the kitchen for a canteen of water, a parchment of soft cheese, and a handful of walnuts. She packed everything into her bag then threw it across her body before leaving through the backdoor.

She passed through Milly's vegetable gardens, entered the forest and began following a path she'd bore down to hard earth years ago.

Her footsteps were swift as she walked along the pathway but Isabelle quickened her pace when she thought yet again about missing him.

60

Clasping her bag to her side, she started running down the forest path, ducking beneath low hanging branches and leaping over downed trees as she persevered, galvanized by some force at her back driving her fiercely towards the sea.

Though fit from years of dance lessons and riding horses, Isabelle's body wasn't prepared for this much exertion on her restful Sunday and her legs grew heavier with each earth-pounding step. Her lungs begged for breath. She was nearly on the edge of collapse when she finally heard the distant sound of waves lapping the shore.

Isabelle slowed her pace as the forest opened up to patches of tall grass blowing listlessly on the sandy dune. Huffing down that fresh sea air, she limped onto the peninsula. Her eyes searched the waves for any sign of him, but there was nothing — not one boat in either direction.

Crippled by a splitting pain in her side, Isabelle hunched over in exhaustion and hobbled to the dune's sandy ledge.

There on the beach below sat a solemn wooden rowboat pulled well up on shore with Jon leaning against it, fiddling with something in his hands. Heavy breaths caught his attention and he looked up to see Isabelle doubled over, panting and holding her side. "You came!" he shouted as he pushed himself off the boat.

Trying not to look like a dishevelled mess, Isabelle stood tall while still squeezing the pain in her ribs. "You waited," she replied through laboured breaths.

Jon smiled as he walked to the sandy edge she stood upon. "For you, I would've waited all day."

"It's a row boat," Isabelle pointed out in surprise.

"You were expecting the Barrington?" he laughed.

"No, but after learning of your love for sailing yesterday I suppose I was expecting a mast and sail at the very least."

"I built this boat with my father." Jon looked to the simple wooden vessel. "He used to say, sailboats build character but row boats build strength."

Looking back at Isabelle, Jon extended his arm to help her down the sandy dune, causing her to smile at the coincidence as this was indeed the second time today she had watched him offer his hand.

Accepting his help, Isabelle stepped off the loose sandy edge, but with her legs weak from her unexpected run through the forest, she quickly lost her footing and slid down the dune right into him!

Catching her slender frame easily, Jon lowered her safely to the ground. "See," he smiled at the cradled woman in his grasp, "strong arms."

Slightly embarrassed of her own clumsiness, Isabelle grinned as she gently pushed herself out of his embrace.

"Does this mean you'll be joining me today?" he asked with a hopeful smile.

"I suppose I have a little time to spend on Horseshoe Island."

"Horseshoe? I didn't know it had a name."

"It doesn't. Mr. Tilly called it that," she explained as they walked towards the boat. "He would row us out there when I was a child and we'd spend all afternoon exploring. It's been quite some time since I've been back there, but the sky is clear today and I trust you to be a skilled captain of your own vessel."

Jon flashed a reassuring smile. "I'll bring you back here whenever it pleases you." He reached in his boat and retrieved a small trinket. "I made this for you while I waited — I thought you may like it."

He handed her a small wooden carving. "If not, you may toss it in the sea. Just please do it when I'm not looking."

Isabelle glanced down at the palm-sized carving to discover Jon had cleverly whittled a piece of sun-bleached driftwood into a miniature white stallion, complete with a flowing mane and tail.

"It's so thoughtful," she replied with a smile. "Thank you, Jon."

Touched by her sincerity, he grinned. "Tuck it somewhere safe and let's get you aboard."

Chapter 8

SEA AND SAND

Isabelle never expected to feel so calm in such a little boat. Seated on the stern bench, her body felt surprisingly at ease. She peered over the water to the distant shores of Horseshoe Island, reminiscing about her visits as a child and the days when her life felt much simpler.

Stroking rhythmically along the coast, Jon watched a delicate smile slide to Isabelle's cheeks as she gazed into the distance, and felt grateful for whatever blissful memory was now making him tingle as well.

Astonished to have whisked away this untouchable woman, Jon's belly was uncharacteristically whirling. "I must admit, I've never had a woman of such pedigree in this boat before."

When Isabelle glanced at him, her childlike smile suddenly appeared sly. "Have you had many women in your boat, Jon?"

His answer was short. "Not this boat."

With a slight lift in her brow, Isabelle smirked. "Have you had many boats?"

Unsure whether the curiosity in her voice was playful or concealing jealousy, Jon chuckled. "No, she's my one and only. I'm more loyal than you might think."

Isabelle's sceptical eyes glanced back over the water only to discover Jon's strong arms had moved them along the coast much faster than Mr. Tilly's ever did. A twinge tightened her chest when she realized they were quickly approaching the fast current.

"I'll cast a line here before we cross," Jon said, interrupting Isabelle's spiralling thoughts. "I caught my supper here last time. I thought I'd try my luck again."

Bobbing safely in the calm water, Jon let go of the oars then reached into his sack. He pulled out a metal pail, a fishing line with a hook at one end and a tiny bell knotted near the other, and a small rectangular tin filled with slithering worms.

After shoving the rusty hook through an unsuspecting bait, he cleaned his hands, filled the pail with seawater and nestled it safely in the hull.

Jon gathered up the fishing line then pushed himself off the wooden thwart. "Pardon, my lady," he said before leaning over Isabelle, catching her gaze as he slowly brushed past her face.

Isabelle leaned aside to give him the space he needed but the boat was quite small and his firm body still pressed gently against hers as he tied the line to the stern.

If he were any other man, Isabelle would've likely made a huge fuss and moved entirely out of his touch, but for some reason she felt completely comfortable against Jon's strapping body and was left wondering if he'd notice that she was blushing.

"There we are," he said as he retook his seat and gripped the oars again.

"Do you often eat fish?" Isabelle asked, hoping to distract herself from the fact that Jon had started rowing them directly towards the current.

"Aye, Mr. Tilly may have taught you how to live off the land, but Tom and I have learned to live off the sea."

"Is Thomas your brother?"

"In all ways but by blood. His parents died when he was young then he lived with an old miser who gave him nothing but scraps from the table. We'd walk past him on mum's way to work. Sometimes we'd bring him food and clothing but as we got older..." a sly grin appeared, "we'd find ourselves in heaps of trouble together." Jon chuckled as though recalling some rambunctious memory. "We've been through a lot."

"Is he your oldest friend?"

"Aye, and when we boarded the Barrington a couple years back, we found the rest of our brothers. We've braved storms together, fought off pirates, visited more countries than even the King himself." His smile left a hint of pride in his eye. "I'd give my life for Tom...or any one of those men."

"Well, you may get your chance once your ship is called," Isabelle casually reminded him.

"I don't expect that to be any time soon. The Barrington's refit has yet to begin. They're using her as a training vessel for now."

Isabelle tried to pay attention to his words but when she glanced over Jon's shoulder and realized how quickly they were drifting, panic began to rise in her throat.

Not now, she silently told herself.

Just breathe.

Jon pulled his oars a few more times before he noticed Isabelle trying to steady herself. "Are you alright?" he asked softly.

Isabelle nodded as she slowly exhaled. "I told you, I don't like the open water," she replied before shutting her eyes.

Even though she had crossed this channel a number of times as a child, her nerves seemed to have worsened as she grew older and Isabelle suddenly found herself feeling quite vulnerable in this tiny creaking old boat.

Her heart started racing. She swore she could feel the wood splitting apart beneath her!

Sensing her fear, Jon glanced over his shoulder and pulled harder through the fast water. "We're almost there," he offered just as the tiny copper bell started ringing in the stern.

The high-pitched jingling startled Isabelle enough to shake the anxious state from her body.

Knowing Jon couldn't possibly drop the oars in this current, she turned in her seat and started pulling the line in.

"Don't bother, Izzy. If we lose it, we'll catch another."

But Isabelle was desperate to take her mind off her nerves and continued reeling. She trolled the line alongside the boat, turned back around on her seat, yanked the flailing fish into the hull and dropped it at Jon's feet.

"Well done!" he exclaimed in disbelief as their new stow away flapped at his heels.

But Isabelle wasn't finished just yet — she held the line up, slid her hand over the fish, making sure to press down the fins and gills, then took a gentle hold of the creature.

After carefully removing the hook, she placed the fish in the pail then leaned over the boat to clean her hands in the water that had finally begun to calm once again.

Jon was gobsmacked. Did a noblewoman just clear his line without a single squirm or squeal?

Noticing his ruffled brow, Isabelle asked playfully, "Is something the matter?"

"Will you ever cease to surprise me?" he answered with a smirk.

A prideful grin slipped to Isabelle's lips while she dried her hands on the hem of her cotton skirt.

Jon glanced over his shoulders as the small rowboat entered the shallows. "There's a beautiful beach 'round this point here. Once we get ashore, I'll find us some firewood before it gets dark. Are you well to stay for the sunset?"

"That sounds lovely," she replied as they entered the crest of Horseshoe's tranquil beach.

Jon pulled his boat ashore, helped Isabelle safely to the ground, then they set out to explore the marshy island together.

Struck by the island's palpable nostalgia, nearly every one of Isabelle's steps sparked another forgotten memory. She showed Jon the jagged rocks that twisted her ankle when she was ten, and the spot where Mr. Tilly taught her how to catch frogs, and the hollowed log where she once spotted the biggest spider she'd ever seen!

Trailing at Isabelle's heels, Jon revelled in her juvenile excitement. He was starting to see who she really was when free from prying eyes and his casual enchantment was beginning to flow precariously into forbidden waters.

"Come on," he said with a smile as he watched her skip jovially across some rocks, "we've got plenty of dry wood. Let's head back and I'll get that fire started."

Chapter 9

BURIED EMBERS

They returned to the beach to find it basking in the saffron glow of a sun slowly being stolen by the earth. Though Isabelle shared the sand with someone who could ruin her life with the simple utterance of her name, she felt weightless, almost childlike as she whirled around in the last golden rays.

She pointed to a spot just a stone's throw from the shoreline. "And this is where we would have our fire and watch the sunset."

"It's perfect," Jon announced, elated to drop their collection of dry wood. "I'll start us a fire so we can eat."

He walked to his boat to retrieve the fish and returned to find Isabelle digging in the sand with a piece of driftwood. "May I ask what you're doing?"

She didn't stop or look up. "We're building a fire, are we not? We'll need a pit to bury it when we're finished."

Jon leaned down to take the piece of wood from her hands. "*I* will build us a fire Lady Isab...there's no need for you to get dirty."

"I'm quite well, thank you," she snipped, moving the wood just out of his grasp. "Clothes can be cleaned, and so can I."

"As you wish." Jon decided to leave her to it and went to clean the fish at the shoreline.

While filleting their catch, he caught Isabelle smiling to herself as she placed each stick with precision and wondered what sorry state he'd find the pit in when he returned.

"Alright then," Isabelle brushed her hands together as Jon came walking back. "Do you happen to have a flint somewhere in that sack?"

Laughing in surprise, Jon knelt down next to her. "I didn't realize you were going to light it too." He placed the fillets on a flat rock while casually inspecting the pit. To his surprise, he was impressed with her fire lay. It looked worthy of a strike without altering a single twig.

He pulled a flint from his bag and handed it to Isabelle who set her tinder ablaze with a single strike. He watched her move the flame to different parts of the pit with a focus on her face that surely would've made Mr. Tilly proud.

As the flames grew taller, a satisfied smile slowly parted Isabelle's lips but she never looked to Jon for gratification — she kept her gaze locked on her growing fire as though memories of her childhood lingered amongst the flames.

"A noblewoman who catches fish and starts her own fires. You wouldn't be lying to me about who you are now would you, *Lady Isabelle?*"

Unable to tell if he was serious, Isabelle looked up to read his face and was suddenly struck by how handsome he looked in the glow of her fire. "What on earth would I have to lie about, Jon *of the Sea?*"

Her facetious tone made him laugh. "I've known quite of few noble ladies in my day and none of them have known how to cook a meal let alone build a fire." His laughter made Isabelle beam with a tremendous sense of accomplishment. "Are you sure you're not a servant of the manor? A daughter of the Tilly's perhaps?"

"If only." Isabelle looked hopelessly back to the fire, forever wishing the Tillys were her real parents instead of the self-centered, emotionally absent pair she had become such a burden to.

"Well, I hope you're hungry because I'm faring to make us the tastiest bit of fish you'll ever eat."

Isabelle looked at the fillets just as Jon swatted a fly off. "Oh, thank you but I've never had much of a palette for flesh. Mr. Tilly always ate whatever we caught. I brought some things from home. Please do enjoy it all yourself."

"But you've never had fish the way I make it." Jon reached into his bag again and pulled out an ornately carved rosewood box. He slid the lid off to reveal smaller compartments of brightly coloured spices. "Take a smell," he said, holding it out to her, "but don't get too close, you don't want this in your nose."

Isabelle leaned in to sniff the earthy spice mixture. "Oh my word!" she exclaimed at its pungency before covering her nose with her wrist.

"You don't like it? It's from India. A woman there made it special for me."

"One of your port women?" Isabelle asked playfully as she reached into her satchel.

"No, a woman from a market there. She took a liking to me."

"Sounds like many women have taken a liking to you," she said to jab him a bit, or perhaps to cover up her fear that she too was becoming one of them.

"It's much easier to move through life if people like you." Jon sprinkled a few different spices over his fish then placed them in the pit to cook.

"So, tell me," Isabelle said as she cracked into her walnuts, "if you do make it out of this war, what is it you plan to do afterwards?"

"Tom and I have talked about sailing to the New Americas. We've seen so much of this side of the world. We want to head some place new. We heard the Duke of York has captured New Netherland. Perhaps we'll start there."

"New Netherland?" Isabelle asked, surprised she was about to be schooled by a lowly seaman.

"The Dutch colony on the east coast — perhaps the Duke will rename it New Gillingham now."

"The King's brother seems determined to conquer the entire world," Isabelle sneered, disgusted by the young Duke's endless tyranny. "He would never name one of his conquests after this small town. He'll likely name it after himself."

"New James?" Jon asked with a smirk.

"Or New York perhaps. The pride of a man laying siege will leave trails of himself everywhere."

"Well, thanks to the Duke and his fleet, England now has another safe port on the other side of the world."

"And that is lovely for someone like yourself, but it's of little use to those of us who prefer horseback."

Jon leaned down to retrieve his hot dinner from the pit. "Do you know I've never even ridden a horse."

"How is that possible?"

"We were poor when I was young, our feet carried us everywhere. The rest of my life has been spent at sea — any animals on board were never my duty. I had no reason to learn I suppose." Jon shoved a bite of hot fish in his mouth. "Are you sure you don't want some?"

"I'm well, thank you," Isabelle politely replied. "You really should learn to ride one day, Jon. You say you've seen this side of the world when really it seems you haven't been beyond the shore. A horse could help you discover places you've never been without having to sail to the other side of the world for it."

Jon let out a small laugh. "I suppose you're right," he said before popping another morsel in his mouth.

As the last bit of crimson sun dipped beneath the earth, Isabelle realised she'd spent most of the afternoon going on about herself and hoped to learn a little more about her unusual companion. Leaning towards him, she threw the last of her walnut shells in the fire. "Are you up for a game, sailor?"

"I'm not ordinarily fond of games," he said dryly before stretching out in the warmth of the fire.

"Well, this is just something silly. It's called two truths and a lie. Have you heard of it?"

He shook his head.

"We'll each tell three stories about ourselves, two of them will be truthful and one, a lie. Then the other person has to guess which story is dishonest."

"I've never looked into a woman's eyes and lied to her before. I fear I won't be much good at this game." He raised an inquisitive eyebrow. "Are you a good liar?"

"I suppose I am when I need to be."

"You don't feel it's better to always tell the truth? Isn't that what they teach you in church?"

"One might beg to ask what makes a lie an evil thing." A gust of wind swept a lock of Isabelle's hair across her face. "Some lies protect the truth," she answered, tucking the strand behind her ear.

"And why would the truth need protecting?"

Flames flickered in Isabelle's amber eyes. "Because the truth is delicate...its life changing. It can be both damaging and beautiful. Perhaps not everyone is ready for, or...worthy of a moment like that." She glanced back to Jon. "I try not to be deceptive with my words but simply asking me a question is not necessarily a worthy cause to hear my truth."

Noticing the assured stillness in her eyes, Jon was grateful for her honesty. "Well then, since you're a beloved player of the game of dishonesty, you go first."

"Alright, let's see." Isabelle twirled a piece of hair in her fingers. "I was born in France, in the court of Louis XIV. My father had arrived with the other royalists taking refuge during Cromwell's war. He met my mother who was a courtier there and I came along shortly afterwards."

"You're French!?" Jon shouted in surprise.

"Perhaps — or perhaps not," she casually replied.

Jon was suddenly intrigued. Engaging in her game of lies meant she would also be revealing some of her truth as well.

"Secondly," Isabelle drew a breath, "I was not always an only child. I had a younger brother who perished at sea when we were children."

When Isabelle's gaze dropped to her lap, Jon finally understood the root of her upset in the open water. Losing a loved one to the sea was something he was quite familiar with. He realized then, they were connected by the waves in a way he never would have imagined.

Isabelle took a cleansing breath. "And lastly…my first kiss was with the Dauphin of France when I was just four years old." She watched a modest smile inch across Jon's face. "Now you choose which one is a lie."

"If you truly were born in the French palace, I suppose you may have kissed the Dauphin," Jon said with a jealous smile, one that quickly faded when he realised what his other choice was. "I'm sorry to hear about your brother," he offered sincerely. "How old was he?"

"Two years old." Isabelle sighed as her gaze dropped to her lap. "We were travelling aboard the HMS London when a storm blew in. Everyone was ordered below deck, but I…I wanted to dance in the rain."

She looked to Jon with guilt in her eyes. "I snuck away and my brother followed. I remember laughing with him as the ship tossed us about in the waves. When our governess finally found us — she was furious. She nearly had my brother in her grip…when the ship listed. A wave thrashed aboard and washed us all off our feet. I was caught by the rail but my brother was so little…he slipped right through the posts," she whimpered. "By the time the crew turned the ship…he was gone."

She turned to the crackling flames. "I'll never forget the sound of my father's voice when he yelled at the crew to come about. My mother was at the rail, wailing over the sea." Isabelle pulled her legs to her chest. "She was never the same after that day."

In the glow of the fire, Jon watched tiny golden pools come to rest upon Isabelle's lashes.

He shook his head. "I'm surprised your father didn't have that governess thrown overboard for letting you out in swells like that."

Isabelle didn't look up from the flames. "He did," she said dryly, "and I was sent here to live with my grandparents."

"You say this happened aboard the London?"

Hypnotized by the fire, Isabelle silently nodded.

"That was my father's favourite ship. She moored in Jersey when I was quite young. I don't remember it but my father talked about her for years. He would always say 'Everyone was so distracted by her shiny brass guns, they missed the beauty of her sails.' When I heard she was being refit in this dockyard I went to find her, and when I stood there and looked upon her, it felt as though my father was standing right there next to me."

Stoically, Isabelle spoke only to the flames. "Yes well…the London holds many ghosts."

"He told me the London was carrying Royalists to France when she stopped in Jersey. Was your father aboard it then?"

"Perhaps," Isabelle replied. "He fought loyally for the King but left with the others who managed to escape England with their heads still attached."

Finally breaking her fiery trance, Isabelle turned to look upon his face. "Alright, it's your turn now."

Sitting up to summon his creative juices, Jon rubbed his hands together then began his first tale. "We were new mates aboard a ship a few years back when a real sod on the crew started hazing Tom. They were about to keel him, but I saw the fear in Tom's eyes. I fought the bastard and untied him. I thought they'd throw us both overboard in the middle of sea but the captain had half a heart and dropped us at a port instead."

"Mmmhmm," Isabelle hummed without giving away her suspicions. "Next."

Jon smirked and looked back to the fire. "Two days before Arlington showed up, I was offered a position as a second mate aboard a fluyt heading to the New Americas. It was a good purse. I thought on it for a full day, but I couldn't leave Tom behind, nor my mates. The thought of sailing away from them...it crushed me."

When the sullen sailor looked over, Isabelle read his honest eyes easily. "You're right Jon — you're not very good at this game," she said with a teasing smile. "Do you have any stories of your life in Jersey?"

Crossing his legs, Jon let his elbows rest upon his knees. Grateful for her heartbreaking honesty tonight, he felt he owed her a dark truth of his own. "Do you remember me telling you of the man my mother remarried?"

Isabelle nodded. Jon's description of the bulging-eyed toad man would haunt her thoughts forever.

"Well, he had this...consuming obsession with fire. He'd come home late at night, reeking of ale then fire his tools red hot. He loved the smell of burning flesh...but not his own. He'd chase after my mother, but I'd do anything I could to get him to come for me instead...and he did."

Jon's shameful gaze looked to the innocent woman sitting next to him. "My body is covered in scars."

In a silent state of disbelief, Isabelle woefully stared back at him. She and her father had a fiery relationship of their own but he had never laid a hand on her — ever.

Jon planned to end his dark tale there but the truth he'd buried seven years ago was suddenly clawing its way out. He turned his gaze back to the flames.

"One night, Tom and I were walking home, it was nearly dawn. We'd had a fair bit to drink and were right pissed," he said with the slightest laugh. "I waved him off and went inside. The fire was still burning, and then I saw him...in the shadows...hunched over the ground, breathing like some wild beast. The air in the room was thick...the smell was so familiar."

Jon's jaw clenched. "When I walked over...I saw my mother on the floor." His voice cracked as sorrow tightened itself around his throat. "He'd held her down in the coals — she couldn't get away on her own."

Jon's words trembled from his lungs. "She was dead...she was still burning."

Isabelle looked away when Jon became overwhelmed. She had never seen a man shed a tear in her presence and her heart broke for him.

"I wailed so loudly, Tom said he heard me from down the street. I pulled her from the fire while he just sat there...glaring at me. The evil that filled that room — it took me. I leapt and drove my fists through him over and over. I couldn't stop. I didn't hear Tom come in, but he was there when I grabbed the hot iron poker from the fire...and thrust it clean through that bastard." Jon's words grinded through his teeth. "I wanted him to feel every last bit of pain he'd ever inflicted on her."

A branch cracked in the fire, breaking Jon's hell-bound trance just enough for him to take a breath. "Flames were spreading through the house when Tom finally dragged me out of there. We ran to the docks, got in my boat, and haven't been back to Jersey since."

Isabelle watched a tear fall to Jon's navy pants when he dropped his gaze. She suddenly felt completely ashamed of herself. She had spent so much of their time together complaining about being told what to do, and how to act — she'd even complained about wearing silk for God's sake — but her litany of problems seemed so trivial now that she knew exactly what Jon had traded for his admirable life of freedom.

Lost in his sorrow, Isabelle asked gently, "May I see them?"

He looked up in confusion. "See what?"

She answered softly. "Your scars."

Jon's veins surged with all the guilt and anger he'd buried years ago, but Isabelle's eyes — those innocently wild tawny eyes glinting back at him offered a tiny glimpse of solace from his plaguing nightmare.

His hands trembled as he slowly pulled his white cotton shirt from his waistband. He lifted it off with shallow breaths, allowing Isabelle to look upon his graveyard of mutilated childhood memories.

Entranced by zagging lines and mounds of scarred skin, Isabelle leaned closer. It pained her to think that each scar likely represented its own horrific memory stored deep within Jon's flesh.

Her fingers floated to his chest and gently skimmed the longest scar running straight across his heart.

Feeling everything and nothing at all, Jon didn't take his eyes off her. He wondered what she must be thinking — the girl with the impossibly perfect life, running her fingers over the remnants of evil that lives within the hearts of all men.

The tiny hairs on Isabelle's arm stood straight up as Jon's rippled flesh passed beneath her fingertips. She could feel the pain of every lashing he'd ever taken locked tightly away yet still quivering just beneath his skin. The fact that he still smiled so fully at her with all this pain hidden beneath a layer of cotton revealed a strength about him that suddenly captivated her.

"I'm sorry you had to feel this," she whimpered before looking up to meet his eyes.

"Every scar on my body was one less on hers."

Jon wore his truth like a badge of honour, but seeing the weight of his darkest secret reflected in Isabelle's eyes was becoming too much for him to bear. "Perhaps we should be getting on," he said abruptly before leaning away to pull his shirt back on.

Isabelle hoped her forwardness hadn't caused his upset. "I'm so sorry, Jon. I didn't mean to—"

"No," he replied calmly. "This is something I carry with me from long ago. It's been quite awhile since I've spoken about that night, that's all."

Isabelle found the truth in his broken eyes and nodded silently.

"Let's get you home before we lose the twilight," he said with a soft smile.

Jon lit the lantern hanging from the bow, buried their fire then pushed his boat into the blackened sea.

With everyone fast asleep after a long restful Sunday and no moon in the sky, the world was quickly fading to darkness as they made their way back to the grassy pier.

Jon rowed them aground in the same place they'd departed from, but the air felt different now. It was heavy, and raw.

82

"Are you sure you're alright to walk through these woods alone?" he asked while helping Isabelle onto the sand.

"There's nothing to fear, I know these woods better than anywhere else on this earth," she said while staring into his ocean eyes. "Thank you for today, Jon. I needed that more than I knew." Isabelle shrunk slightly as the reality of her life came flooding back. "And please don't speak of me to anyone. I'm not asking you to lie but perhaps you could...protect my truth?" she asked lightly before glancing to the sand.

Not wanting to leave her in such a vulnerable state, Jon gently lifted her chin. "You have my word."

Years of rules and restrictions whirled through Isabelle's mind as she gazed up at him. When Jon slid his hand into her hair and leaned in, she closed her eyes. She was ready to feel his lips against hers...but her eager mouth was left empty when Jon softly kissed her cheek.

With her eyes still closed, Isabelle tenderly grasped his wrist, and felt his fingers tighten beneath her touch.

Struggling to contain himself, Jon was becoming more aroused than he should ever be in her presence, but he understood his position in her life and was not about to compromise her integrity for his own selfish desires.

He summoned his willpower in one breath and slowly slid out of her embrace. "Have a wonderful rest my Lady, and perhaps if luck is in my favour, I'll see you again." Slipping away with a smile, he pushed his boat into the water and hopped in.

"Travel well, Jon of the Sea."

Taking advantage of the moonless night, Isabelle stayed hidden within the dune's shadow until the warm glow of Jon's lantern slowly faded away.

Chapter 10

DANCING ON MARBLE

The heavy fog that had settled upon the dockyard overnight was just beginning to lift as Jon came above board. Walking to the bow in the morning twilight, he kept his eyes on the eastern horizon. It was his favourite time of day — the last moments of darkness.

Ready at his post, Jon awaited Captain's orders as he glanced around the marketplace that was gradually beginning to stir. Shop owners swept their thresholds, and carpenters gathered tools. Three ships off the Barrington's bow were being loaded with provisions by men who had awoken this morning to find their ships had been deemed fit for war and their time for departure had come.

Jon watched the soldiers bid farewell to their families before boarding their ships with brave faces and swords at their sides. As the men climbed the gangplank in single file, Jon wondered if their feet would ever touch dry land again.

Looking to the country road he'd accompanied Isabelle down just days before, Jon pictured her wrapped safely in her satin sheets, completely unaware of the men who'd just left to fight for the protection of her blissful innocence.

A familiar urge to leap from the ship began to swell inside. He wanted to run down that dirt road and wrap himself with her in swirls of satin. He'd kiss her passionately while her long golden hair tickled his—

"CAST OFF!"

Captain's orders jolted Jon back to his place on the bow.

Echoing the order to his mates, Jon cast his line and the Barrington began her journey down the Medway just as the first few rays of sunlight pierced the sleepy horizon.

.   .   .   .

The delicate china rattling on Milly's silver tray sent an effervescent chime through the hall. She had selected Isabelle's favourite tea set for breakfast this morning; yellow primrose blossoms hand-painted like tiny polka dots on crisp white bone china.

The old woman woke Isabelle the same way each morning. She would step lightly through the darkened bedroom, open the floor length curtains slowly, making sure to rouse her gently, then serve Isabelle a light breakfast before getting her ready for the day.

But the loyal housekeeper found an odd sight when she pushed the door open this morning — Isabelle's room was already filled with sunlight.

Startled by a sight never seen, Milly placed the breakfast tray on the side table then inspected Isabelle's bed.

Her sheets were strewn but she was nowhere to be found.

Milly looked up to find the balcony doors wide open with the drapery billowing into the room, but the fresh air did little to quell the pit of terror growing in her stomach — Isabelle never slept with the doors open.

She rushed to the opened doors and stepped onto the balcony where she spotted Isabelle standing safely at the railing peering over the sea with her floral silk robe ruffling lightly in the breeze.

"My word, child, you nearly stopped my heart!"

Lost in a daydream, Isabelle startled at the sound of Milly's voice. She turned to see the woman hurrying across the balcony in a bit of a tizzy.

"I thought you'd disappeared during the night! Why on earth are you out here?"

Still half-asleep, Isabelle looked back to the sea. "I thought I'd watch the ships sail past this morning."

Milly's confusion scrunched her brow. "Are you ill?" she asked, placing her hand on Isabelle's cheek to check for fever.

Isabelle smiled and raised her hand to Milly's wrist just as she did with Jon the night before. "Do not fret. I have never been happier."

Milly took the young woman by the hand and smiled. "Come then, let's get you dressed. Your first appointment will arrive shortly. We've no time to waste."

Isabelle's tight schedule began with needlepoint in the conservatory followed by tea at Countess Huntingdon's estate in the afternoon. She then spent the remainder of her week being shuttled from one side of town to the other, meeting every appointment dressed to absolute perfection and handling herself immaculately — even during a society luncheon at the Wellington Estate where guests prodded about her engagement to William while other women at the table covered their mouths and sneered.

Steady breaths, she told herself.

With no time set aside for casual visits to the square, Isabelle hadn't seen Jon all week yet fantasies of him followed her everywhere. The curiosity nagging her heart had left her splintered, as though a small piece of herself was bobbing somewhere in the North Sea while the rest of her sat here, in the back of the carriage, en route to yet another required appointment.

Frustrated by her fractured sensibility, Isabelle tried to convince herself that her afternoon with Jon was meant to be nothing more than a blissful memory for her heart to draw upon once she found herself married to a controlling womanizer.

Surrendering her fantasy, Isabelle's breath came a little easier just as Mr. Graham drove the coach through the ornate silver gates of the infamous Davenport Manor.

Surrounded by acres of perfectly mowed fields, the manicured evergreens lining the lengthy driveway were the only trees in sight. In Davenport's insatiable quest for elaborate ostentation, he had built a gargantuan white marble manor that looked more like a palace than a home. No less than thirty servants could be found within the household at any given time; footmen, butlers, chambermaids and kitchen staff worked tirelessly to ensure the manor, and those within its walls, were kept in a constant state of opulence.

Isabelle took a deep breath and straightened her posture just as one of the many Davenport carriage-hands opened her door.

A butler escorted her up the white scalloped staircase then into the palatial ballroom where Isabelle thanked him and left him at the door.

Her heels clicked along the marble as she made her way towards eleven of Victoria's friends and sisters excitedly huddled around their new dance instructor.

Monsieur Bouffie was a loud flamboyant overweight Frenchman well known for living on the leading edge of fashion and influence. Gold floral appliqués covered his knee-length white overcoat, and his white periwig, piled high with impeccable curls, framed his heavily powdered face perfectly.

His gold staff echoed off the marble floor when he tapped it to gather the girls' attention. "Ladies!" he announced in a thick French accent. "Monsieur Davenport has requested a choreographed piece for Victoria's birthday masquerade at summer's end." He turned to Victoria. "If I understand correctly, your theme is From the Sea?"

Those three words stole Isabelle's breath and sent her mind whirling again. Shaking Jon's face from her thoughts, she tried to stay focused on the spirited man in front of her.

"That leaves me eight weeks to turn you into beautiful creatures from the sea." He rapped his staff again. "Suivez-moi!"

Bouffie led the young women to the center of the ballroom. "My dear friend, Monsieur Lully, has composed a beautiful piece of music." He pointed to the youngest Davenport. "Victoria! You will be a heartbroken girl stricken with grief after your lover's death at sea." Bouffie swirled around as he animated his story. "Stones in hand, you will throw yourself into the water in a desperate attempt to end your life and return to your lover."

Victoria exchanged a look of confusion with Isabelle.

"But the sea witch," he twirled around and pointed to Anne, "who has watched you for years and grown jealous of your youthful beauty, will send her slithering army to capture you and steal your virtuous spirit."

He sashayed towards his assistant. "However, before she steals your last breath, a swarm of mermaids will come to your rescue!" He plunged his hand into a bag of costume fabric.

Grabbing a spool of silver taffeta by the frays, he whirled around the girls, draping them in iridescence. "They will wrap you in a magical pearl and carry you back to the surface where you will emerge as a stunning Princess of the Sea!"

Still holding the shimmering fabric, Bouffie twirled into the center of the group, spread his arms to the side and bowed deeply.

"That story makes no sense at all," Anne quipped, brushing the taffeta from her shoulders.

Bouffie locked his eyes on her as he rose.

Clicking his heels together, he marched over to address her. "Though a certain level of intellect is certainly required for one to comprehend why they chose this broken girl for their princess, I suspect only an uncultured swine would have difficulty with the interpretation, *ma chérie.*" He tapped his staff once then turned his back on her.

Bouffie had a reputation for being cutthroat with his words, and it seems Anne may have just met her match.

The next few hours passed quickly to the monotonous rapping of Bouffie's staff. Isabelle's legs lagged in lethargy when she finally heard the jingle of a small bell, signalling the end of their first lesson.

While most of the young women left to fulfill the remainder of their appointments, Victoria, Anne and Elizabeth made their way to the Davenport's towering solarium for tea and sandwiches served on the manor's finest china.

When Isabelle returned from the powder room, she joined her friends at the circular table.

"I'm glad you're finally here," Anne said as Isabelle took her seat next to Beth. "Perhaps you can set her straight."

"I'm quite well, thank you," Beth piped up. "Besides," she turned to Isabelle, "you of all people should understand that true love can exist between different social classes."

Beth's comment caught Isabelle off-guard. "Why would you presume I would know anything about that?" she asked, slightly fearful she was about to be called out for her secret island tryst with Jon.

"Because of your book!" Beth replied.

"Oh…yes of course," Isabelle said sheepishly.

"A royalist and a parliamentarian. Their love may not be permitted but it would still be love," Beth pointed out.

"Forgive me," Isabelle shook her head in confusion, "what are we talking about?"

"Seems our Beth here has fallen in love with a sailor." Anne snickered then sipped her tea.

"Thomas?" Isabelle asked, remembering the tales of Jon's oldest friend.

"Yes! We've spent every evening together. You have to help me convince my mother to let me marry him."

"Marry him?" Isabelle blurted out, shocking everyone at the table. "Have you gone mad? You barely know him! Are you really going to throw your entire future away for some wayward sailor? Your mother would lose her wits if she heard you speak this way!" Isabelle shouted, likely projecting her own personal frustrations more than her friends would ever know.

The young ladies stared silently back at Isabelle, trying to figure out what exactly had roused the usually poised young lady this afternoon.

"She's right Beth," Victoria said. "Your mother would never allow it. She wants a better life for you than anything a merchant sailor could offer."

Isabelle looked down at her lap, disheartened by a truth that had just struck her as well.

"Where will you live?" Victoria jeered. "In his bunk on the Barrington?" Both she and Anne exploded in boisterous laughter.

But Isabelle didn't join in their amusement. She looked over at Beth with a woeful heart, understanding exactly what her friend was feeling. Even though she and Jon had only spent a small amount of time together, he had consumed her thoughts all week and she too found herself falling victim to an impossible love.

"I don't need fancy things," Beth said lightly.

"Says the girl who will be taken home in a satin lined carriage," Anne laughed.

Isabelle placed her hand on Beth's arm. "You do need to stop these thoughts, Beth. This is dangerous ground for your heart to tread."

Beth ignored Isabelle's plea. "He said they will be attending the Solstice Festival tomorrow. Perhaps you could speak with him then? You will see for yourself how gentlemanly he is." Beth searched her friends' eyes for any sense of approval but found none.

"Pardon the interruption." The Davenport's butler looked exceptionally tall standing next to the man he'd just escorted into the room. "Mistress Anne, you have a visitor."

Anne looked over to find a short wiry character with pluming white ruffles sprouting from the collar of his fancy blue overcoat. "Ah, Sir

Barkley, I was wondering when you would turn up." She rose from her chair and accepted his welcoming embrace.

"I wanted to make sure the lovely Davenport ladies were quite alright," he announced, pulling her close.

Towering over him, Anne wrapped one arm around his shoulders then placed her other hand on his chest. "Of course we're alright. Why wouldn't we be?"

"Reports in London say the plague is spreading beyond pauper streets. Some believe servants have brought it into their master's homes, others are saying it's some type of warfare from the Dutch."

"Are we blaming everything on the Dutch now?" Isabelle interrupted, disgusted by the propagandist rumours.

"I've not hired any servants from London this summer," Barkley continued. "I have filled my household entirely with help from Gillingham and cancelled all visitors coming from the city. One can never be too careful."

"You sound quite precautious," Anne coyly replied. "Our father is accompanied by his household from London each weekend and we are all well here. There's nothing to fear." She pushed her exposed cleavage into him. "I'll protect you."

"I think we'd fair better if I protected you, Mistress Anne." Barkley ran his hand down her décolletage and over her breasts. "We wouldn't want this delicate skin turning black now would we?" he said with an obvious squeeze of her flesh.

Isabelle turned away in disgust. How could a proper woman allow herself to be mauled in front of half her household and a table of guests?

Completely appalled, she rose from her seat. "If you'll please excuse me, I believe it's time for me to leave."

Chapter 11

SOLSTICE AND SIN

Tiny rocks clinked against the carriage as Mr. Graham rolled along the dirt road. He despised this road. Every plink was another spot for him to polish away later, but Isabelle had specifically requested that he take the coastal road to the Solstice Festival this evening and he was obliged to obey.

He'd just rounded the corner and started along the main dock when he heard Isabelle shout from within the carriage.

"This is fine here!"

Confused, he halted the horses, climbed down from his seat and opened her door. "The festival is not at the square, my Lady. It is being held in Gander's Field."

Holding the hem of her dusty-rose gown, Isabelle squished the puffy skirt and full petticoat through the door and saw herself safely to the ground without taking his hand. "Yes, I am aware," she said, running her hands down her dress to smooth it out. "I am meeting a friend here first. Please carry on without me."

Mr. Graham bowed his head. "Yes, my Lady." He climbed back up to his seat then obediently rolled away.

Isabelle kept her eyes glued to the back of the carriage as she walked towards the square, but the moment it disappeared down the hill, she turned on her heels and walked back towards the dock.

Soldiers aboard the Barrington were disembarking while the crew hustled to unload crates and artillery, lower the sails and secure their ship for the evening.

With everyone merrily distracted down at the festival, Isabelle searched the ship for Jon but soon realized she may look like one of those port women he spoke so tastelessly of and decided it might be best to continue to the festival before anyone noticed her.

Isabelle walked away deflated. She'd thought about Jon every day that week and although she knew they could never be together she—

"Izzy!" A loud voice boomed from behind her.

Isabelle turned around to find Jon leaning over the stern railing.

"It is you!" he shouted. "I barely recognized you in that poofy dress," he said with a laugh, knowing how much she detested bouffant gowns. "Are you off to the festival already?" he asked as he watched her slowly saunter back to the ship.

"I am," she hollered. "Will you and your crew be joining us?"

"Our week was long, we're knackered...but knowing you'll be there may change my mind," he added with a grin.

A cheeky smile crept upon Isabelle's face but she placed her hands on her hips and shook her head, letting him know she wasn't falling for his charming advances quite as easily as his other portside conquests.

Jon threw his head back with a laugh. "Stay there a moment, I'll come down."

Still smiling, Isabelle watched him pick up a crate and start making his way off the ship.

"Ah, Lady Isabelle," a man cooed from behind her.

Isabelle's shoulders tightened the moment she heard his voice.

A shudder trembled through her body as she turned to find her future husband walking towards her in his knee-length red overcoat with black satin edging. His curly black periwig and mahogany staff made him look much older than his twenty-two years.

"My Lady, was that sailor yelling at you as though you were some vagrant street hound?"

Choosing to protect her truth, Isabelle tried to distract him. "What brings you to the square this evening, William?"

"We were on our way to the festival," he motioned to a group of friends he'd left at the edge of the square, "but it seems the Solstice is blowing the winds of luck in your direction my dear. We will be the talk of the night when you arrive with me," he said, offering his arm.

"Thank you," Isabelle shifted to spy Jon out of the corner of her eye, "but I was just about to meet a friend. Please do go on without me. I will see you there — I'm quite sure." Her words held more disdain than she'd hoped to reveal.

"Who are you meeting?" William asked, completely unfazed by her slight. "Do I know her?"

Isabelle had watched Jon grab an apple from the crate and walk to the bench where they'd first met, occasionally glancing over while also trying to seem completely unaffected by the periwig-wearing pompant who'd just stolen her attention.

"No," Isabelle looked back to William, "it's no one you know."

"I hear your father will be in town to re-launch the London in a fortnight. Perhaps he'd like to join me for a hunt at the Mason Estate while he's here?"

"I do not conduct my father's schedule. I implore you to extend the invitation to him directly. Now, if you'll excuse me, I must be getting on." She turned to walk away but William darted in front of her.

Taking a firm grip on her arm, he glared down at her. "Women are not usually so eager to leave my side," he sneered.

"Then you are a lucky man to have so many beautiful women fawn all over you," Isabelle added lightly. But the sarcasm slipping so easily from her tongue only fueled William's indignation.

"Will," his friends called from a distance, "let's away!" The group of men had a cluster of sloppy women hanging in their arms.

Isabelle smiled. "Ah, you see, there are some now." She prayed the drunken women were enough to distract his attention, but William's eyes fell back upon her and he stepped closer.

Towering over her, he lowered his head to look directly in her eyes. "You are soon to become my wife." The stern words spit from his lips. "It would serve you better to show more appreciation of my attention."

Unfazed by his aggression, Isabelle stood firm in her desire to be rid of him. "If what you say is true, should you not be over there showering your attention on those lovely women before you are vowed only to me for the rest of our lives?" she replied confidently.

William released his grip. His brow furrowed as he straightened up. "You believe I'll stop bedding other women once we're married?"

Glaring up at him in silence, Isabelle watched a spine-tingling grin slither to his cheeks.

"Even the all-righteous King has his mistresses, my dear."

Without another word, he walked back to his friends before turning to take one more look at his future bride.

"I'll see you tonight, Lady Isabelle," he jeered before being swallowed up by the arms of drunken women.

Though pleased to be rid of him, Isabelle's stomach churned as she watched him walk away. She wondered if she was more upset by William and his promise of betrayal, or in herself, for keeping her virtue so sacred only to be forced to give it to such a smug self-serving snake.

A hopeless sigh slipped from her lips when she realized the rest of her evening would be filled with hundreds of others just like him.

But for now, a handsome sailor was awaiting her attention on a bench nearby. She happily turned and started straight for him.

"I apologize for making you wait," she offered, unaware that William had stopped just before the hill to turn back and watch her.

He saw her speaking with the sailor from the ship but the persuasion of the drunken beauties on his arm defeated his curiosity. Succumbing to their prodding, he left Isabelle behind and continued down the hill.

"Was that one of your father-approved suitors?" Jon asked through a mouthful of apple.

"He's certainly been trying to charm his way into my father's good graces lately," Isabelle casually replied, not ready to reveal just how close their contract was to being signed. "But I didn't come here to speak about him, and I really don't have much time." Hoping to seem inconspicuous, Isabelle walked around the flower planter, taking a seat on the other side of the planked bench to face the square.

Trying to avoid any obvious eye contact, she kept her gaze on the clasped hands in her lap. "I wanted to thank you again for taking me to the island last Sunday. I haven't felt like that in quite a long time."

Jon grinned at her gratitude. "It was my pleasure to have you there, and it would please me even more if you'd join me again tomorrow."

Touched by his invitation, Isabelle felt confident to move forward with a proposition of her own. "While I would love to join you again someday, I thought perhaps you'd like to try something different with your leave tomorrow."

Jon's eyebrow raised in curiosity. "I'm listening." He took another bite of his apple then leaned back against the stone planter to face her more easily.

"It was so generous of you to take me to the island. I'd like to repay you by teaching you how to ride a horse," she offered, glancing at him for the first time since she sat down.

"A horse? I have no need to ride a horse."

He laughed but Isabelle persisted. "Oh, nonsense. We don't know where life will take us Jon. You said you'd like to explore the New Americas when this war is over. Were you planning to do it all on foot?"

"Horses are big strong animals that should be tied to a wagon. They surely have no desire to have me bouncing around on top of them."

"Horses are brilliant wild creatures that we've tamed and shackled," she replied. "But they have their own souls too. You can see it. When you look in their eyes — they look right back at you. Ships don't do that."

"Aye! A horse has a mind of its own! How am I to control something like that?"

Isabelle chuckled. "Traditionally, there are two ways to control a horse. Either you can use force to bend the horse to your will, or you can be gentle and let it find trust in you. However, horses broken by force always seem a tad more tempestuous than the others. They tend to toss their riders for no reason at all."

Jon's eyes widened at the idea of being thrown from a huge animal. "Tell me then, how does one earn the trust of a horse?"

"I suppose the easiest way is to be pure of heart."

Jon laughed. "Oh, that simple is it? Do you know anyone like that?"

"No, but a horse can certainly sense our integrities. They sense our fears as well. They're quite intelligent animals. The fact that we feel in control of them at any moment is a nod to our own ignorance."

"You believe in my integrity enough to trust the horse won't toss me?"

Isabelle flashed a sideways grin. "I believe in the integrity of my horses enough to let you upon their backs."

He smirked. "And where would this lesson take place?"

"On my family's estate. I give our servants full leave on Sunday and even if they do return to the property, they never venture out to the coast. I can meet you at the peninsula."

Jon thought about her offer but the idea of being at the mercy of a large animal between his legs sounded terrifying.

Sensing his discomfort, Isabelle offered a small reprieve. "I promise to keep you safe," she said with a smile.

Not wanting to look like a pansy, and certainly honoured by this exclusive invitation, Jon decided he'd be a fool to turn her down. "Alright," he leaned over to peer into her eyes, "but if that horse throws me and breaks my arms, you'll have to run the rigging 'til I'm well."

Isabelle looked over her shoulder to the Barrington then back at Jon. "You'll be fine," she said with a reassuring smile before rising from the bench. "I'll meet you tomorrow, just passed midday. Now if you'll excuse me, I must get on with this laborious event." With that, she walked off to begin her dreaded evening of social intercourse.

Jon popped up and rushed to her side. "If I come tonight, will I get to speak with you, or will you pretend not to know me?"

"Je ne sais pas," she replied with a smile. "Au revoir, marin."

Jon took a deep breath as he watched her saunter away. Isabelle had been running through his mind since he'd left her a week ago. It took everything within him not to run after her and take her passionately right there in the street. Instead, he drove his teeth hard into the apple and watched her glide gracefully down the hill.

The steady rumble of bodhrans rolled up the forest pathway as Isabelle wound her way towards the riverside field. Mandolins and flutes soon accompanied the rhythm, followed by shrieks of joyous laughter.

When she finally reached the festival, Isabelle found it swarming with townsfolk and nobility alike. Strings of glowing lanterns hung in the trees and fire pits burned bright. Merchants from the square had set up booths to sell food, ale and souvenirs as people of all ages melted together in celebration of what would hopefully be the start of a prosperous season for all.

Isabelle was just beginning to think she may actually salvage a good time out of this chore when a fury of puffy red satin came bounding straight towards her.

"Well, I see you've finally arrived!" Anne bitterly announced. "Who were you talking to?"

"When?" Isabelle asked while maintaining her perfect poise.

"On the bench at the docks just now. Cecily Mercer said she saw you speaking with a sailor. That wouldn't happen to be the same sailor from the square last week, would it?"

Isabelle didn't bat an eye. "I was speaking to William Cunningham at the docks. Perhaps Cecily should have her eyes *and* her mouth checked," she snipped, not at all impressed that it had only taken half a heartbeat before someone had started interrogating her.

"Well, I should certainly hope that was the case. We wouldn't want your impeccable reputation tarnished so closely to your betrothal now would we?"

Her rhetorical question fumed with acrimony but Isabelle scoffed at the idea of taking advice from Anne. Any remaining morals this woman managed to hold were questionable at best and Isabelle wasn't about to let a comment like that slide tonight. "I manage myself quite well, thank you. You should run off to find Sir Barkley, is he here? Perhaps he needs a tit in his hand." Isabelle raised her chin just slightly. "Good evening, Anne."

Leaving her gobsmacked friend behind, Isabelle walked off to find someone more pleasant to talk to.

But her hopeful mission was quickly snuffed when nearly every step was interrupted by someone else brimming with questions about her father.

Will he be attending tonight?

When will he be arriving in town?

Will the King be coming with him?

If Isabelle was given a pound each time someone mentioned her father, she could've amassed a small fortune and started a new life all on her own.

In an effort to dodge any more questions, Isabelle strolled to the river's edge where she spotted Victoria and Elizabeth seated next to one of the burning fires.

"Izzy!" Beth popped up with excitement at the sight of her friend walking over. "I haven't seen you all night!"

"Actually, I was just thinking of leaving," she replied.

"Lady Isabelle! Lovely to see you here."

Isabelle turned to find Charles Rhemy, yet another childhood acquaintance, appear seemingly out of nowhere. "Good evening, Charles. It's been quite awhile since I've—"

"I heard you were here tonight and I was hoping to catch a moment of your time. William told me your father will be re-launching the London in name of the King. Do you suppose he could see me aboard the ship for its voyage up the Thames?"

Isabelle realized he was not interested in speaking with her at all — he was just another man trying to raise himself with a bit of her help. "My apologies, no. That voyage is reserved for friends and family of Admiral Lawson exclusively. My father will only give a speech. I do not believe even he is sailing to London. You will have to watch from the dock with everyone else I'm afraid," she answered politely.

He shook his head in disappointment. "I thought you'd be more help than that." Without another utterance, he turned and walked away.

"That was rude," Victoria remarked.

Isabelle took a seat next to her friends. "I've been dealing with this all night."

"Are you really leaving?" Beth asked sweetly. "Thomas has not yet arrived. I was hoping you would have a moment to speak with him. I know you'll love him as much as I do," she pleaded. "I really need your help, Iz."

The sun had set long ago and Isabelle felt like she'd spoken to nearly everyone of importance tonight. She had been there long enough for her presence to be noted; should any remarks find her father's ears, he'd hear of what a poised young lady she was, eloquently conversing with everyone in town.

And now — she was done.

"I'm sorry, Beth. I'll speak with him another time." She rose from her place. "Besides, Victoria is here with you. I trust her judgment and so will your mother."

When Beth only stared back in silence, Isabelle leaned in to kiss her pouting friend on the cheek. "I'll see you at church tomorrow," she offered before slipping away.

With only a half moon above, the forest path back to her carriage seemed eerily dark. Though normally quite comfortable in the woods, a sudden rustle in the forest froze Isabelle in her tracks.

Squinting through the darkness, she was shocked to spy someone's bare white bum thrusting back and forth in the moonlight. She laughed quietly when she realized she had stumbled upon a couple getting rather well acquainted in the woods.

Unable to look away, Isabelle watched in silence. She'd heard Anne ramble on about her sexual liaisons quite a bit, but this was the first time she'd ever witnessed it in the flesh. Although, the way Anne described her lustful encounters sounded much more erotic than the jackrabbit thrusting she was witnessing now.

As Isabelle was about to turn away, the moaning man threw his head back in ecstasy, exposing his face. Without his black periwig

Isabelle hadn't recognized him at first, but it was William and one of his drunken whores from the dock!

Instantly nauseated, Isabelle turned away. She covered the sudden pit in her stomach and hurried down the rest of the pathway. Fighting back tears, she climbed into her carriage without a word to Mr. Graham and plunked herself down on the seat.

Free to take whichever road home he pleased, Mr. Graham chose the smooth cobblestones back to Bluefields while the rambunctious crew of the Barrington started along the docks, singing and thrashing cups of ale as they made their way towards a night of debauchery that was only just beginning.

Chapter 12

HEATHEN AND EARTH

Church bells chimed through the air as Mr. Graham helped Isabelle out of the carriage. With her social card filled from the night before, she decided conversations were acceptingly avoidable this morning and snuck in just before the arched doors closed.

Sliding into the last pew, she took a seat next to an elderly man who tipped his chin to welcome the youthful beauty at his side. Isabelle smiled politely then turned her attention to the sermon, pretending not to notice him rib the equally wrinkly chap to his left to show off his good fortune in church today.

With an afternoon of excitement ahead of her, Isabelle felt the service ran exceptionally long today, but the moment it ended she popped up and headed straight for the door. A slight hesitation nipped her heels when she remembered promising Beth a visit at church today but she had run out of patience somewhere around Matthew 2:21 and was eager to get to the stable. She was almost at her carriage when she heard Beth shout her name.

"Every time," she mumbled before turning to face her friend.

Expecting to be torn apart for slipping out on her promise, Isabelle was surprised to find Beth beaming with excitement as she came bounding into her arms.

"Goodness!" Isabelle shouted while being spun about.

"He kissed me Iz!" Beth struggled to keep her voice low.

"Thomas? He did? Did anyone see you?" Isabelle couldn't believe her virginal friend had been so careless with her decisions at such a public event.

"No, no, we were in the woods. It was just before dawn. I know it now, I truly do love him," she swooned.

Isabelle took a hold of her friend's shoulders. "Beth," she looked straight into her eyes, "you must get a hold of yourself."

Unfazed, Beth continued. "They all arrived just after you left. The entire crew, even their captain — I met everyone!" She bounced in her Sunday best. "Jon was there as well," she added, catching Isabelle's attention. "He asked about you and got quite upset when I told him you'd just left. They were all liquored by the time they arrived and he was ready to chase your carriage down the road." Beth burst into giggles as she recalled the moment they all tried to convince him not to drunkenly chase after her.

Hoping Jon's drunken state hadn't led to a loose tongue, Isabelle pressed her friend for answers. "Did he say anything else about me?"

"No, but Anne followed him around all night."

Isabelle snickered at Anne's audacity.

"He didn't speak to her though, nor any woman really," Beth added. "Once the rest of the crew left, Thomas and I spent awhile together before he had to be back on board. Captain said he only has one rule about staying out, be back on deck before sunrise or get left behind. He said—"

"Well, if it isn't the elusive Lady Isabelle," William interrupted, moving right in between the girls with his back rudely in Beth's face. "I heard you attended the festival last night. It seems you spoke to everyone but me." His tone seemed to imply that he was genuinely upset but Isabelle knew he was definitely not a lonely man last night.

"As far as I'm aware, I am not your wife nor are we betrothed, and therefore you are owed none of my time," she curtly replied before glancing away.

"You left my heart aching for your company," he said, sliding closer.

Beth interrupted to call his bluff. "Didn't I see you with Catherine Spencer last night, *and* Lady Olena?"

William spun around to shoot Beth a look that sent a shiver down her spine.

"I believe I've had enough conversation for today," Isabelle stated. "Excuse me please." She brushed by William.

"You're not coming to lunch again?" Beth whined as she watched her friend walk away.

"Not today, and you two should go home to rest as well. It sounds like neither of you got much sleep last night!" she yelled before climbing into her carriage.

When she arrived home, Isabelle quickly changed into her riding clothes, packed some supplies then made her way to the stable where she cheerily greeted her horses.

"Hello you two. I hope you're ready," she said while stroking their muzzles. "You're both coming with me today."

Chapter 13
MATE AND MARE

Peering though her wispy windblown locks, Isabelle stood upon the grassy pier watching corduroy swells roll in. It felt like hours had passed and there was still no sign of Jon. She knew he was a tad anxious but never thought he would bail completely.

Slightly disgruntled, she was just about to gather her grazing horses and leave when she spotted a small rowboat in the distance.

Jon's pace seemed sluggish as he stroked towards the peninsula and there were more grunts than usual as he pulled his wooden vessel ashore. "Forgive me for being late!" he shouted through laborious groans. "This was not an easy morning."

He secured his boat, walked to the dune Isabelle stood upon and looked to the woman above. "The only thing that saw me through was knowing I was coming to see you," he said with a smile. He lumbered up the sand to meet her. "But truthfully...I'm not looking forward to the horse bit." Coming to Isabelle's side, Gryphon let out a loud snort of resentment.

"I heard you had a fair bit to drink last night," she teased.

Jon grinned. "Have you been asking about me?"

Isabelle raised her chin. "Stories of drunken sailors were passed around church today."

Smiling silently, he waited for the truth.

"Beth told me."

Jon chuckled as he recalled the many conversations he'd shared with Beth last night. "Tom has been running off with her quite a bit. He said he's really falling for her."

Shaking her head, Isabelle glanced to the grassy dune. "Yes well, if they're not careful, they could wake one day to find both their hearts torn to pieces."

Jon found her tone innocent enough, but when she looked up, her eyes seemed to sear that warning to his heart as well.

Gryphon dispelled the tension with a long-winded whine and shook his head. Isabelle rubbed his neck to calm him. "Alright Gryph, you've been quite patient. Jon, I'd like you to meet Gryphon, and this is his mother, Buttercup."

As Isabelle handed the mare's reins to Jon, she noticed his hesitation. "She's an old lady now, she'll be gentle with you, sailor. You've nothing to fear."

"I'm not afraid." Jon snatched the reins. "I've harnessed winds blowing faster than she could ever run."

"You may trick the wind into moving your ship but how will you fair with the soul of a living creature — one with its own free will?"

Avoiding her intimidating question, Jon searched for reassurance. "Any tips from Bluefield's Master of Horse before I get up there?"

"It's called mounting, and yes, just as a sailor must sense the wind upon his face, you must sense the animal the same. Watch her ears as she observes the world around her. Did her muscles tighten with fear or was she listening to you laugh? Is she gliding freely beneath you, or is she questioning your leadership?"

Jon had hoped her instructions would calm him but they only escalated his apprehension.

"Your first step though, is to place that foot into this stirrup here. Come on then," she commanded in an effort to rile the lethargic sailor.

Jon gathered his confidence and placed his foot in the stirrup. Grabbing a hold of the saddle, he pulled himself onto the horse, swung his leg to the other side and took a seat.

"Were you lying when you said you've never done this before?" Isabelle asked in awe of his seamless mount.

"I've seen men do that hundreds of times. If that was the hardest part, this'll be a breeze."

Isabelle adjusted his stirrups as she instructed him. "Now, before you move forward, one must know how to stop. First, place your thumbs under your reins and grip them from above."

She watched Jon do exactly as she asked. "When you want her to stop, you're going to pull straight back and shout, whoa! She's not terribly fond of running anymore therefore you shouldn't have much trouble getting her to stop."

Jon watched Buttercup's ears turn — she was listening to Isabelle's instruction. "Aye," he said while practicing gently.

Isabelle placed her foot in her stirrup, gracefully pulled herself up, threw her other leg over the saddle and sat down.

Jon peered at her but tried not to seem obvious. "I've never seen a woman sit on a horse like that," he said bashfully.

Surprised by the slight shyness in his voice, Isabelle took a moment to reply. "Yes well, I only ride like this when I'm alone."

Jon's eyes were inquisitively inviting. "But, you're not alone."

"I suppose I'm beginning to trust you with my secrets," Isabelle offered with half a grin. "When you're ready, give her a slight tap with your heels."

A gentle knock to Buttercup's side was all it took to start them at an easy pace. They walked along the coast for quite some time before Isabelle noticed Jon start to relax — a sure sign he was beginning to trust the animal between his legs.

"Are you comfortable at this pace?" she asked.

"I'm just sitting here. If this is horse riding, I'd say I've got it nabbed."

Isabelle chuckled at his naivety. "This is not exactly all there is to it. Even a dead man could ride a horse at this pace." She glanced over the flat earth before them. "Would you like to run her?" she asked, looking back to Jon.

"Shouldn't you be asking her that question?" Jon leaned forward to stroke Buttercup's neck. "What do you say old girl? Promise not to toss me if Izzy makes you run?"

Buttercup looked cautiously over at Isabelle.

"You'll be fine," she assured them both. "First, get a good grip on your reins, squeeze tightly with your legs then give her a good hard kick."

The moment Jon drove his heels into Buttercup's side she took off down the coast like she'd been shot from a cannon!

Not expecting her old mare to be so responsive, Isabelle laughed at the sight of Jon bouncing around on his saddle. Collecting herself quickly, she nudged Gryphon and took off after them.

The lightning-fast colt caught his mother easily then obeyed Isabelle's rein to ease up, allowing her to shout instructions to the novice rider at her side.

"Sit up straight Jon! Push down with your bottom — it will help keep you in your saddle. Squeeze your legs together! Right! Now follow her stride!" With a few corrections, Isabelle noticed Jon had found his knack and she pushed Gryphon harder.

Leading them away from the coast, Isabelle checked back frequently and found herself pleasantly surprised by their stamina.

The scent of turned earth filled Jon's nose as he chased Isabelle across the open fields all the way to the forest's edge where she stopped at the head of a trail and waited patiently for him to catch up.

"Whoa!" Jon yelled, pulling straight back on the reins, bringing Buttercup to a halt at the tip of Gryphon's nose.

"You did well, Jon. I dare say I'm quite impressed."

"That was incredible," he stood in his stirrups to rub his painful backside, "but I fear I won't be able to walk tomorrow."

"We'll take it slow from here," Isabelle offered with grin.

Sunlight and shadows leaked through the rustling canopy as Isabelle led them down the woodland path towards her favourite spot on the property.

"Why is it called Bluefields?" Jon asked, glancing to the windblown woman next to him. "The fields looked green to me."

"Yes well, you've never seen them in the moonlight," she replied with a smirk. "My grandfather would stay up all hours of the night painting the grounds from his balcony. He would always use the same shade for the fields — Moongrass Blue," she said with a smile.

Jon noticed how exceptionally beautiful Isabelle appeared every time she spoke about something she loved. He was beginning to learn the tell-tale signs of her true happiness.

Golden rays from the low hanging sun slipped through the forest as Jon and Isabelle followed the trail onto the cape where the sea lapped at them from all sides.

A smattering of trees offered the solace of their shade while the breeze passing through the tall grass echoed the soothing sound of the breaking waves.

"It's so peaceful here," Jon said, glancing over the shimmering sea.

"It's the only place on the property where one can view a proper sunset. I try to come out here every evening." Isabelle gazed over the waves to the glowing horizon. "There's something so tranquil about a setting sun...it seems such a pity to miss one."

She looked to the man at her side. "Alright Jon, it's time to dismount, I'll show you. Place your reins in this hand, swing this leg to the ground then pull your foot from the stirrup," she instructed as she gracefully slid off Gryphon.

Jon copied her movements perfectly but howled the moment his feet hit the ground. "Bloody hell!" he yelled before limping towards her. "I think I broke my arse."

Isabelle laughed as she took Buttercup's reins. "You'll be alright sailor. Shake out those sea legs."

Still rubbing his behind, Jon looked to the inviting water. "I fancy a swim," he said before glancing back at her. "Care to join me?"

A hundred responses whirled though Isabelle's mind but only one made it to her lips. "Not today," she politely replied. "I loathe the feeling of wet clothes against my skin, and swimming nude doesn't seem appropriate given my company this afternoon."

"You swim naked here?"

"Yes, it's much calmer on this side." She pointed to the soft dune-filled beach to their right. "I walk in right over there."

"Right there?" Jon pictured her smooth naked body wading into the glistening sea.

When Isabelle noticed him lost in a daydream, she gave him a good shove with her elbow. "Get on with it then."

Jon looked to her with a smile then started down the sandy ridge.

"Do you often picture your friends naked?" she yelled as she watched him scoot down the dune.

Landing on the soft beach below, Jon spun around with a toothy grin. "No, but I've never had a friend that looked like you before!" he shouted before dashing towards the sea.

Isabelle chuckled to herself as she finished securing the horses.

Stopping just shy of the shoreline, Jon undressed down to his white cotton braies before looking back to see if he had an audience.

Catching his glance, Isabelle quickly looked away but her cheeks had already begun to blush.

With a half-witted smile Jon glanced back to the water. Sending sprays of sunlight splashing through the air, he charged in and dove through an incoming wave.

He took a few strokes then flipped onto his back. Gazing at the sky above, he felt grateful for the loyal water beneath him. He was finally off that horse, and back in the sea.

In the shade of her favourite Ash tree, Isabelle had laid down a blanket, unpacked their snacks and started a small fire. Wondering what was taking Jon so long, she decided to walk down to the beach where she found him kneeling in waist deep water, covering himself in mud.

"What on earth are you doing?" she exclaimed with laugh.

Jon opened one eye to find Isabelle standing on the shore with her hands on her hips. "If you dig a bit through the sand, it's all clay here. They sell this to you in your expensive lotions but you can get it for free if you know where to look."

He dipped beneath the water, thrashed around to rinse then stood up with his eyes still closed. "Did I get it all?"

Isabelle watched the muddy water ripple down his muscular chest. "Not quite. Have another go at it," she chuckled.

Slipping back under water, Jon scrubbed a little more then made his way to the beach.

As he bent down to retrieve his dry clothes, he looked to Isabelle with a smirk. "I know you're not keen on wet clothes, but what would happen if I drenched you right now?"

Raising his arms high in the air, Jon stomped towards her growling like a ravenous sea monster.

"Jon, don't you dare!" Isabelle leapt out of the way just as he was about to pounce!

Her shrieks of laughter echoed over the water as she weaved through the dunes trying to lose him. When she finally reached the sandy hill, instead of scurrying back up to safety, she turned to see where he was.

"Gotcha!" he yelled as he leapt at her.

But Isabelle quickly jumped out of the way and Jon landed face down in the dune.

He rolled onto his back to discover he was covered head to toe in sand. "Shit!" he shouted, causing Isabelle to spin around.

Laughing hysterically, she collapsed next to him and playfully splashed more sand onto his chest.

"Oh, you think this is funny?" Jon asked through heavy breaths. "Now I have to wash again."

Still giggling to herself, Isabelle threw her arm over him and planted it in the sand, caging him in like a prey she'd just conquered.

Hovering above him, a cheeky grin appeared. "You brought this upon yourself," she teased, as long strands of golden hair began to slip from her shoulders and dangle around them.

Reflecting off the water, the sun's rays crept though Isabelle's wispy veil each time her untamed locks caught the breeze.

Entranced by a speck of sunlight dancing across her lips, Jon was slow to reply.

He raised his hand to her cheek. "Then I'd happily do it a hundred times again," he said with a smile as his thumb gently traced the golden fleck.

A battle of love and fear whirled in Isabelle's chest as she watched his ocean eyes drift across her lips. A lifetime of etiquette and expectations blared in her head, but a soft voice within was urging her to surrender.

When Jon looked up to meet her gaze, Isabelle pressed her cheek deeper into his palm.

There, cradled in his hand, safely hidden within the dunes of her sunset cape, Isabelle slowly leaned down…and kissed her sailor.

Jon quivered in surprise the moment he felt her lips. After a few gentle kisses, Isabelle opened her mouth and let her tongue gently explore his, causing him to purr as he welcomed her unexpected embrace.

Jon had craved her velvety lips since the first day they met, but never believed he would ever get to taste them.

They were soft, like early autumn plums — supple and sweet. He wanted to taste every inch of her but pulled his own reins when he felt her pull away.

Still holding her head in his hand, Jon slowly opened his eyes. "You *are* French," he said with a sarcastic grin.

Isabelle laughed at his revelation then playfully pulled herself from his grasp. "Go clean yourself and come join me. I've started us a fire."

Jon washed for a second time, collected his clothes then climbed back up the sandy hill where he found Isabelle seated on the blanket, fervidly writing in her notebook.

Searching for a private place to change, he deemed his trusty steed to be a perfect divide. He passed by Isabelle, ducked behind Buttercup then removed his sopping braies.

As he pulled his dry pants on, Jon peered over the old mare's back to spy Isabelle still writing with such a focus she hadn't seemed to notice that he'd walked right by her.

He stole a few more moments of admiration but he knew, like the distant moon, Isabelle was untouchable. His heart sunk as he suddenly became aware of the eternity he'd spend coveting her from afar.

He finished dressing then joined her for the sunset. "You wouldn't be writing about me, would you?" he asked while sprawling out next to her.

"Not unless you are a twenty-year-old woman living in 1641 who believes the King's head should be rotting on a spike," she casually replied.

Consternation lifted Jon's brow. "Why would a genteel lady such as yourself choose to write about such gore?"

"Because that is what people wish to read," Isabelle answered matter-of-factly. "Destruction, war, heartache. Why do you suppose Shakespeare only wrote tragedies?" She dipped her pen to complete her sentence then laid the book down to dry.

"Have you written many stories?' Jon asked while helping himself to a slice of cheese.

"No, this is my first but I believe I'm beginning to enjoy it more than painting...it feels like I'm betraying my grandfather by saying such things out loud."

"What's so wonderful about writing that it makes you speak such blasphemy?" Jon teased.

Catching his sarcasm, Isabelle grinned. "Because I can control an entire world with the stroke of my pen," she answered readily. "If I want it to be a clear day, then it is. If I want her mother to never touch a sip of wine, so be it. I make the decisions. It's empowering to have this much control." She glanced to her book. "I imagine this is what it must feel like to be a man."

Jon looked to the setting sun. "Well...sometimes men don't always make the best decisions," he admitted softly. "Sometimes they sign up for a war before knowing what they'd be leaving behind." When he looked to Isabelle, he thought he saw a hint of despair in her eyes before she glanced away to the blazing horizon.

What was she doing, Isabelle thought to herself. If her father knew she was out here kissing some merchant sailor, he would end both their lives as they knew them.

Wrapping her knees to her chest, she glanced to Jon and contemplated telling him right then exactly who her father was. But when he looked at her, and their eyes met, she decided not to spoil their precious time together with unsolicited confessions and kept their conversation light, hoping not to wake any demons tonight.

As the fuchsia sky began to fade, Isabelle knew they had to start heading back. "I must return the horses before we lose the twilight," she said while packing up. "The Tilly's don't sleep until I'm home."

Confused, Jon respectfully popped up to help her. "Didn't you say you'd spend all night in the forest?"

"Yes," Isabelle replied with a grin, "but they don't know that."

Jon met her at the horses. "Home before twilight, out again in the moonlight?"

Isabelle only offered a sly smile as she handed Buttercup's reins to Jon. "Time to get back on the horse, sailor."

After an easy walk back through the woods, Isabelle stopped for a moment at the edge of the forest. She looked at Jon in the glowing dusk and saw no sign of fear in his eyes as he peered over the open fields, knowing exactly what was coming next.

Feeling her eyes upon him, Jon glanced at her.

"Catch me," she said with a grin. A swift kick to Gryphon's side sent her charging away.

Jon hunkered down in his saddle with a cheeky smile then took off after her.

Knowing they were losing the light quickly, Isabelle chose a faster path back to the peninsula. She led them over the fields then dipped into the forest where she eased up to give the horses, and Jon, a bit of a break.

Walking at an easy pace, Jon spotted something on the other side of the trees. "Are those gravestones?" he asked, looking to Isabelle.

"Yes, that's our family plot. My grandparents are buried there. I hope it will be my final resting place someday as well. I wouldn't care to spend my eternity any place else."

Jon looked back to the graves with a grievous heart. From the day he left Jersey, his life had felt so fleeting. He was ready to leave this earth at any moment...some days, he begged God for it. But something changed the day he met Isabelle. The thought of her laying beneath this soil while he might still walk this earth without her sent a chilling shiver through his scars.

He looked to the beauty riding at his side. Their time together was a gift, he knew it, but a sudden pit in his stomach had him weary of when that time might run out.

Dusk was quickly fading to darkness when they arrived back at the grassy pier, leaving it awash in a muted misty light. Needing no instruction this time, Jon dismounted without so much as a grunt.

"Well done," Isabelle said before sliding off Gryphon. She walked over to take his reins. "You did well today Jon, much better than I expected."

"That was better than you expected?" He laughed while rubbing his backside.

"There is room for improvement of course. Would you care for another lesson next Sunday?"

"I'd love nothing more than to spend every Sunday afternoon with you until the day I die," he said with a smile, "but Arlington placed us on assignment. We'll be at sea for the next two weeks."

Isabelle tried to speak through the sudden lump in her throat. "Has your ship been called?"

"No, we're training a crew early in the week then Arlington's sending us to Spain to collect a shipment from the Far East — he knows we're still the fastest crew in this yard," Jon added with proud smile.

"What on earth do they need from the Far East that is so crucial it requires retrieval by a naval ship in the middle of a war?"

"Artillery for Admiral Lawson. They're filling the London with arms before she's sent to base. I may even get to board her while we're loading," he added with a giddy bounce.

"But we have an armoury here in England. Why would he send you to Spain?"

"Perhaps he fetched a fairer price elsewhere," he shrugged. "Once the London sets sail, I may take my leave." Stepping closer, Jon slid his hand into Isabelle's silky hair. "May I see you then?"

Gripping his waist, Isabelle looked up to his eyes. He'd be gone for two weeks. This would be her last chance to tell him who her father was before he would see them together at the ceremony. Once Jon knew the truth, he would likely never bother with her again.

Isabelle's gaze dropped to the earth. "You know I'm not permitted to be seen with you."

"Aye," he lifted her chin, "nor are you permitted to be in my arms, yet here we are." Feeling free to walk a line already crossed, Jon leaned in to steal one last kiss.

Happy to receive his lips again, Isabelle slipped her hands beneath his loose shirt then slid them slowly up his back.

Jon knew he needed to pull himself away but when Isabelle opened her mouth, he couldn't resist — he pulled her closer.

With the sensation of her body against his, her hands pressing into his flesh, Jon felt himself growing aroused and conjured all the willpower he possessed. Even if he woke tomorrow full of regret, he respected her virtue and was not about to place an inappropriate hand where it was not permitted.

Reluctantly, he pulled his lips away but left her head cradled in his hand. "I've met a fair number of women in my travels," he let his forehead rest against hers, "but I've never met anyone like you," he said with a smile.

Melting in his hands, Isabelle's secrets burned within. She wanted to tell him everything but the welling truth lodged in her throat.

"Turn that ship quickly," were the only words she could muster.

"I'll make sure of it," he said with a grin. "Thank you for today. You've taught me more than you know." Jon turned to Buttercup. "And thank *you* for not killing me," he said while stroking her neck.

Isabelle watched him slide confidently down the dune. "Please be safe."

"Always," he shouted while pushing his boat into the sea.

As she watched Jon row away, even though she stood upon firm ground, Isabelle felt something within her begin to fall.

Chapter 14

FAREWELLS AND FAVOURS

Once known for her impeccable focus, Isabelle's concentration seemed non-existent lately. Living somewhere between fantasy and reality for the last two weeks, she had tried desperately to rid her thoughts of her impossible situation, but it seemed everything now reminded her of Jon; her horses, her yellow silk dress, her sunset cape, the docks, the sea, the sand — everything. He was everywhere, yet he was nowhere.

Each time a storm blew in, Isabelle prayed the Barrington was sheltered in a safe port somewhere, which then caused her to worry about any portside women who may be waiting to comfort the weary sailors blowing in. What if Jon fell in love with one of them? What if he never wanted to see her again? Isabelle's mind had been spinning for two weeks straight, but deep down she knew none of this mattered anyhow. Her betrothal to William would likely be announced any day now and Jon would have to be removed from her life just as swiftly as he'd entered it.

With the London's re-launch on her schedule for tomorrow, Isabelle knew the Barrington had to be back by dawn at the very latest.

As she sat in the Davenport's solarium, half-listening to Victoria yammer on about something, Isabelle made her decision — tomorrow she would head to the square before the ceremony started, tell Jon who her father is, then bid him a fond farewell.

Shaking any remaining lustful thoughts from her head, Isabelle tried to focus on Victoria who seemed to be complaining about the royal family she was marrying into.

"I've been told their King has twenty-two wives!" she whined. "And I cannot speak the language. I sound preposterous when Mr. Mudrais makes me try."

"Oh, enough!" Anne slammed her teacup on its saucer. "Father has arranged for you to become a princess for God's sake. You will have your every desire handed to you for the rest of your merry life while the rest of us stay here, and become nothing."

Slightly resenting Anne's remark, Isabelle's eyes dropped to her lap when she realized the brutally honest woman's words might actually be true.

"It is true," Beth added. "My mother could very well disown me once Tom and I are married. We really could start our family with absolutely nothing."

Victoria shoulders dropped. "Well perhaps I would rather have true love over titles and tiaras," she huffed before slumping back in her chair.

Beth noticed Isabelle's gaze lost in her own lap. "Izzy," she nudged the distracted friend at her side, "are you even listening? We hardly see you anymore and you've barely been present all afternoon."

Isabelle turned to her friend. "Forgive me, I have a lot on my mind," she politely replied. "I should really be getting home to prepare myself for the ceremony tomorrow." She elegantly rose from her seat and bid her friends a good evening.

· · · ·

Rising before the sun the next morning, Isabelle wondered if she'd even slept at all. With no appetite today, she picked at her breakfast on the balcony then Milly dressed her in the beautiful golden gown her father sent from London, and curled her hair as tight as she could get it.

Staring into the vanity mirror, Isabelle felt repulsed by her own reflection. She looked exactly as her father would expect — like every other girl in Gillingham — hair curled tight, waist cinched tight, mouth shut tight.

The house rumbled beneath them as her father's household from Whitehall scurried to prepare the manor for their noble master's impending arrival.

Startled by a loud crash below, Milly's hands jolted from Isabelle's curls. "I swear it, Iz, they're gonna tear this place apart," she moaned before affixing the final bow in Isabelle's hair.

"Alright, I'm going down there to see what all the fuss is about." Milly backed out of the room gathering dishes and linens as she went. "The ceremony starts at mid-day but you must find your father before then. He has requested you by his side while he gives his speech," she said, kissing the air in Isabelle's direction as she left the room.

With time to spare, Isabelle decided to work on her story before heading to the docks. As she took a seat at her desk, a hopeless smile slipped to her lips when she spotted Jon's carving next to her writing pen.

Shaking his face from her mind, she reached for her pen, dipped it and began writing.

> *"You're hurt! "Charlotte shouted.*
> *"Nay, a scratch." Gareth collapsed on a hay bale. "All is*
> *well. No frets now."*

Another crash below shattered Isabelle's focus.

Suddenly aware of clanging pots, shouting orders, and even the occasional animal noise, Isabelle decided to leave her fantasy world behind and start making her way towards the square to face the gloomy truth of her reality.

She left her room and walked down the servant's staircase, pausing at the kitchen entrance just as Milly shouted to some palace hand—

"You can't bring that in here!"

Isabelle stepped into the room to find a man with a white lamb on a lead, but Milly was close at his heels and chased them both out the backdoor.

"Oh good! You're here!" Milly darted towards Isabelle. Latching their elbows, she hurried the young woman across the bustling kitchen.

"S'cuze, ma'am." A servant brushed by with a bushel of potatoes who was quickly followed by another lad carrying a stack of porcelain plates.

"Those go in the dining room!" Milly shouted, grabbing the young boy's shoulders to redirect him. She turned back to Isabelle. "One of your father's messengers was looking for you. You're requested at dinner tonight. Seems your father has something he wishes to discuss."

Milly backed up to let another servant pass by then rushed Isabelle out the door. "Have fun today, love. And remember to be back well in time for supper!"

Isabelle followed the flat stone path to the front of the house where her perfectly polished carriage sparkled in the sunlight with Mr. Graham waiting patiently at the door. He looked particularly groomed today and greeted her with a smile.

"Good morning, Lady Isabelle," he said while helping her into the coach, "your father is awaiting your arrival."

As the carriage rolled down the laneway, Isabelle peered through the window at palace hands ripping out tender weeds and replacing broken cobbles.

Exhaling a deep sigh, she leaned back in her seat. She was dreading everything about this day; her talk with Jon, her appearance during the ceremony in front of hundreds of people, and possibly worst of all — dinner with her parents. Watching her mother drunkenly slumped in her chair, forever sipping her wine, while her father bestowed whatever message, punishment or order he had in mind. This entire day would require an insufferable amount of patience and self-control, both of which Isabelle seemed to be running short of lately.

The ceremony wasn't scheduled to start for another hour, but the square had already sprung to life. Beaming like a prideful peacock, the King had spent a fair purse to create quite the spectacle for his subjects. Colourful flags hung from one side of the square to the other, musicians strummed their lutes and banged their drums. Tourists popped in and out of shops purchasing food and souvenirs before they set sail for the journey to London.

Isabelle sauntered through the crowd that seemed to be mostly Admiral Lawson's friends and family as there was no one she immediately recognized — which may aid in her favour as she was hoping to have a private word with Jon before the festivities began.

That was of course, if she could find him.

The crowd was thick but Isabelle knew if there was ever a permissible time to be seen speaking with a sailor, the ceremonial launch of a royal vessel would surely be one of them.

Hoping to find the Barrington tied in its usual place along the main dock, Isabelle's heart dropped when she reached the end of the square.

Moored in the Barrington's place was the ship that had haunted her since childhood.

She gazed upon the HMS London in all its enormity. From the outside, the second-rate ship didn't look much different than she remembered. A tad smaller perhaps but just as intimidating.

The London's seventy-six brass guns gleamed under the midday sun. Reminiscing about the time Admiral Lawson took her to see one up close, a hint of a smile broke Isabelle's grim gaze.

Entranced by the glimmering cannons, a rush of blissful memories came flooding back. Her time aboard that ship wasn't entirely horrible. It was mostly a time when she still viewed her father as a great protector of his family, and her mother hadn't yet taken to wine with her breakfast.

But then...she spotted it.

The wooden railing her brother slipped through in the storm.

The wooden railing that was supposed to save him from the sea.

The wooden railing that changed everything.

132

Isabelle's stomach churned and she pulled her eyes away. Her gaze fell to the stern of the ship where a seaman was rolling a barrel up the plank and into the hull.

It was Jon! The sight of him evaporated any looming ghosts and Isabelle started straight for him.

He had already made his way off the ship and was starting to roll another barrel along the dock when Isabelle hopped directly in his path.

"Christ!" he yelled, grabbing the barrel to stop it from running this person over.

"I thought you said you turned ships quickly," Isabelle said playfully.

Jon looked up to find the woman he'd been fantasising about for the past two weeks standing right in front him. "Izzy!" he exclaimed, nearly jumping into her arms before realizing he might actually lose his hand if he touched her in this crowd. "I mean...my Lady," he said with a respectful bow as a Vice Admiral walked by casting a steely glare in their direction.

Once his superior passed, Jon stepped closer hoping to quench the insatiable hunger that begged for another taste of her. "I'm not allowed to touch you, am I?" he asked with a grin.

Isabelle shook her head as she gazed upon his full lips. She'd spent so many nights dreaming of having his mouth upon her again...but she tried to stick to her plan and cleared her throat—

"Ah, Lady Arlington!" Admiral Highbury shouted at the sight of his superior's daughter.

Isabelle squeezed her eyes shut hoping Highbury might not notice her if she didn't look directly at him.

Jon's brow wrinkled in confusion as he stared back at Isabelle. "Arlington?"

The boisterous and bloated Highbury didn't hesitate to walk up and throw his heavy arm around Isabelle's shoulders. "Yes! Lady Isabelle!" he shouted, even though he was standing right next to her. "Is your father about? I heard your family was sailing with us today."

Isabelle tried to concentrate on Highbury's words while her eyes searched Jon's face for any understanding that for all this time, he had secretly been courting his boss's daughter.

Arlington had bought the Barrington and her entire crew. He had secured nearly every ship that entered and departed this dockyard. He could turn a young sailor into an Admiral, or end his career — or his life — with a single stroke of his pen.

Managing to remain calm in the Admiral's presence, Jon only returned Isabelle's silent gaze.

"I have not seen my father today," Isabelle said before turning to look upon the overly assertive man she found herself squeezed against. "However, I do not believe we are sailing with you today, Sir Highbury."

"Nonsense! You will join us today. This voyage needs more beautiful women such as yourself. Your father will have the carriage meet you in London. You will be back at the palace by midnight!" he announced loudly as he started leading her towards the ship. "Come, let's away!"

"Oh, um—" sliding out of his grasp, Isabelle pulled her shoulders back and raised her chin. "Sir Highbury, this man is a sailor with the Royal Navy. He was just telling me how he has admired this great ship since he was a child on his father's shoulders, and how he would be honoured to serve as crew aboard your voyage this afternoon. Should you require more skilled men for your short journey, I believe he would be a lovely fit." Isabelle knew Jon was likely furious with her, and rightfully so, but she hoped he would see this gesture as the peace offering it was intended to be.

Highbury looked the strapping lad up and down, taking note of the sweat on his brow that proved he was, at the very least, a dedicated worker.

"He's a sailor with the Barrington," Isabelle persisted. "I've been told they are the most skilled crew in this yard. You would be lucky to have one of her men aboard your voyage," she added confidently — like the young noblewoman she truly was.

"We've had a few men fail to turn up today." Highbury looked at Jon. "Grab another one of your best men and I'll be back to see you both aboard shortly." He turned to Isabelle. "Come now Lady Arlington, let's see you aboard." As Highbury whisked her away, Isabelle glanced back at Jon with a tepid fear in her eyes.

Standing silently in the bustling crowd, Jon's gaze was locked on his golden beauty as he watched her slide from his life once again.

But not all hope was lost today. Highbury may have stolen Isabelle away, but he was taking her aboard the London. Not only was Jon about to crew a vessel he never thought he'd get the chance to board — Isabelle would be there as well. The woman he'd been fantasising about for weeks was about to watch him in the rigging as he helped bring this massive ship up the Thames.

Hoping he might be able to sneak another kiss upon their voyage, half a grin raised Jon's cheek. Her father may have the power to sink him and his entire crew but Isabelle had stolen his heart, and he was ready to risk everything.

Chapter 15

LOST IN FLAMES

"Duke! What are you doing out here?" Isabelle asked the brown and white pup bounding down the forest path. The sight of her father's beloved cavalier spaniel was a sure sign her parents were lurking deep within the manor only a few hundred yards away. She scooped him into her arms. "It's getting much too dark for little dogs to be out. The foxes are sure to gobble you up," she said playfully as he lapped at her neck.

Isabelle had managed to slip from Highbury's grasp just as he was about to haul her aboard the London. Every step she took towards that dreaded ship had sent anxiety coursing through her veins. She knew she couldn't gather enough poise to stand next to her father during his speech — and she was certainly not about to step foot upon that ship whether Jon was aboard it or not.

Instead, she walked home while Mr. Graham, and everyone else in Gillingham, was preoccupied at the square.

She changed into her riding clothes, stormed out to the stable, quickly tacked Gryphon, then charged across the open fields, pounding her panic into the earth as she rode.

She expected her father to be furious with her, it seems he always was, but Isabelle had her story ready. With Duke in her arms, she was nearly through Milly's vegetable gardens when she heard a low hum emanating from within the normally sedated manor.

Isabelle pushed the door open to find the kitchen a flurry of coordinated chaos. Pots boiled and fires roared as a sea of servants, nearly stumbling over each other, scrambled to prepare a proper dinner for Lord Arlington and his family.

"You're home!" Milly darted across the frenzied kitchen the moment she spotted Isabelle.

Seeing the alarm in Milly's eyes, Isabelle placed Duke on the floor who immediately hurried back outside the moment another servant came rushing through the door.

Isabelle sighed at the sight just as Milly grabbed a hold of her shoulders to stop herself from flying past. "You were supposed to be back here hours ago, *Lady Isabelle*," Milly chided.

"I'm sorry. It took everything within me to return at all," she sombrely replied.

Milly plucked through Isabelle's windblown tresses. "They're nearly ready to be seated, we must hurry." Wrapping her arm around Isabelle's tiny waist, she rushed the young woman through the kitchen.

When Isabelle went for the servant's staircase as she always did, she felt Milly tighten her grip. Their home was filled with outsiders who knew a proper nobleman's daughter would never take the cramped hidden staircase meant only for lowly servants. Isabelle would have to play the part of a real Lady tonight.

Milly led her out of the kitchen, down the grand hall then up the imposing dark wood staircase lined with red carpeting and endless spindles as thick as William Cunningham's ego.

"This way is so long!" Isabelle huffed, as her shoulders that were loose mere moments ago, grew tense once again.

Milly ignored her complaints. "There's no time for a corset now," she said as they rounded the top of the stairs. "We'll put you in your tightest bodice and hope he doesn't notice."

Seated at the head of the table, Arlington rapped his heavy fingers on the embroidered tablecloth as he waited for his incorrigible daughter to join them for dinner. Having taken his seat only moments ago, the King's favourite was not keen on being kept waiting, especially by someone as insignificant as his only child.

He sipped his wine in the antiquated dining room that had been decorated immaculately for the nobleman's supper this evening. Elaborate tapestries hung on the wall, exotic drapes covered the windows to shut out the ever-changing light, and priceless paintings brought in from Whitehall hung within eyesight of the Lord for him to gaze upon during his dinner.

Silver vases, overflowing with red and pink roses plucked from Bluefield's gardens lined the center of the table while tiered candelabras warmed their petals, sending their sweet scent wafting through the room.

A single bead of perspiration slid from beneath Arlington's grey periwig as he glanced at his wife seated next to him, who was already having her empty glass refilled by her personal steward's endless carafe of wine.

The jewelled combs holding her blonde curls sparkled in the candlelight when she dipped her head, happily bringing the full glass of wine to her lips again. Long strands of white pearls swallowed her emaciated frame as she leaned against the side of her towering chair silently returning her husband's sultry stare.

The sound of heels clicking down the hall stopped the moment Isabelle appeared at the doorway in a bouffant champagne satin gown. At the sight of her parents already seated, she drew her shoulders back, clasped her hands together then gracefully walked to the chair being pulled out next to her father.

"Isabelle, I didn't know you were here," her mother slurred from across the table as she watched her daughter take her seat.

"Where were you today?" her father grumbled without looking at her.

Expecting his interrogation, Isabelle had her reply ready. "I attended the ceremony as you requested. It seems your speech was well received," she said confidently just as three servers entered the room, each carrying a steaming plate of food.

In one perfectly synchronized motion, they placed the meals in front of the noble family.

Without acknowledging his staff, Arlington picked up his sparkling silverware and sliced through his meat. "I requested you by my side during my speech," he stated before shoving a bite of food in his mouth. He immediately began cutting another piece, all without looking over at Isabelle.

Remembering the little white lamb in the kitchen earlier that day, Isabelle stared down at her plate of steaming flesh with a woeful heart.

She drew a deep breath, raised her chin and looked directly at her father. "I was on my way to find you when I was accosted by Sir Highbury who—"

"Pardon the interruption, my Lord," a butler announced with a bow. "A message has come from Whitehall."

The hair on Isabelle's arm stood straight up as she watched a young messenger walk into the room and remove his cap.

"Out with it, boy!" Arlington demanded, without giving the lad a moment to take a breath.

"It's the London, my Lord. She has exploded inside the Thames estuary. Her powder magazine ignited. The decks have been reduced to shreds." He dropped his gaze. "No survivors have been recovered."

Isabelle's chest seized.

Jon was on that ship.

He was only on that ship because of her.

No survivors have been recovered.

The words rang through Isabelle's skull as she turned to her father for some direction or comfort, but she only found him staring stoically into the candlelight.

The messenger continued. "There is speculation this was a plot by the Dutch. The King has requested your assistance at the wreckage, my Lord — immediately."

Still frozen in the flame, Arlington's gaze went unchanged.

Isabelle's breath quickened as she awaited her father's response — a reaction, a blink — anything. She was on the edge of hysterics, how was he staying so calm?

Arlington finally looked to the young messenger. "Yes," he replied slowly, "yes, of course." He rose from his seat and kissed his wife on the forehead. "I'll see you back at Whitehall tomorrow," he said before leaving the room.

"I'll go with you!" Isabelle blurted.

Stopped by her outburst, Arlington turned to glare at his daughter. "You? What good would you be?" he asked in utter disgust.

Isabelle had no answer. She had no plan. She only knew she had to get out there. She had to find Jon — she needed to make sure someone was there looking for him!

"I could help," she meekly replied.

In a daze of confusion, Arlington scoffed at her suggestion then stormed out of the room.

Left quivering in her seat, Isabelle's thoughts whirled in the sudden mania. She knew that ship was cursed! Why did she push to get Jon aboard? He'd still be alive if it wasn't for her!

Drowning in guilt, she looked to her mother for reassurance but found her still blissfully sipping her wine as though she hadn't heard a word of what had just transpired.

When Isabelle realised this woman was not about to be any source of comfort tonight, she felt more alone than ever. Her burning eyes dropped to her untouched plate of lamb. "I need to be excused," she announced before pushing herself up with whatever grace she could muster.

With a sloppy smirk, the Countess raised her glass in a silent toast to her daughter as she watched her run out of the room on the verge of tears.

Chapter 16

APPARITIONS

No survivors.

The words rattled through Isabelle's mind as she raced back up the formal staircase, doing her best to keep her composure as she passed by servants from Whitehall.

When she finally reached her bedroom, she slammed the heavy door closed and let the wails of anguish explode from her lungs.

Startled from her duties, Milly spun around. "Good Lord!" she shouted.

No longer able to withstand the weight of her heartbreak, Isabelle collapsed to the floor.

Milly dove to her side. She scooped Isabelle into her arms and pressed her tight to her bosom. "What's the trouble, child?"

"It's the London!" Isabelle's breath stuttered between every word. "It exploded...shattered...no survivors!" she cried.

Milly held her tight as Isabelle sobbed into her chest. She knew that ship held horrid memories for this family. The loss of so many more lives must have overwhelmed the poor girl. "All will be well child." She gently stroked Isabelle's back. "They are all with God now — no longer burdened by the treachery of this world."

But Isabelle couldn't hear a word of Milly's comforting prose. Her soul was far from this room, floating somewhere with Jon, reliving every moment she'd spent with him, every decision she made; accepting his escort home, their trip to the island, pulling her lips away in the golden cape when her body so fiercely craved more.

A few...more...breaths.

In the silence, Milly noticed Isabelle had calmed in her arms. "Come love, let's get you changed for bed." She stood first then reached down to help Isabelle rise.

As though waking in a living nightmare, Isabelle looked up to Milly's outstretched hand — she must want her to take it.

Accepting her faithful servant's help, Isabelle's weightless body rose from the hard wooden floor. With Milly's arm sturdily around her waist, she walked to the chaise and disrobed.

A haunting silence filled the room as Milly helped Isabelle into her long white nightgown with floral lace along the scooped neckline and hems. She tied the white ribbon upon Isabelle's chest then used her apron to dab her cheeks. "Have no fear, love — all is well here," she said with a smile.

Her warm intentions did provide a small sense of solace, but Isabelle couldn't bear any more words tonight, not even from her loving housemaid. "Thank you, Milly," she replied, "but I would like to be alone if I may."

"Of course," Milly kissed her cheek. "Sleep well, love." She gathered some linens for the wash as Isabelle took a seat at her vanity.

Stopping at the door, Milly offered a few last words of comfort. "Don't you worry dear...everyone you love was safe here in Gillingham." The old woman smiled then closed the door behind her.

Left to stare at her own blank reflection, Isabelle's pulse began racing again. If Milly's words were true, why did it feel as though her heart had shattered right alongside the London; bits of it now floating at the mouth of the Thames calling her to come collect them.

No survivors.

This was all her fault!

The panic still lurking in Isabelle's chest seeped to her veins while her head whirled with guilt and nonsensical solutions. She could feel the scalding flames from the London tickling her flesh, burning her skin beneath the delicate lace.

She glanced up to discover all the windows were shut tight. Gasping for air, Isabelle pushed away from her vanity. She clutched the lacy petals beneath her throat as she trudged towards her balcony.

Her bedroom felt like it was flooding.

She couldn't breathe — she was drowning!

Slamming through the doors, Isabelle flung herself onto the balcony. She ran to the railing and crashed hard against the thick stone as she sucked in the fresh country air and willed herself to calm down.

She sipped a few more breaths then closed her eyes as her exhausted body slid to the floor.

Exhaling her surrender, Isabelle slowly opened her eyes to gaze through the stone posts into the bewitching forest below.

Rustling leaves and seductive shadows were luring her in; their dark lullaby calling her to run deep into the woods as she did as a child.

Only tonight...she wouldn't come back out.

She could slip away from this earth — become a shadow in the forest never to see another light of dawn. The trusty blade resting in her grandfather's desk could end the curse that had plagued her since childhood, and now followed to her Bluefields. There was no safety from its evil grip — no sanctuary here on earth.

Her silent resignation filled Isabelle with a sense of peace she'd never felt. For the first time in her life — she was in control of her own destiny.

But first, she needed to pull herself off this floor.

Gripping the cool railing, Isabelle pulled herself up, but just as she turned to fetch her dagger, a flicker in the forest broke her eerie trance.

She watched a golden orb float delicately through the woods, ducking behind trees and illuminating leaves.

Was it a ghost? An apparition set free from the burning ship come to haunt her last breaths? Was it Jon seeking his revenge for sending him aboard the ill-fated ship? Or perhaps it was her young brother, finally free from the grips of the London, coming to play with her in the woods.

But her haunting thoughts eased when the orb drew closer and Isabelle realized the mesmerizing apparition was nothing more than a flickering lantern. Beth must have heard about the explosion and come to tell her, but Isabelle had some distressing news to share as well — Thomas was likely the only person who came to mind when Highbury asked Jon to choose a mate for the journey.

Fearing Beth's heartbreak may keep them out all night, Isabelle turned to grab a shawl but just as she glanced away, the white glow of a sailor's shirt caught her eye.

She peered through the trees.

It wasn't Beth at all.

"Jon!" she yelled into the darkness.

Isabelle's voice rang like church bells in Jon's ears as he stepped to the forest's edge.

When Isabelle found his smile in the glow of the lantern, a surge shot through her body like a million fireflies tickling her from within.

Without another breath, she began spiralling down the staircase. She ran across the dining terrace then down the last set of stairs, but every step felt like an eternity to reach him.

Her delicate nightgown billowed behind her as she dashed through the rose garden, setting velvety pink and red petals free in her wake.

Jon's eyes brimmed with tears as he watched Isabelle come dashing towards him. She looked like an angel in her white nightgown; her loose curls blowing behind her. The heavenly sight left Jon wondering if they did in fact die on the London tonight, as surely such a beautiful sight could not be contained on this earth.

He placed his lantern on the ground just as she came barrelling into his arms.

With Isabelle wrapped tightly to his chest, he let his chin rest upon her head, closed his eyes and let the sensation of her body pressed safely against his, sear deep into his soul.

His hand slid up her back, grateful for the very touch of her flesh. She was alive, she was struggling for breath in his arms, but she was alive.

Isabelle felt him squeezing so tight she could barely breathe. "You're alright," she whimpered into his chest.

Leaning back to look in his eyes, her voice shook. "Jon...I thought you were dead. I felt something...lift out of my body when I heard the news. I thought I'd never see you again — it was all my fault!"

"Hush," Jon's voice was calm as he tucked her close. "Even if I did board that ship — my fate is not in your hands, Iz. We all make our choices in life. I'm alright," he said with a long exhale. "We're both alright."

Pulling back, Isabelle looked at him in confusion. "Why is it you weren't aboard?"

"Highbury never came back for us. We went to look for him but they wouldn't let us board."

Isabelle sighed, suddenly grateful for the Admiral's empty promises.

"And what of you?" he asked. "I lost sight of you once Highbury shuffled you off. He didn't get you aboard either?"

"I was not stepping foot upon that ship whether ordered by an Admiral, my father, or even the King." Stopped by her own words, Isabelle suddenly realized Jon now knew exactly who 'her father' was in all her stories and felt awful for deceiving him all this time.

"I'm sorry I did not tell you who my father was sooner," she offered shamefully.

Jon silently stared back at her, not wanting to ruin this sought-after moment of peace with talk of something that seemed so trivial now.

"I was afraid," she continued. "I know it could have cost you your place with the Navy, your entire future...I could have ruined you."

Seeing she was becoming overwhelmed, Jon pulled her close again. "You owe me no apologies, Isabelle. It doesn't matter who your father is."

A smile found its way to his lips. "You are the noblewoman who catches fish and builds fires." He brushed a golden lock from her cheek then slid his hand into her hair. "The woman who rides horses like a man...who is poised to pull a dagger on me at any moment," he

148

chuckled. He gazed into her eyes as she smiled up at him. "The woman I..."

Finally ready to face the truth he'd fought so hard against, he let the words slip from his lips. "The woman I think I've fallen in love with."

Spellbound by his proclamation, Isabelle was speechless. This entire day had worn her completely through.

She took a moment to gather her thoughts before a gentle smile slid to her cheeks. "Do you have leave to come somewhere with me?" she asked kittenishly.

Looking deep into her eyes, an enchanted smile parted Jon's lips. "Anywhere."

"Good," Isabelle picked up his lantern and held it towards the dark forest. "I want to show you something."

Chapter 17

RIPPLES OF MOONLIGHT

Holding the lantern out in front of her, Isabelle silently led Jon deeper into the forest. Her other hand was clasped with his — fingers intertwined in a perfect fit.

The earth was forgiving underfoot as Jon followed behind her, meandering through a part of the property he had not yet seen. There were no hoof prints on this path — it was wild and overgrown.

With the landscape saturated in silvery-blue moonlight, Jon felt lost in a dream. This woman was untouchable, yet her hand was in his, palm to palm.

But his euphoric daze quickly dissipated when he remembered exactly whose property he was indeed trespassing upon. Every day he'd spent at sea he longed to be back by Isabelle's side, yet now with his fantasies manifesting in front of him, all he could think about was Arlington castrating him like one of her horses.

When panic trembled to his fingers, Isabelle looked back with a soothing grin. Jon made his decision right then — whatever she had planned for him in this forest would absolutely be worth any punishment he might have to endure.

A subtle bubbling in the distance grew louder when Isabelle swept aside the thick boughs of an old willow tree. Opening them like a curtain, she welcomed Jon into her moonlit lagoon.

Veiled by weeping willows and huddled evergreens lay a modest spring-fed pond mirroring the silver moon to near perfection. The scent of damp earth filled Jon's nose as Isabelle led him towards an old wooden crate covered in pine boughs.

She placed his lantern on a rock next to the box, pushed the knotted branches off then pulled the creaky lid open.

Jon watched her remove a fur blanket and lay it on the soft ground. "May I help you?" he asked, quickly moving to offer his hand.

"Yes," Isabelle replied while digging through the box again.

Lifting out a pile of logs already split and dried, she dropped them in his arms. "You may start us a fire."

"Aye, you're letting me build the fire tonight?"

"I'll be right here should you require any help." She winked before turning back to her chest of treasures.

"Do you have any—"

"Here you are." Isabelle tossed a tinderbox on the logs then pointed to an area next to the blanket. "Just here is fine."

Digging through the wooden crate, Isabelle pulled out a quilt, laid it on top of the fur then reached in again to retrieve a few cloth pillows, puffing each one as she dropped them into the little nest she was making.

While Jon readied their fire, Isabelle plucked the stubby candle from her tinderbox and set it ablaze with the help of his lantern.

Moving silently, Isabelle lit small glass lanterns hanging in the trees around them.

As Jon continued stacking logs, he watched the tranquil lagoon illuminate before his eyes. Dragonflies darted around velvety bulrushes, and moss-covered knolls encased nearly the entire pool. Towering evergreens lining the distant edge of the pond created a wall that nearly climbed to the stars.

Beneath the trees, rocks smoothed by centuries under the flowing spring let the fresh water trickle over them into the pool below.

He watched Isabelle blow out the candle as she sauntered back towards him. "Is this your secret hideaway?" he asked.

She laid on the blanket as tiny flames emerged in the fire. "Yes. It's the only place on earth where I don't feel eyes upon me."

Beautifully sprawled in her nearly sheer nightgown, Isabelle looked like a fallen angel in the fire's warm glow. Fighting every urge to rip the delicate fabric from her soft skin, Jon reeled his desires with a deep breath then dropped into their little nest.

Rolling onto his side, he came face to face with his golden-haired beauty. "Well, you have eyes upon you now," he teased, leaning in so closely he could feel Isabelle's steady exhale on his cheek. "And you're soon to have lips upon you as well." Jon ran his hand through her fallen curls before leaning in to taste her silky lips — but Isabelle stopped him and pulled back slightly.

"I am truly sorry I did not tell you who my father was sooner," she offered.

"I told you — you owe me no apologies for your choices."

Isabelle smiled, grateful for his acceptance, but the weight of her only remaining secret dropped her gaze. "I'm afraid I have another confession as well."

Looking up to meet Jon's eyes, Isabelle finally spoke her truth. "My father is finalizing my betrothal to the man you saw me speaking with the night of the Solstice. We are to be married this fall."

Jon's gaze fell to the blankets while his heart burned with only one question.

"Do you love him?" he asked quietly before looking up to search her eyes for the truth.

Isabelle shook her head. "It takes all I have not to completely despise him. Our marriage is meant to be a symbol of unity between crown and council. Blending our families will see the King with more power in parliament than ever...all thanks to my father," she added spitefully.

Sliding her hand beneath his white cotton shirt, she let it rest on his waist. "He will never have my heart."

Her words landed softly but Jon felt no reassurance. Even though her hand was on him — he suddenly felt so far from her.

Hoping a kiss would soothe any ills she may have caused, Isabelle pressed her lips to his, but when she pulled back to meet his loving gaze, his eyes fell again. He could barely look at her.

"Is something the matter?" she asked softly.

Sensing her concern, Jon was hesitant to speak his truth. He didn't want to disrupt any moment of passion he was granted with her, but this sensuous stirring within was becoming too much for him to carry.

He looked up with gentle eyes. Needing to anchor himself, he slid his hand into her hair. "I'm mad for you, Iz," he said through a heartbroken smile that did little to mask his frustration. "I've found myself in love with a woman I'm not permitted to touch."

154

A grin slipped to Isabelle's lips. "You're touching me now," she lovingly pointed out.

Jon rested his forehead against hers. "I want to touch more than just your cheek, Isabelle," he replied honestly.

As she stared into his eyes, a sultry smile slowly crept upon her face.

"Alright," she elegantly replied.

Sliding away from him, she stood up at the end of the blanket where he could look upon her completely.

In the warmth of the small fire, Jon watched Isabelle pull the lacy ties of her décolletage, gently loosening her nightgown as she sweetly looked down at him.

As she untied the ribbon, she turned away and began walking towards the moonlit pool. When Isabelle reached the water's edge, she lifted the hem of her nightgown and swooped it over her head, letting it slowly drip to the ground, finger by finger.

Mesmerized by her perfectly curved body, Jon stopped breathing when Isabelle glanced over her shoulder with a salacious smirk.

"So come touch me then," she said before turning her inviting eyes back to the water.

Jon was gobsmacked. Was he dreaming? Did he truly die on the London? Either way, he wasn't about to decline her offer. He kicked off his boots while undoing his belt and never took his eyes off her.

Isabelle dipped into the water then turned to see what Jon thought of her invitation. She chuckled when she found him half-naked, struggling to get out of his of pants while also trying to cover his manhood.

Once free of his clothing, Jon calmly made his way into the tepid pool with his hands still hiding his only remaining secret.

Slipping beneath the surface, he opened his eyes into a lucid dream. Amid the clear water, Isabelle's naked body glistened in the moonlight.

Like a fish to a gleaming hook, Jon swam towards the shimmering skin then popped his head up just in front of her. Letting his eyes rest silently in hers, he searched for any apprehension — any doubt — but there was none.

A seductive smile appeared in her eyes as she leaned in to kiss him, but Jon playfully pulled away with a grin and stood up in the waist-deep pool.

Faced with his rippling stomach, Isabelle watched the water glide down Jon's body. When he lifted his hands to wipe his face, silver droplets dripped from his arms like diamonds in the moonlight.

Isabelle looked up to meet the ocean eyes gleaming down at her then leaned in to kiss his stomach gently.

Weakened by her touch, Jon's muscles quivered beneath her lips. He softly took Isabelle's head in his hands then closed his eyes as she kissed her way up his chest, allowing the gentle branding of her lips to seep into his scars.

When she finally reached his lips, Isabelle wrapped her arms around his shoulders and kissed him deeply, letting her tongue play against his as the sound of water slipping from their naked bodies tinkled into the water below.

With a coy smile, Isabelle pulled herself away and sunk back into the water. Resting on her knees, she leaned all the way back to look up at the night sky as she felt Jon's hands slide beneath her.

Feeling completely at peace in his arms, Isabelle lifted her feet from the earth and let her body float gently. When she arched her back to dip her hair beneath the water, her breasts glistened in the moonlight.

Accepting her subtle invitation, Jon ran his lips over her dripping skin, kissing every silvery speck from her chest.

Lost in the tranquil night sky, Isabelle realized for the first time in her life, she felt completely comfortable in the presence of someone else. With all her secrets bared, she trusted him with every part of who she truly was. Welcoming his soft kisses as they reached her lips, Isabelle wrapped her arms around him.

Jon lifted her out of the water. Kissing her passionately, he carried her over to the soft mossy knolls next to the trickling stream and laid her down gently.

Isabelle ran her hands down his firm body, finding him eager for her embrace. In a blissful state of disbelief, Jon pulled back to look into her eyes.

Her hands were on him — he wasn't dreaming.

Needing nothing more than her permission, Jon was nearly breathless when he felt Isabelle slip him inside her.

He pressed his mouth to hers as their bodies slowly began to move together.

When he pulled his lips away, Isabelle let out a sensual gasp. She'd never felt anything like this. A pulse shivered through her entire body each time Jon thrust himself inside her. He was gentle, yet strong. His mouth moved along her neck while their hands explored each other's flesh.

Feeling completely free, Isabelle reached her arms over her head and arched her breasts to the sky.

Seeing her hard nipples shimmer in the moonlight quickly became too much for Jon to witness. He buried his face in her neck and exploded in ecstasy.

With an exhausted sailor nuzzled on top of her, Isabelle smiled at the sound of his laboured panting. She wrapped her arms around him as his heavy chest rose and fell against her body.

When Jon finally gathered his strength, he pushed himself up to gaze into her eyes.

Of all the men in this world — she had given herself to him.

Silently thanking God, he slid his hand onto her cheek and kissed her velvety mouth again.

"I've done that once or twice in my life," he confessed with a grin, "but it's never felt like that before."

Lost in her own euphoria, Isabelle had a whimsical smile on her face. Her entire body was tingling. She wanted to stay there forever. They could sink right into this spongy earth and spend eternity in each other's arms. But time stops for no one — not even for a young woman whose virtue had just dissolved in the moonlight.

Jon kissed her again then pulled himself from her. Taking Isabelle's hand, they slipped back into the water and made their way to the shore.

Snuggled beneath blankets warmed by the burning fire, the young lovers talked a little while longer then blissfully drifted off to sleep, wrapped safely in each other's arms.

Chapter 18

CONFESSIONS

Explosions erupted whilst Charlotte searched London's bloodstained streets for red coats. Her stomach churned each time she rolled another dead soldier while praying not to find her lover's lifeless eyes staring back at her.

"Charlotte!" A voice cried from the shadows. She turned to find Gareth collapsed in the alley, his white shirt leaking blood. "NO!" she hollered, as she ran into his arms. "Cromwell's men have the King," Gareth winced. "The war is lost. I must leave tonight."

"Izzy!" Milly shouted, bounding into the bedroom in her usual state of borderline panic. "Are you still writing, love? You're expected at the Davenport's shortly. Monsieur Bouffie will have a fit if you're late for the last rehearsal."

Without looking up, Isabelle continued scribing. Truthfully, she was in bit of a tizzy of her own today. She had intended to spend this summer alone writing at the cape or sketching landscapes under the moonlight, but everything changed the night of the London's ill-fated journey.

She had awoken the next morning just before dawn to Jon's gentle kisses on her shoulder. He had to return to his ship but didn't want to leave without waking her.

Isabelle felt filled with him. His sea-blue eyes flowed through her as he returned her loving gaze. She had never felt so still. It was as though every bit of her bones had found their peace during the night while she slept in his arms.

No longer having to protect her virtue, Isabelle gave her body to him again in the budding twilight as the forest around them slowly began to wake.

Before leaving for the Barrington, Jon promised he would return — and he did. From that day on, Isabelle spent every possible moment of leisure with her sailor. They would ride to her golden cape and make love as the sun slipped into the earth; their moans of passion lost to the breaking waves.

Jon had managed to become quite a skilled rider under Isabelle's instruction, now easily keeping up with her as they raced along the coast.

Other days he would row them to the island where they were free to explore each other with nothing surrounding them but the lapping waves. No longer fearful of the fast water, Isabelle had found her courage in Jon's strength. She trusted him, and she knew if anything were to happen, he was certain to keep her safe.

Nearly every night, once the darkness settled, she would see Jon's lantern flicker in the forest calling to her to come play. They would slide into her secret lagoon and sleep beneath the stars wrapped in each other's arms, both secretly wishing the earth would stand still, and this moment would become their eternity.

Though Isabelle felt herself slipping, she was constantly aware of the future they would never share. She gave her body freely but kept her cautious heart well guarded. Through all the conversations they shared, they never once spoke of their future.

As it was, *they* didn't have one.

Instead, the young lovers chose to linger longer in their precious moments of sunsets and skin.

However, Isabelle now feared she may have lingered just a tad too long. While enjoying her lustful trysts with Jon, she failed to notice how quickly this summer was approaching its end. Victoria's masquerade was tomorrow evening, the bon voyage celebration was only four days away, and Isabelle was about to flounder on the one promise she made to her dear friend — to finish her story before Victoria left for Calvaria.

"I understand," Isabelle replied, turning to face Milly. "I only wish to finish this last bit. I need a few minutes more."

With the Earl and Countess arriving in a few days for the bon voyage party, Milly had a hundred tasks she needed to complete and easily gave in. "I'll return in two shakes of a lamb's tail," she said before slipping out the door.

Gathering her focus, Isabelle got back to her story.

> Charlotte pleaded, "How can you leave me here?" Tears streamed down her face. "I will die without you." She crumpled to his bloody chest. "Please stay with me."

"I'm sorry, love," Milly came rushing back through the door with a kitchen cloth strewn over her shoulder. "Mr. Graham is waiting. Let's get you away."

Isabelle's carriage pulled up to the Davenport Manor while it was being transformed from a stone-faced country home into a grand Calvarian palace. The scalloped staircase had been covered with elaborate purple and gold carpets, swathes of drapery sent from the Calvarian crown hung from the eaves to the ground, and ropes wound from pure gold lined the staircase all the way up to the doors.

Entering the manor on the arm of her escort, Isabelle even passed by a camel on a lead while a team from Calvaria methodically converted the manor's interior into an Arabian dreamscape.

In the ballroom, drapes of indigo hung from the ceiling as hired hands worked tirelessly to turn it into a starry desert night sky.

Lost in the silvery constellations glinting above her head, Isabelle felt something whisper within...

"This party would be the beginning, and the end, of everything."

"Izzy!" someone shouted, shaking Isabelle from her starry trance.

She looked over to find Victoria in full costume, running by on the arm of Monsieur Bouffie who quickly glanced over at Isabelle. "You're late mademoiselle," the Frenchman quipped without stopping. "See François for your costume. Rapidment!"

Once properly dressed, the girls swirled about in their iridescent gowns. Angelic mermaids and evil sea nymphs — one side fought to steal the young girl's soul while the other battled to set her free.

It only took a few raps of Monsieur Bouffie's staff before Isabelle realized Beth wasn't looking at her. In fact, it seemed Beth was making a point of looking completely in the opposite direction.

It became even more apparent during their partner work when Beth was supposed to look Isabelle directly in her eyes while they battled for the sea princess, but Beth's angry stare glared right past her.

Isabelle was perplexed — she'd barely seen Beth all summer. What could she have possibly done to make her this upset?

They ran through the entire routine three more times before Bouffie signalled François to ring the gold bell.

"Bravo ladies! Leave your costumes in the parlour. I will return tomorrow evening for the festivities. I will be dressed as the sea mother since I have created all of you." With that, he tapped his staff, clicked his heels together and sashayed out of the room.

A slew of Davenport staff helped the young women out of their costumes and back into the gorgeous gowns they had arrived in, but the moment Beth finished dressing, she quickly said goodbye to every other woman in the room then walked right by Isabelle without a glance in her direction.

"Are you not speaking to me, Beth?" Isabelle asked bluntly as her friend strolled past.

Beth didn't flinch at the sound of Isabelle's voice. She kept walking, her cinnamon curls bouncing bitterly with every step. She was almost out the front door when she heard Isabelle call again.

"Beth, stop!"

But Beth quickened her pace. She was halfway down the purple staircase before Isabelle finally took a hold of her arm, stopping her in her tracks.

"Please tell me what I've done to make you this upset!" Isabelle shouted in a huff.

Suddenly aware of their public outburst, both girls looked up to find two butlers, six coachmen and entire crew from Calvaria staring at the two young women having an obvious row in the middle of the grand entrance.

"Come with me," Isabelle said, taking her friend by the wrist.

She led Beth down the rest of the stairs to a small marble bench far away from prying ears.

"I haven't seen you all summer!" Beth yelled the moment her bottom hit the seat.

"I'm sorry. I had no idea you were so upset by it."

"A lot has happened this summer Iz, and you were nowhere to be found. You haven't been to the square, you run away after church—"

"I have seen you at the Davenport's every Friday since summer began," Isabelle pointed out. "What held your tongue?"

"I didn't want to speak in front of them." She motioned to the snarly Davenports within the walls. "I miss it being just us, like when we were children."

Her eyes dropped as she sighed. "My mother can no longer afford our Gillingham estate. She has decided to sell it," she confessed before looking up.

"That's dreadful news, I know you how much you love it there. You'll miss it terribly."

Beth shook her head. "Seems I won't miss it at all actually."

The sadness in her voice left Isabelle confused.

"My mother made a deal with the man interested in buying it."

"Well, that's wonderful, then."

"Not exactly," Beth replied. "Instead of selling the house — she has sold me. She offered my hand in marriage so the house would stay in our family."

"She traded you for a house? Oh Beth, I'm so sorry."

"Don't be. She's arriving in a few days for the bon voyage party, and I'm going to tell her then."

"Tell her what?"

Beth's sullen face finally sprouted a grin. "Thomas asked me to marry him last night."

"What?" Isabelle blurted.

Beth nodded. "When he returns from the war, we're going to get married. My mother can stuff that house."

"But your family's reputation...she will disown you!"

"I no longer care!" Beth shouted. "Thomas has lived on nearly nothing his entire life. We will get by just fine on the wages he has now." Beth's hopeful face turned sombre again. "I'm more upset that I didn't have my closest friend to speak to about all this — and I know you're keeping something from me too, Iz. Why have you been hiding all summer? Where have you been?"

Isabelle had no words. How did she fail to see they had both found themselves in exactly the same dilemma this summer?

No longer able push her feelings aside, Isabelle decided to be honest with Beth — and herself. "I suppose I've been..." her gaze dropped to her lap "...in love," she added softly.

"I beg your pardon," Beth quipped. "In love with who...yourself?"

"No," Isabelle answered meekly before looking up to meet Beth's eyes, "...with Jon."

Beth's mouth gaped open when she realized who Isabelle was talking about. In a sudden burst of excitement, she wrapped her arms around her friend. "I knew it!" she yelled as her mouth passed Isabelle's ear. "Thomas told me Jon would always head out in the same direction." She pulled back to look in Isabelle's eyes. "I knew it was towards your coast, but after the way you scolded me for falling for a sailor, I never believed you would allow one to steal your own heart."

"I don't know how it happened. I don't even know...when...it happened. I ..." Isabelle's voice began to quiver.

"You really are telling me the truth, aren't you?"

Barely able to speak, Isabelle nodded silently.

"Aren't you tired of hiding, Iz?"

Shamefully, Isabelle looked down at her lap and shook her head. "I've been hiding my entire life," she replied. "I'm beginning to think it's the only thing I'm quite good at."

Beth squeezed Isabelle's hands and leaned in with a cheeky grin. "Send Mr. Graham home and come with me. I have an idea."

Chapter 19

LOVE IN RUINS

"Stop here please!" Beth shouted abruptly from within her coach as they passed along the main dock.

The carriage rocked a bit as she stepped to the ground while Isabelle stayed seated within.

Staring through the small window, Isabelle watched her friend inconspicuously slip a note to a member of the Barrington's crew before climbing back into the carriage.

"Follow the river towards Reynolds. I will tell you when to stop," Beth instructed her coachman.

The girls were halfway to the next town when Beth spotted an opening in the forest up ahead. "Here please," she commanded.

The coachman helped the young women out of the carriage near what looked to be the remains of a worn out stone path leading deep into the woods. "We are going to sit by the river for some time. Keep yourself amused," Beth instructed as she took his hand to exit the carriage.

"Watch your heels," she mentioned to Isabelle as she led her down the broken path. "I've had to send two pairs away for repairs this summer."

Isabelle stepped lightly but skipping over broken cobbles was nothing new for this noble.

She followed Beth through the forest as it slowly opened to the ruins of an ancient stone castle. Half of it remained while the rest lay in rubble. Hundred-year-old trees had grown straight through the collapsed ceilings. Wild vines covered mounds of crumbled grey stone.

One turret still stood — a tower overlooking the river. Isabelle wondered if it once held a prisoner, or perhaps a heartbroken woman who sat by the window waiting for her lover to return from the sea. "Where are we?" she asked in awe of the untamed beauty.

"I'm surprised you've not heard of this place," Beth replied as they followed the path to the backside of the castle. "It's called Reynold's Ruins. They say Scottish nobles held it centuries ago but it was destroyed when they were driven out of England. I've met Thomas here nearly every night. He asked me to marry him right over there." Beth pointed to a quiet spot on the river bank.

Though genuinely happy for her friend, Isabelle suddenly found herself growing jealous of Beth's new gumption. She was ready to start a future with her sailor and had no fear of what that life may look like.

Beth stepped over a few broken stones as she led Isabelle into a room with half a ceiling still intact. Reaching into the remains of an old fireplace, Beth pulled out a large basket then laid a blanket on the floor.

The two women chatted in the shade of the old ruins until a small wooden rowboat appeared on the river. "Ah, there they are," Beth said with a smile before standing and making her way to the water's edge.

Following her friend into the sunlight, a grin appeared on Isabelle's face when she spied a red headed sailor on her usual seat in Jon's boat.

168

The moment Thomas felt the earth beneath him, he leapt from the boat and ran straight into Beth's arms.

Isabelle smiled as she watched her friend kiss the man she would one day call her husband.

She then looked to Jon who had pulled his boat ashore and was bounding straight towards her with a beaming smile.

She wrapped her arms around his shoulders as Jon's exuberance lifted her off her feet. He carried her into the privacy of the ruins before leaning in to kiss her deeply.

Sliding his hand up the back of her neck, he pressed his forehead to hers. "You told her the truth about me?" he asked with toothy grin.

"I couldn't keep it from her any longer," Isabelle replied. She glanced to the rubble beneath her feet. "And now...I need to be honest with you as well." Taking his hand, she slid it out of her hair.

She looked into his awaiting eyes. "Do you remember when you asked me if I'd ever felt the fate of my life shift in a single moment?"

Jon nodded, but the distress in her eyes filled him with concern.

"Well...I felt it," Isabelle finally confessed. "I felt it when I watched you leap from that ship, I felt it when you invited me to the island...I feel it every time I look at you...and I fight it constantly," she admitted before dropping her gaze.

Craving those tawny eyes, Jon gently raised her chin to look into her soul as the truth poured from her lips.

"I love you, Jon," she said quietly, "and I'm terrified of what that means."

Her beautifully heartbreaking revelation left Jon speechless. With a gentle smile, he pulled her safely to his chest.

Wrapping his arms around her, he let his chin rest on her head while he searched for any words of reassurance...but found none.

"Izzy!" Beth screeched as she came bounding towards them with Thomas in hand. "I have another brilliant idea!"

Knowing Isabelle was trying to compose herself, Jon replied for her. "Let's hear it then," he said with a smile, still cradling Isabelle in his arms.

"I'll have Victoria draw up two more invitations to her masque tomorrow night. One for the Baron of Giveny," she said, looking to Thomas, "and one for his business associate from Paris, Monsieur...De La Mar?" she added with a smile."

"You want to sneak them into the party?" Isabelle asked in surprise. "Everyone in town will be there."

"It's a masque, Iz. No one will know who there are." She turned her attention to the two men. "The theme is, From the Sea. Most of the men will be dressed as pirates or admirals. I'll send a note to the shop in town and ask them to hold two admiral costumes on my mother's account." She looked to Thomas. "Just make sure you turn up once everyone's a bit drunk," she added with a wink.

Chapter 20

MASKS AND SHADOWS

Eight servants helped Victoria prepare for her masquerade; layering one costume over another, snapping things into place, tying ribbons and bows — and that was just her clothing. Strings of pearls swirled around her neck while other attendants buffed her nails and rouged her cheeks. Skilled hands affixed sparkling jewels in her platinum curls for the perfect finishing touch, all while Victoria stared blankly into the mirror.

With her billowing costume already complete, Isabelle sat back and watched her friend in silence. When she noticed a tear stream down Victoria's cheek, she stood up and walked to the vanity in a noisy swathe of sea-foam taffeta.

"Please leave us," she politely commanded the room before kneeling in front of her friend.

Having the highest rank in the room, Isabelle's orders were followed and the chamber cleared quickly. She grabbed a small cloth and dabbed Victoria's cheek. "What could possibly be troubling you on a night like this?"

Finally breaking her hopeless gaze from the mirror, Victoria looked down at her friend. "I can't walk down those stairs, Iz. Walking down those stairs means the beginning of my end here in England."

Clasping Victoria's small hands, Isabelle felt them trembling.

"I don't want to be shipped off like barrel of silk," Victoria whimpered. "I cannot speak the language. I won't be able to talk with my own husband!"

"You're not going anywhere," Isabelle assured her. "Not tonight."

Victoria blinked away a few budding tears.

"Tonight, we're just walking down those stairs. The same staircase you've walked down hundreds of times. We are going to perform the dance we've been rehearsing all summer and then we're going to celebrate you becoming a real princess."

Victoria did her best to feign a grin.

"You're going to live in a beautiful palace Vic, with the most luxurious fabrics, and endless servants to tend you—"

"I'd rather have love," Victoria interjected with a sniff.

Two months ago, Isabelle would've told her forlorn friend that love wasn't real; that it only existed within the fictitious world of daydreamers and the lustful eyes of men.

But saying those words now would be a lie. Isabelle felt it. She held it within her even now as she stared into her friend's tearful eyes. Her love for Jon was real. It woke her every morning, inspired every decision, engulfed every one of her thoughts, and broke her heart every time she thought of what was next for them.

Isabelle tightened her grip on Victoria's hands. "Love only ends in someone's broken heart," she grimly replied. "You may count yourself fortunate that you will never have to feel that."

Spotting an unfamiliar sadness in her friend's eyes, Victoria wondered how Isabelle had suddenly come to know so much about heartbreak.

A butler called from the doorway. "Your guests await, Mistress."

"We're just walking down the stairs," Isabelle said with a reassuring grin. She squeezed Victoria's hands then helped the future princess rise to her feet.

Joining the rest of their iridescent draped friends at the top of the stairs, they exchanged a friendly smile and slipped their masks on.

At Bouffie's signal, the orchestra began and an entourage of Gillingham's most beautiful young women gracefully followed Victoria down the grand staircase then onto the dance floor.

Bassoons bellowed as the girls swirled about, tossing Victoria back and forth in the waves. Beautiful mermaids fought evil nymphs before the crimson sea witch slithered into the fray.

Capturing her innocent sister, Anne raised her silver trident high in the air then plunged it down as the girls quickly turned to throw spirals of red satin into the crowd.

Victoria's lifeless body sunk below the waves while the mermaids and sea nymphs continued to battle for her soul.

Beneath the swirling taffeta, Victoria worked quickly to release the snaps on her first costume, letting it fall to the ground moments before the victorious mermaids lifted her high in the air to display their sparkling princess to an eruption of tremendous applause.

Accepting their praise with heavy breaths, the girls safely lowered Victoria to the ground as shouts of "Bravo!" erupted from the crowd.

"Well done!" the audience cheered as the young women took their bows.

Dressed in an extravagant costume of his own, Bouffie smiled at his shimmering sea princess and proudly dipped his head.

As Victoria rose from her final curtsey, the crowd before her slowly began to part. She watched as a tall olive-skinned man dressed in gold linens and an amethyst sash confidently emerged onto the dance floor followed by four burly men at his heels.

His dark hair was quite luxuriant for a man. His teal eyes were clear and peaceful.

The room fell silent when he stopped directly in front of her.

Even though Victoria had never seen this man before, her heart knew exactly who he was.

The Calvarian Prince smiled at the sight of his future bride glistening in the candlelight. He gently took her hand, knelt before her then looked up to her sparkling blue eyes. "I am humbled by your true beauty." His accent wasn't perfect but his words were clear.

"You speak English?" Victoria uttered in surprise.

"I have studied English since the day your father left Calvaria. I have come to see you safely to your new home...if you will have me," he offered.

Anne's jaw nearly hit the floor as it dropped open in jealousy, but Victoria paid her no attention — she was blissfully lost in the inviting eyes of her handsome Prince.

"I will," she replied with a smile.

Delighted by her answer, the young Prince rose to his feet and escorted her off the dance floor.

Isabelle watched the gleeful sea princess saunter past Beth whose eyes were filled with tears of happiness then by her sister Anne, who was scathing with a mixture of disbelief, jealously, and a hint of self-loathing before she stormed out of the room.

Though Victoria had disappeared from her own party, the celebration still roared on in her honour. Guests enjoyed trays of wine and spirits. Tables were stacked high with delicious tarts, cheeses, and fruits. Isabelle was already on her third glass of wine when she realized how late it was and Jon still hadn't turned up.

Had he grown weary of appearing at his first society event? She knew he wasn't fond of lying and wondered if he'd changed his mind about attending all together.

Glass in hand, Isabelle decided to head upstairs to Victoria's room for a touch up, but as she strolled by Anne's bedroom, she overheard the familiar sounds of pleasure leaking through the crack of a nearly closed door.

The copious amounts of wine she'd swallowed earlier had loosened her inhibitions and she curiously crept towards the glowing sliver of light.

Peering into the candlelit room, she spied Anne and another woman from the party intimately sprawled across the red satin bedding. Two other men wearing nothing but their black velvet masks soon joined their lustful embrace.

The mystery woman stroked a pluming black feather over Anne's breasts, causing her to moan with pleasure and turn her head towards the door where she spotted Isabelle watching from the dark hallway.

Anne stared straight back at Isabelle as one of the men kissed his way down her stomach — then kept going.

Isabelle saw no shame in Anne's eyes. No fear of what would happen to her reputation, or what her father, or anyone else might think if they stumbled upon this orgy of flesh and feathers.

For the first time in her life, Isabelle found herself jealous of this salacious woman — for Anne was truly free. She shamelessly enjoyed her desires while noble Lady Isabelle still lurked in the shadows.

When the other masked participant shoved his manhood in Anne's open mouth, he moaned in satisfaction and Isabelle instantly recognized the sound. She'd heard the same one earlier that summer in the forest the night of the Solstice Festival.

It was William. Her future husband was thrusting himself into the welcoming mouth of one of her oldest friends.

Completely repulsed, Isabelle turned away. With Beth determined to marry Thomas, William engaged in lewd acts right in front her, and Jon nowhere to be found, she suddenly felt helplessly alone. This is exactly what the future held for her — hiding in the shadows while everyone else was free to enjoy to their lives of pleasure.

Isabelle swallowed the last of her wine as she backed away. No longer interested in primping her worthless self, she stormed back downstairs, lifted a full glass of wine from a servant's tray then gulped down a very un-ladylike sip to help satiate her sudden feelings of inadequacy.

Through her mask, Isabelle glanced around the room. The night was getting on and the crowd was getting sloppy. Guests threw their heads back in laughter while their hands slid onto areas that, at any other time of day, would've been considered an absolute sin.

"Bonsoir, ma cherie." A voice whispered softly in Isabelle's ear.

She recognized that horrible French accent immediately but kept her gaze straight in front of her — even after a few glasses of wine, she was still able to keep herself from flinching in a room full of onlookers.

"Bonsoir, marin," she replied as a smile crept to her lips. "I was beginning to think you had deserted me," she said as Jon stepped in front of her.

"My apologies, but getting all this on was a bloody nightmare," he exclaimed, looking down at his constrictive admiral's uniform.

Isabelle laughed at the sight of him in a black periwig, three-point hat, red jacket, and black buckled boots.

"You look…" she glanced up his body, stopping when she met his eyes behind the black mask. He was still there, though buried beneath this ridiculous costume, his eyes still swept her away "…handsome," she finally said with a drunken smile.

"Am I allowed to kiss you?" he asked, stepping closer. "I am an admiral after all."

She leaned in, nearly touching his lips. "If William were to see some other man kiss me, he would likely demand your head right here in front of everyone."

"Then take me some place where we can be alone and I may devour you in peace," he said, sliding his hand up the soft skin of her back.

"Alright, follow me."

Isabelle led him through the crowd of dancing aristocrats, but as they were about to leave the room, she spotted a tiny woman with wispy grey hair and a purple turban seated at a table draped in exotic tapestries.

Noticing the crystal ball and deck of cards laid out before her, Isabelle turned to stop Jon. "Is that one of those gypsy women you spoke of?" she asked before glancing back at the woman.

As though sensing eyes upon her, the wise woman shifted her gaze to meet Isabelle's inquisitive stare.

"Aye...perhaps. Should we ask if she can see our future?" he asked, nuzzling into his love's ear.

"I'm not sure I want to know." Isabelle replied, trying to stifle the doom she felt upon hearing his question. They shared a look of disparity knowing their future together had always been uncertain and perhaps both their destinies were better left unknown.

"It couldn't possibly be worse than what we expect," Jon said with a cheeky grin.

He took Isabelle's hand and led her to the gypsy's table. "Are you a fortune-teller?" he asked as they approached.

"It's not always about fortunes," the wise woman replied with a raspy foreign accent.

"Pull one, Iz," Jon insisted, motioning to the cards laid face down on the table.

The woman looked to Isabelle then passed her open palm across the spread, giving her permission to reach down and choose a card.

Running her fingers lightly across the deck, Isabelle stopped just as she neared the end. She slid a single card towards the woman who flipped it over with her ring-filled hand.

It pictured a white dove perched within an opulent golden birdcage shrouded in a sheer cloth. "The Veil," the gypsy woman announced. "You live in a cage of lies."

"I'm not sure I'd go that far," Isabelle replied, slightly insulted.

"You don't show who you really are. You hide your truth from the world."

"I don't suppose that's much of a secret." Isabelle chuckled as she looked to Jon.

"Not yet." The woman added sternly — sending a shiver down Isabelle's spine. "Secrets hold resistance and fear. You will never be free while you live in a cage of lies."

Locked in the woman's swirling grey eyes, Isabelle found herself stunned for words. She was never given a chance to explore the truth of her own life — what could an old woman from some far away land possibly know about *her* truth?

"Alright," Jon announced, breaking the tense silence, "my turn." He reached down, chose a card without hesitation then flipped it over.

"The Vow," the woman announced with surprise. "This card is only drawn in the presence of true love."

Her words caused Jon and Isabelle to smile as they sheepishly caught each other's glance.

"Will you two soon be married?"

"Not to each other," Isabelle quipped before taking another sip of wine.

Jon started to fidget. "Well...there is something I need to ask you."

Isabelle shook her head in disbelief. "Jon, we, I couldn't possibly—"

"No....not that," he replied with a heartbreaking smile. "Thank you for your time," he said to the fortune-teller before pulling Isabelle out of the room.

The wise woman stayed seated at her table as she silently watched the secret lovers take their tryst back behind the veil.

After winding down dark hallways, Isabelle led Jon into a sitting room lit by tiered candelabras. He pushed the door closed behind him but this wing of the house was old and the door didn't quite shut all the way.

Isabelle sat on the creamy satin lounge covered in tasseled pillows then lifted her mask off. "What did you need to ask me, Jon of the Sea?" she teased as she watched him remove his jacket and take a seat next to her.

A hopeless sigh slipped from Jon's lips as he removed his mask. He looked to the beauty at his side. "I've spent this summer training hundreds of men. So many mornings I've stood on the bow watching them board their vessels and leave the dockyard...but I haven't seen a single one return."

Jon reached into his pocket. "I don't own much, everything I have is aboard the Barrington. If we do go down in this war, it all sinks with me."

He pulled out a small cloth bag, untied the ribbon then slid a silver ring onto his palm. "My father gave this to my mum a few years before his ship went down. I took it off her finger the night I left Jersey." Jon looked to her amber eyes. "I would die at peace knowing this ring was safe upon your finger."

Isabelle glanced to Jon with a smile. "It would be my honour to wear it."

He gently took her hand and slid the ring onto her finger.

It was a perfect fit.

Admiring the modest piece of jewellery, Isabelle noticed two tiny circular rubies embedded in the silver band and a small indentation between the two stones.

"There were three rubies when my father gave her this ring, one for each of us. He had it made special for her, but she lost one of the stones somewhere along the way. I understand if you don't want to wear it, but it would mean the world to know it was safe with you."

Looking down at the ring, Isabelle sensed the heartbreak already contained within these stones and feared she may have just inherited a new curse. "I promise to it keep it until you return."

She banished any looming worries with a deep breath and looked to Jon while his thumb lightly grazed the ring now resting on her finger.

"Perhaps we should go back and ask the fortune-teller if she grants wishes," he said hopelessly.

"What would you wish for?"

"I know that I'll love you forever Isabelle. My wish would be that my forever includes you."

Lost in Jon's somber eyes, Isabelle leaned in and pressed her lips to his. Her only intention was to ease his heartache with a few secret kisses but the wine coursing through her veins moved her hand down his stomach then onto his pants.

Jon pulled his lips away in surprise. "What if someone sees us, *Lady Isabelle*?" he snickered.

"I no longer care," she said confidently as she pulled Jon's shirt from his belt and started undoing the buttons.

Jon leaned back on the chaise, shocked by her forwardness in a house filled with hundreds of guests who knew exactly who she was — masked or not. "Are you mad?" he asked with a surprised smile as she kissed her way up his chest.

"No," Isabelle reached up to fling his hat and periwig to the floor, "I'm in love," she teased before leaving his lips empty.

Lost in a whirl of their own passion, they made love deep within the Davenport manor without a single clue they were being watched.

Chapter 21

WINDS OF CHANGE

Sunlight seeped through the slits of Isabelle's sleepy eyes as they opened with a few blinks to greet the new day — but a sudden pounding in her skull shut them quickly again.

Shielding her eyes from the scant bit of sunlight trickling through the draped windows, Isabelle rolled over in Victoria's enormous bed to find Beth still asleep with her mouth drooped open, snoring like a wild goose.

Isabelle chuckled at the adorable honking sound but soon realized it would be impossible to fall back asleep next to the spontaneous bursts. She decided to face the short journey home where she could enjoy the quiet seclusion of her own sheets.

Knowing young Lady Arlington had drunkenly fallen asleep in her costume, a servant came scurrying over with a light dress in her arms. "Good morning, Lady Isabelle. Would you care to change your dress now?" she asked while pouring water into a crystal glass at the bedside. "You were quite firm about us leaving you be when you arrived to bed early this morning."

Isabelle's stomach turned at the thought of how rude she must've been to this poor woman last night but still held her convictions. "No. I am well in this until I arrive home." Her dry mouth felt like the Arabian dessert. "However, I will have the water, thank you."

Bringing the crystal glass to her wine-stained lips, Isabelle gulped down every last drop as the chambermaid looked on in amazement.

She huffed a few breaths as she placed the empty glass back on the side table. "Do you know if my carriage has arrived?" she asked while squeezing the throbbing pain in her brow.

"Yes, he's been waiting outside since just after dawn."

"And what time is it now?"

"Nearly two o'clock, my Lady," she replied while refilling the empty glass.

"Thank you. Please tell him I will be down in a moment." Isabelle pushed herself up from the marshmallow bedding. "I just need to..." she crinkled one eye before sitting back down. "I just need to get myself together first."

"Let me help you, Lady Isa—"

"No, no I'm quite well on my own. Please tell him I'll be right down," she said firmly as she reached again for the full glass of water.

The chambermaid curtsied before leaving Isabelle to her privacy. "As you wish." She left the room, closed the door behind her and started down the enormous staircase, her hard-soled shoes echoing down every step.

The Davenport Manor was a bustle of activity this morning as the servants removed any sign of last night's party and prepared the mansion for its next celebration — Victoria's official bon voyage in a few days.

The chambermaid had nearly reached the front entrance to deliver Isabelle's message when she heard her name called from behind.

"Mary!" A small voice echoed through the marble foyer.

Mary quickly turned to find the newest employee at the Davenport residence running towards her; a young dark-haired kitchen maid who had just begun to learn what silver service really meant.

Mary waited for the young woman to approach before scolding her. "I understand that you are new here, but this is a grand estate. We do not run about shouting at each other, do you understand me?"

"Forgive me," the young maid replied insincerely, "but did you hear about the men who snuck into the party last night?"

"No," Mary replied, suddenly intrigued.

"Two sailors from the dockyard. It's been said that one of them was quite handsome," she added with a smile. "I told you I could've donned a mask and celebrated with them all night. No one would've known it was me."

Mary scoffed at such nonsense. "My dear, you were not hired to celebrate with these people, and if you keep trying to find ways out of your duties, you will soon find yourself back in that tavern from which you came. Now get back to work!" she ordered.

The startled servant bowed her head then hurried away.

"Oh," Mary shouted softly, catching the young maid's attention, "do tell Phillip about the sailors. He may want to count the silverware again."

.   .   .   .

Isabelle's sleepy eyes peered through the window of her coach. Hypnotized by billowing clouds and swaying trees, she rested her clammy forehead against the cool glass.

The seasons were beginning to change. The rustling leaves were crisp in the trees; the air was no longer humid. The thought of the impending autumn, or perhaps the swaying of her coach, began to turn Isabelle's stomach. She took a few deep breaths and tried to focus on the cozy bed she planned on climbing into the moment she arrived home.

As the carriage made its way through Bluefield's gates and up the laneway, Isabelle's short-lived moment of serenity ceased when she passed a fleet of wagons lined all the way up to the front door.

Coachmen lifted their caps as the Lady of the manor rolled by. Her parents were expected in a few days for the bon voyage party, but sending their entire household to prepare this early seemed a tad unnecessary.

Mr. Graham stopped at the front steps then helped Isabelle out of the carriage. Still feeling slightly woozy, she welcomed his sturdy hand as she stepped to the ground.

"S'cuze, m'lady," A servant scurried up the stairs then into the manor through the propped open doors.

Isabelle felt like she'd suddenly found herself in the middle of an ant line as servants darted in and out the house carrying silverware, oversized candelabras, tapestries, crates of wine and of course, Duke perched upon a satin pillow.

As Isabelle started up the stairs, she heard Milly call from inside the house. She looked up just as the old woman came charging through the doorway.

Nearly running into a lad carrying a towering flower display into the house, Milly pinned herself against the door allowing him to pass before bounding down the stairs towards Isabelle. "Your father's here, Iz...Lady Isabelle," she said with a curtsey knowing they were both under watchful eyes at the moment. "He's not happy about something, Iz," she whispered as she linked Isabelle's arm and accompanied her into the house. "You'd better get yourself looking nice for supper or he may actually blow tonight."

"Ah, Lady Isabelle. How lovely of you to join us," a tall plain woman interrupted as they approached the grand staircase. The high collar on her well-tailored grey dress nearly touched her chin. Her clasped hands rested on her immaculately pressed white apron, and her black hair, pulled so tightly into a bun, left her with a devilish glare.

"I am Lady Elenore of your father's household at Whitehall. He has tasked me as your chambermaid this evening," she said while unlatching their arms. "Thank you, Moira. I will tend the girl from here. Go see if you could be of use somewhere else," she said coldly.

Giving Isabelle an apologetic glance, Milly curtseyed to both women then walked back to the kitchen.

Lady Elenore wrapped her arm around Isabelle's waist and escorted her up the stairs. "Your parents would like you to join them for dinner. Your father mentioned you were not corseted the last time you dined with him and found it unacceptable. He has asked that you be dressed to his highest expectations for dinner this evening."

Isabelle said nothing as she listened to the woman drone on. The last thing she felt like doing in this state was eating, especially alongside her parents, and now in a corset as well? She had visions of staring into a juicy lamb shank while her drunken mother leered at her from across the table, and her father scowled because Isabelle was not his son.

Her legs began to wobble. The whirlpool welling in her stomach was about to erupt. Her body heaved as they reached the top of the stairs.

Tossing the woman's arm off her, Isabelle ran to a nearby potted plant and threw up all the water she had so elegantly chugged from the crystal goblet earlier.

Caught off guard, Lady Elenore quickly dashed after her charge and held Isabelle's hair back from the vomit. "Perhaps we'll start with a bath."

Chapter 22

BETROTHED

A soothing ginger tea and a warm bath had Isabelle feeling like herself again, but her newfound tranquility didn't last for long.

Lady Elenore laced her into a bone corset, pulling so tightly with each latching Isabelle wondered if it were an ordered punishment. The stone-faced woman then tied a petticoat around Isabelle's waist and helped her into the ivory gown her father brought from the palace.

The elaborate red floral appliqués sewn into the bodice flowed onto the shimmering skirt in a peppering of tiny rose buds. Lady Elenore fluffed the obnoxiously puffy sleeves while Isabelle stared down at the cleavage bursting from her scooped neckline.

Knowing there wasn't enough time to wash, dry and curl Isabelle's hair, Elenore tried to bring some bounce back by running a light salve through her loose curls, but it was no use. She tied both sides up with ivory satin bows before looping a strand of pearls around the young noble's neck.

Isabelle stared blankly into the vanity mirror as this woman struggled to make something magical out of the dehydrated, sleep deprived mess she was presented with.

Embarrassed by the porcelain doll staring back at her, Isabelle mumbled under her breath, "I look like one of the spaniels."

She glanced to Duke who was watching from the chaise. A quick tilt of his head shook his long curly ears as he curiously stared back at her.

Isabelle looked down at her hand, pleased that Jon's ruby ring matched the scarlet appliqués on her dress perfectly. She was certain no one would notice one missing stone if she kept her hand in her lap as much as possible.

A loud knock on the door startled both women. Elenore responded without looking up from her task. "You may enter."

In the mirror, Isabelle recognized the elderly butler from her apartments at Whitehall.

"They are ready to be seated, my Lady," he announced.

You can do this, Isabelle silently told herself. It's one plate of food. You've done this a hundred times.

She pulled her shoulders back, rose from her seat then elegantly walked over to her awaiting escort.

As she left her bedroom, Isabelle glanced over her shoulder and spotted Lady Elenore bent over the vanity, picking up perfume bottles and placing them in a small wooden box.

That's odd, Isabelle thought. She must tell her father about this. He'll want to have that woman checked before she leaves the property.

After being escorted back down the staircase, Isabelle entered the dining room to find it filled with the same elaborate candelabras and the same tapestries draped over the windows. The same vases of pink and red roses lined the entire table even though it was only set for three. Her parents were already seated and enjoying their wine as Isabelle's escort pulled out her oversized chair.

190

Her greeting was sullen as she took her seat. "Good evening. With the extravagance of my dress tonight, I presumed we were entertaining guests."

Perched with his elbows on the table, his head resting on his clasped hands, Arlington stared stoically into the candlelight. "There's certainly more room at the table," he said without moving. "Who would like to join us?"

His tone sliced Isabelle like a dagger. She knew there was more to his sarcastic question and waited patiently before replying.

"Yes," her mother slurred from across the table, "a young sailor perhaps." The Countess slowly stroked her pearl necklace across the top of her cleavage. "We should invite him for dinner," she said with a sensuous smile.

A predictable plate of lamb was placed before each of them as Isabelle replied. "Any particular sailor you had in mind, mother?" Her words reeked of disdain as she peered across the table.

"Yes," Arlington said matter-of-factly, glancing at his concupiscent daughter, "the one you were with at the Davenport's last night."

His words blew a hole through Isabelle's chest.

Completely blindsided, she knew she had to come up with something quickly. Admitting to his accusation would undoubtedly seal her fate here at Bluefields and possibly end Jon's life entirely. "I don't know what you're talk—"

"Oh, enough!" Arlington slammed his fist on the table causing Isabelle and her lethargic mother to jump in their seats. "I've heard rumblings of you running around with him all summer. From a ship I brought into this harbour, no less!"

The ridges of Arlington's snarling face caught the candlelight, terrifying Isabelle to her very core. Someone had clearly tipped him off.

Blood surged through her body while her mind searched for an answer...a lie, a convincing fib...a tale of how it must've been someone else.

But then, something within her finally snapped.

She couldn't bring herself to lie anymore. She was a grown woman about to embark on marriage and motherhood and more importantly, she was still slightly ill from the night before and didn't have the stamina or wherewithal to uphold this facade any longer.

"Oh, what does it matter to you?" she shouted in a huff. "I'll soon be married to William, you will get your deal for the King, and you'll all live happily ever after!" she said as she popped up from the table, ready to bolt to the comfy bed she'd been craving since she first woke up.

"Well," Arlington calmly replied, "if William wants you for his bride, he'll first have to see you divorced from your husband," he said before sipping his wine.

Isabelle's brow wrinkled in confusion. "My husband?"

"Yes, I believe I've found a much better match for my promiscuous daughter than those pompous Cunninghams," he sneered.

Isabelle's legs went weak — she slowly sat back down. "Who?"

"The Baron of Beaumont is desperate for an heir. Since you seem to have developed a new penchant for sexual leisure, you'll be happy to know he's likely to take you every night in his desperation for a son." He cackled as he raised his glass in a toast to himself — he had finally found the ultimate punishment for his eternally incorrigible daughter.

Glancing to her lap, Isabelle tried to figure out who her father was referring to. The only Baron of Beaumont she knew of was a seventy-year-old shipping magnate who lived hundreds of miles away.

"But he is an old man!" Isabelle yelled, completely disgusted by the thought of having to give herself every night to someone old enough to be her grandfather.

"Yes," Arlington answered with a laugh, "he is! Even still, he has yet to produce an heir. Three wives...no children."

"Perhaps he's cursed." Isabelle quipped under her breath.

"Either way, he's willing to aid the King with a generous fleet to give it another go with you. Should you succeed in producing an heir, your children will be very powerful here in England." He lifted his glass towards his wife.

Receiving her husband's toast to their future grandchildren, the Countess raised her glass without a glance in Isabelle's direction.

"And better still," Arlington continued, "his estate is all the way out in Plymouth. I hope that takes you well enough away from these nonsensical rumours," he added sarcastically, knowing by Isabelle's reaction that everything he'd heard about his licentious daughter was completely true.

Isabelle deflated in her seat. "When?" she whimpered as her eyes fell back to her lap.

"His fleet is underway to the dockyard as we speak. He has also sent a carriage to collect you and whatever you can pack into a few chests. It will deliver you to Plymouth where you will be married upon arrival. You leave at dawn."

"Tomorrow?" Isabelle exclaimed.

"Yes," Arlington replied. "You may be excused to pack your things," he added without looking at her.

Searching for some solace in this sudden nightmare, Isabelle's heart begged for her comforting companions. "May I take the Tilly's with me?" she asked as her face began to flush. "Without me here, they will have nothing to tend but the house."

"No," Arlington answered sharply. "Beaumont has plenty of servants to tend you. They will stay here — you will go."

Isabelle's chest quivered as tears clumped in her throat. She knew she was about to break but refused to let them see her cry.

She gracefully rose from her seat and excused herself from the table.

As she left the room to pack whatever part of her life she could fit into a few chests, a glint of hope did pass through her mind — the thin silver lining to this dreadful punishment was knowing she would never have to lay eyes upon either of these two self-serving people ever again.

Chapter 23

THUNDER AND PROMISES

Isabelle felt herself coming to a boil as she climbed the stairs back to her bedroom, but halfway up, she began to feel light headed and stopped briefly to steady herself against the wall.

When she finally reached her bedroom, she pushed the door open to discover the sunset beaming through her windows left her room aglow in a burning crimson fire.

Was she trapped in a dream?

Had this entire day been a burning nightmare she hadn't yet awoken from?

The gentle luffing of the terrace drapery caught Isabelle's attention. Lured by their hypnotic dance, she floated over then stepped onto the balcony.

In silent awe, she stared at the beauty forming before her eyes. Dense clouds rolled in from the sea; fluffy rows of reds and purples moving against a glowing fuchsia sky. She peered over the scarlet forest below. It looked as though the entire world had been set ablaze by the burning sunset.

Isabelle breathed the warm air deep into her lungs, closed her eyes and prayed to wake in Victoria's bed.

"Oh, Lady Isabelle," a voice chirped from inside.

Isabelle turned to find Lady Elenore standing in the middle of her room amidst a collection of open chests.

"Back so soon?" she spoke again, breaking the young noble from Earth's fiery spell. "I'm still in the middle of packing your things as your father requested."

A steely glare settled in Isabelle's eyes. "Thank you," she replied while wondering if she was the last to know of her impending move. "I can finish the rest. You are dismissed."

"But I—"

"That's enough," Isabelle commanded sternly. "Go see if you could be of use somewhere else," she added in the same condescending tone Milly was dismissed with earlier.

Knowing she was not allowed to speak back to the young woman of the house, Lady Elenore dipped her head in place of a full curtsey and left the room.

When Isabelle heard the door latch, she turned her gaze back to the sky to find it had already lost its enchanting lustre. The deep plums had rolled into dark greys and there was now a slight chill in the air.

Left disheartened by a beautiful sight so quickly lost, Isabelle looked into her bedroom at the open chests then stepped back inside.

How could she possibly be expected to move her entire life to Plymouth overnight — and why the rush?

A buzz began to swell in her chest.

She can't do this.

She won't leave.

In a haze of desperation, Isabelle glanced around her room and made a decision right then — she would not be leaving for Plymouth at dawn. She would pack whatever she could carry and leave on horseback tonight.

But she knew her father wouldn't let his prized trophy slip away that easily — he would surely send his hunters to track her down. She wouldn't be able to fight them all on her own, and looking over her shoulder for the rest of her life sounded eternally daunting.

She would never survive it.

She glanced to her desk with tears in her eyes.

Hidden within the top drawer lay her trusty dagger. The steel blade that had protected her innocent life could take all this pain away tonight.

She didn't have to face a life of servitude and obedience. She no longer needed to bow to the whims of men.

She could take all the power from them in an instant.

Lost in a hopeless trance, Isabelle suddenly craved the cold steel in her hands. Tears rolled down her cheeks as she walked to her grandfather's desk.

Her fingers rested on the drawer handle, hesitating for just a moment, before gripping it and pulling it open. But the old drawer jammed halfway, jolting the desk, sending Jon's hand-carved stallion tumbling to its side.

"Jon!" she blurted.

How could she have forgotten that she was no longer alone in this world. She wasn't a virginal young girl who needed to take orders from her father. She had fallen in love with a man who had vowed to love her forever.

As the heaviness lifted, Isabelle's mind started working quickly; Jon can keep up with her on horseback now — she wouldn't be alone if he was by her side. They could ride to the end of the earth as long as they were together.

Isabelle shut the drawer and picked up the tiny carving. She'd wait until Jon came to visit later tonight and tell him they must leave right away. She could tack both horses while he went back to pack his things. The Baron of Beaumont would have to find some other girl to satisfy his breeding desires.

As the sky dimmed, Isabelle packed her expensive gowns and perfumes to make it look as though she would still be there come dawn, but she also kept a separate pile on her bed for items she would be taking with her tonight.

She tossed the dagger on her bed just as the first lulls of thunder began to roll in the distance. When she realized the window above her desk was still open, she reached out to pull it closed, stopping briefly to appreciate the scent of incoming rain; this storm would not make their journey easy tonight but it would serve to conceal them nicely.

As she pulled the window closed and turned the latch, she spotted a small flame flickering beneath the tree line.

Had Jon come early? She could slip out to speak with him now but wouldn't be able to get the horses out until Mr. Tilly turned in for the night.

She stopped by her vanity and quickly realized her hair was still swept up in two curly ponytails. After untying the bows, Isabelle removed her pearls and dangly earrings then raked her fingers through her newly freed locks.

With everyone tending her parents on the other side of the manor, Isabelle held the hem of her ivory gown as she spiralled down the staircase.

She ran through the garden, spellbound by Jon's longing eyes upon her. The wind blew thorny roses in her path but Isabelle kept running. For the first time in her life, she knew exactly what she wanted, and he was waiting for her just beneath the trees.

Jon placed his lantern on the ground then stood quietly in the forest. The sight of Isabelle gracefully running towards him with a glowing smile caused him to crack a sorrowful grin.

When she finally reached him, Isabelle leapt into his arms and pressed her lips firmly against his. She knew he was her true love long ago but tonight, he would also be her salvation.

Jon raised his hands to her hips as she pressed into him, but to Isabelle, it felt like he was barely touching her. Even his kiss felt empty tonight.

Where was he?

Slipping from their unsettling embrace, Isabelle looked up in hopes of unearthing an answer, but the startling sadness in his eyes made her heart sink like an anchor through a bottomless sea. "What's wrong?" she yelped.

Jon's empty gaze looked to the hopeful honey eyes staring up at him, but he couldn't bring himself to answer. He silently brushed a stray hair from Isabelle's cheek in an attempt to steal just one more moment of innocence from this life.

He couldn't bear to speak his truth while looking directly at her and dropped his gaze to the ground.

Isabelle felt her heart breaking before he spoke a single word. With no breath in her lungs, she just stood there, silently waiting for him to offer something...anything.

"Our ship has been called," he sighed.

His weak hands finally grasped Isabelle's hips in hopes of never having to let go. When the only response he heard was a clap of thunder above, Jon looked up to meet her eyes.

Through no more than an empty whisper, just one word slipped from Isabelle's lips "...no."

Sliding from his embrace, her eyes welled with tears. God had served more than her fair share of disruption today.

"We depart at dawn," Jon continued. His normally sturdy voice cracked through his confession.

"But...your ship has not yet been refit. She carries no guns. How will the Barrington be useful in a war with no cannons?"

Without a proper answer, Jon silently shook his head knowing her fears were completely rational.

"No!" Isabelle said again, this time with more gumption. "It's just...you came early." In an attempt to pull herself together, Isabelle wiped the tears from her eyes. "It's good that you came early because we have to leave tonight."

Confused by which part of his explanation she failed to understand, Jon asked, "What do you mean we?"

"Remember when I told you people are always watching me?"

Jon nodded knowing he was forced to hide his love for her all summer because of it.

"Well, it seems word of our encounters has reached my father's ears, which is likely why your ship has prematurely been called, and why I am now being sent to the other side of England to be married to some old man!" she exclaimed, nearly keeling over in complete emotional and physical exhaustion.

Jon grabbed her arms to stabilize her. "When?"

"Tomorrow morning."

The sullen sailor suddenly sprung to life. "What?" he shouted.

"Shhh!" Using what little strength she had left, Isabelle pushed him further into the forest. "My father's entire household is here. They'll hear you," she shouted softly. "My parents came early to inform me of my betrothal and send me off."

"To where?"

"It doesn't matter to where because I'm not going," Isabelle replied with a sniff. "We need to leave on horseback tonight. We can disappear together."

A hollowed woman in ivory satin, Isabelle had nothing left. She needed him to be more than just her lover tonight; she needed him to be her strength, her protector — her freedom.

Jon's eyes softened as he slid his hand into her hair. "My Izzy,' he said with a gentle smile. Wrapping his arms around her, he let his chin rest upon her head. "Or maybe we could find a way to make this night last forever." Truthfully, he was terrified of what lay ahead and wanted nothing more than to spend what could easily be his last night on earth with the only woman in the world he loved more than himself.

But Isabelle's tempestuous urgency broke their embrace. "I'm serious, Jon," she said, pushing herself from his arms. "I have to leave tonight. You don't have to sail into that war tomorrow. You can start again...a new life...with me," she pleaded as she sweetly leaned into him. "We can turn into strangers...live like gypsies."

Shocked by her invitation that was an absolute impossibility mere hours ago, Jon was speechless. The thought of running away with her had crossed his mind many times but he never imagined a future together would ever truly be possible.

"There are plenty of men to fight that war," Isabelle persisted. "No one will ever notice one missing sailor."

Jon stayed silent as he contemplated her words, but his eyes suddenly grew stern. "My mates will notice," he replied coldly, insulted by her insinuation that he could so easily desert them.

"Didn't you once say they'd understand if they knew you were with a beautiful woman?" she said with a loving smile.

Even as his heart shattered in his chest, Jon managed to hold steady. "Before we ever sailed up the Medway, I swore to those men that I would fight this war by their side. My love lies with you Isabelle, but right now...my loyalty lies with them." His dull eyes returned her hopeful gaze. "I can't betray my brothers, Iz."

"But you can so easily leave me?" Isabelle whimpered before pushing away from him.

"Izzy, please," he grabbed her arm as she turned away. "I will return for you and die a happy man growing old in your arms," he moved closer, "but I cannot abandon my brothers as they sail into a war."

Not able to look in his eyes, Isabelle's gaze was far off in the forest. She heard words coming from Jon's mouth — none of which brought her any comfort.

Lost in a daze of her own exhaustion, Isabelle realized right then — even men who had vowed to love her forever would still abandon her when she needed them the most.

Wind whipped through the canopy above dropping the first bits of rain on Isabelle's cheek as even her beloved forest could no longer protect her from the incoming storm.

She slowly drew a breath and closed her eyes.

With a steady exhale, Isabelle turned to take one final look at the sea-blue eyes of her fractured fairy tale.

"Fare thee well, Jon of the Sea."

Sliding from his grasp, she tuned and started walking away. Tears brewed as thunder rattled the thin earth she walked upon.

"Isabelle!"

She heard Jon yell but she didn't stop. She needed to get back to her room where she could collapse alone and try to convince herself that she never truly loved him anyway.

When she reached the edge of the forest, she felt Jon come up behind her as lightning flashed through the sky.

"Izzy, stop!"

Grabbing her arm, he darted in front of her as the rain whipped at their sides. "I swore my loyalties to Tom and those men long before I ever met you. Once I fulfil my promise to them, I will come back for you." Jon embraced her but Isabelle was too empty to feel anything but despair.

"If they truly are you brothers, surely they will understand," she whimpered.

Jon was completely torn. He wanted to ride off into the night with her, he wanted her forever, but he knew he could never abandon his crew.

Jon bellowed over the wind. "If I left with you tonight, and abandoned my crew, I would despise the man I'd grow to become! It would haunt every day of my life if something happened to Tom because I wasn't there to protect him...then you would grow to hate me too...and then where would we be?"

Isabelle saw him getting upset but had no words of comfort. Emotionally drained, she pulled herself from his grasp and walked into the raging storm.

"I promise I will come back for you!" Jon yelled after her.

In one breath, Isabelle summoned all her thunderous rage and swirled around. "Oh, I won't be here!" she yelled as her tears finally gave way. The pounding rain wilted Isabelle's curls and soaked her gown, pushing her scooping neckline off her shoulders. "I will be a baroness somewhere, with babies in my belly! And you..." spiteful words poured from her tongue, "you will be a corpse. Even if you do return from this war...watching your brothers die will kill parts of you as well."

Her desperate eyes glared back at him. "So you see...everything changes at dawn." She pleaded with him one last time. "Please stay with me."

Jon's eyes welled at the thought of leaving her, but his heart could not be swayed. "I can't, Iz," reluctantly slipped from his lips.

Realizing now that the love Jon had for those men was stronger than anything he felt for her, Isabelle barely nodded.

Completely emaciated, she turned and started walking back to her room.

"I will come back for you!" Jon shouted through the storm as he stepped beyond the trees into the pounding rain. "Isabelle!" he yelled again. "Do you hear me?"

But Isabelle didn't turn around, she started running.

"I promise I will come back for you!"

Jon watched her run across her balcony and into her bedroom, possibly never to be seen through his eyes again.

Beneath the pelting rain, he was left heartbroken and alone. Watching her leave in tears made him contemplate running right up those stairs to tell her that he'd stay — he'd stay with her forever.

But he knew it was hopeless. Their destinies had been set long before they ever met on that dock — not even a beautiful woman in a mesmerizing silk dress could change that.

Jon stayed at the edge of the forest the entire night hoping she would calm down and return to him, but she never did. He didn't even see her again through the windows. It was as though she had disappeared from his life just as quickly as she'd entered it.

When the storm finally let up, he decided it was time to begin the lonely walk home.

Thoughts raced though his head as he slowly sauntered back to his ship. Though he'd been through a heap of training this summer, he was scared of what lay ahead. He had hoped one more night in his lover's arms would ease his apprehension because he knew everything was about to change with the impending dawn.

Chapter 24
DECAY OF WAVES

Each step along the dirt road ripped Jon further from the piece of his heart he'd just left at Bluefields. He wanted to turn back. He wanted to rescue her; to take her away from the life she so despised. They could be together and live blissfully until the day they took their lasts breaths — but the voice of past promises booming through Jon's head drowned the quiet whispers of his heart.

When he finally reached the main dock, the dim morning twilight seeping through the fog made the Barrington a gloomy sight to behold. The market had not yet begun to stir. The dawn had not broken. The world was nearly silent as he glanced around the square for what could possibly be the last time.

The tiny art shop that had thrust Isabelle into his life was shut tight, drapes drawn. Looking upon the square for the last time felt eerily the same as looking upon it for the first time — as though his eyes had never truly seen it before.

The taunting unrest pumping through Jon's veins left him wondering if he'd ever sleep again. Taking one last glance around the square, he started towards the Barrington when he saw Thomas come walking up the road from Gander's Field.

Tom's shoulders were slumped forward, his eyes on the ground — his pace so obviously reluctant to return.

Jon walked straight towards him. When he reached his despondent friend and placed his hand on Tom's shoulder, it felt like he was touching a ghost.

Thomas was empty. He didn't even look up at the touch of his oldest friend. He couldn't face the truth of what lay ahead — or what he'd just left behind.

Their summer of lust and fanciful futures was over. When they cast their lines today, both men knew they might never lay eyes upon Gillingham, or the women they had grown to love, ever again.

Without a word, Jon swung his arm around Tom's shoulders and they walked back to the ship together.

The crew of the Barrington loaded up artillery and provisions, cast their lines from Gillingham, then sailed down the Medway for the very last time.

Chapter 25

THE END OF IT ALL

The Barrington was the only ship to enter the naval base at Lowestoft that day. She joined three-masted barques, fully-rigged brigs, and refit merchant ships that had left the dockyard weeks ago — but she didn't stay moored in the safe harbour for long. Ordered to join a fleet leaving for battle, the Barrington and her crew immediately set sail for the blood-filled waters of the North Sea at first light the next morning.

Having departed the dockyard without a proper refit, the Barrington was left to the mercy of her skilled crew and armed soldiers who did their best to keep her whole in the middle of a raging war.

Her sailors were swift in the rigging, edging her close to wounded Dutch vessels while English soldiers swung to their decks and sliced through the hearts of their mortal enemies.

"Ready about!" Captain shouted.

The crew heaved, braced round forward then turned hard against the rolling swells.

Coming back alongside the sinking Dutch vessel, English soldiers leapt back to the safety of her planks. By the time the sun set on her first day at war, the Barrington's decks were completely stained with blood.

Jon stared at the crimson pools beneath his feet. With everything he'd seen at sea, he had never once seen a ship bleed. He drew a deep breath and looked to the sky for strength, knowing this battle had only just begun.

As the days quickly turned into weeks, other than her bloodstained planks and a few repairable holes in her sails, the Barrington managed to hold steady. Her crew worked together to protect their home, and their lives. They knew every line on this ship better than the fading faces of the families they'd left behind. Though dodging cannon fire and aiding wounded soldiers added new obstacles to their course, the crew of the Barrington were starting to believe they may all make it out of this war alive.

A bitterly cold December forced a slight pause in battle, allowing both sides to retreat and revive. When they sailed back into Lowestoft, Jon had never been so thrilled to step foot upon a dry dock. But the collective elation of England's entire Navy ceased the moment they received some devastating news.

The plague was spreading through England.

What had started as a few sick paupers in London's low streets quickly swept the entire city and beyond. The sickness had stolen more English lives in four months than the Dutch had taken in a full year of war.

While docked in base, members of the Royal Navy were ordered to stay isolated aboard their ships. Though grateful for this time of tranquility, Jon spent every quiet moment thinking of Isabelle — wondering where she was, what she was doing...hoping she was safe.

But as the frost began to ease, so too did this brief moment of peace. News of an approaching Dutch fleet pushed the English Navy back to the waves where the cycle of endless battles began again.

It was late spring when Jon realized his feet hadn't touched dry land in months. His bones ached. Parts of his hands were both calloused and raw. He'd never felt exhaustion like this. Though not overly religious, he prayed for God to end this war. He no longer cared if England held safe passage through some channel to collect goods that no one needed anyway. He was tired of watching men die in his arms only to be ordered back to the rigging by a ball-busting admiral.

He'd seen enough — he was done.

"Brace 'round forward!"

From his post on the aft deck, Jon's body moved automatically at the sound of Captain's orders. These lines had become a part of him. His strong arms heaved the sheet as the Barrington drew alongside a wounded Dutch fluyt with soldiers ready to pounce — but the Dutch commanders were getting wise to their stealthy opponents and this time, had their cannons ready.

"FIRE!" was the last word Jon heard before all five cannon holds exploded into the Barrington's hull.

Jon's world went black. His body fell into the sea, shattered bits of the Barrington sinking with him while the rest of her burned upon the waves.

The whipping breeze quickly swept the blaze across the entire ship, engulfing her sails in seconds. Up in the rigging, Thomas watched his mates burning in the crackling blaze. With flames quickly slithering up the mast, there was no time for courage. He leapt from the highest point of the burning ship into the water below.

Left abandoned and alone, the mighty Barrington burned on the waves until there was nothing left of her upon this earth but splintered bits at the bottom of the sea.

Chapter 26

RIVER ON FIRE

"Open your eyes!"

A mate from an allied vessel knelt over a waterlogged sailor they'd just pulled from the sea. By his side, the doctor onboard plucked chunks of wood from the sailor's body while he was still out cold.

With explosions still erupting in the distance, Thomas sat slumped on the deck in a complete daze. Propped against the ship, his hazy eyes watched the doctor pull blood soaked bits of the Barrington from his friend's flesh. "His name's Jon," Thomas mumbled as he watched his oldest friend slowly turn blue.

"Breathe Jon!" The quick thinking sailor turned Jon on his side and started smacking his back.

Jon's body writhed with each thud but his eyes never opened.

Choking back tears, Thomas watched his friend's life slip away before his eyes.

Just like that, all his brothers — every single one — was gone.

No longer able to withstand the sight of his dead best friend, Tom's burning eyes dropped to the planks.

"Yes!" the doctor shouted. "Cough it out."

Thomas looked up to see foamy water spewing from Jon's mouth as he purged the salty sea from his lungs.

"Breathe lad!" the doctor yelled, propping Jon up to help him catch his breath.

When he checked Jon's eyes, and found the bloody sailor glaring back at him, the old doctor smiled. "We almost lost you there."

Jon's head hung low as he huffed life back into his body.

"I'll write an order for you men to head back to Lowestoft for a few days rest. The nurses there will finish mending you." The doctor pat Jon's shoulder before hurrying off to tend another fallen soldier.

Finally coming back into his body, Jon looked up to find his red haired companion leaning against the side of the ship with a broken smile and tears in his eyes.

They were the last ones alive. Jon knew it. He could feel the souls of his dead brothers pulling at him to come join them.

But Jon wasn't ready to leave this earth just yet. As he returned Tom's stare, he felt his rage brewing within.

No longer driven by a King's salary or oaths of loyalty, both men were determined to bring England to victory, ensuring their brothers' lives were not lost in vain.

After a few days rest at Lowestoft, Jon and Thomas decided to leave their days in the rigging behind. They attained weapons from a Vice Admiral and permission to board a new ship departing at first light.

Having little practice with artillery, Jon's two-handed sword weighed heavy in his hands, but the fiery rage boiling his blood left no room for insecurity. It drove him to the decks of his enemies on an impossible mission to quench his endless thirst for revenge.

Slicing through Dutch flesh, Jon felt nothing but pure satisfaction each time he watched their blood spill to the planks.

Firearm in hand, Thomas had Jon's back. Slaying soldier after soldier, the men fought for their country as they avenged the deaths of their fallen brothers.

Months passed in swathes of bloodshed. After a year at sea, Jon was beginning to feel as though his entire life before this war was a complete delusion. The love of his mother, his life in Jersey, the touch of Isabelle's soft skin — they existed only in his memory. He breathed an entirely different existence now. His hair had grown thick chestnut curls. Left unshaved, his dark beard concealed his dimpled chin. He slept in hammocks once belonging to soldiers who were now dead or captured, and his double-edged sword never left his side.

By the next spring, their voices had worn gruff. Shouting commands and hollering in pain had left their throats hoarse. Both men had let their hair and beards grow wild. Jon's shoulders had grown thick and broad from wielding his heavy steel sword for months without end.

Both fleets were punctured, sunken and depleted when England took formation for what many hoped would be their final victory. But as the naval fleet pushed forward, an officer suddenly spotted something in the distance.

Flying from the mast of The Netherland's lead ship was a white flag of surrender.

A tiny piece of cloth instantly ended years of abhorrent bloodshed. England's soldiers were finally free to lay down their weapons, and return home.

Tom's bushy red hair blew wildly in the breeze as he glanced back at Jon. "Let's go get our girls," his said with a smile.

By the next week, the scarred remains of England's Royal Navy entered the Thames estuary and started their journey back up the Medway. The sun was nearly set as guards lowered the heavy chain barricade, allowing England's fleet back into the dockyard they had departed from nearly two years ago.

With little light left in the sky, Jon noticed how different Gillingham looked from the last time he saw it. Once full of life, the docks were now barren and splintered. There were no billowing flowerpots, no young women awaiting their arrival, no sound of smacking hammers — only a deafening silence shattered by the captain's call to his exhausted crew.

A few men mulling about the square came running to receive lines from the broken fleet as they finally came to rest in the safe haven of the naval dockyard.

Gillingham looked like a ghost town, but when Jon spotted the dirt road at the edge of the square, he suddenly felt like he was home.

Finally able to rest peacefully for the first time in nearly two years, Jon and Thomas decided to sleep on the bow beneath the stars. With less than twenty vessels in Gillingham, the dockyard was exceptionally quiet.

Though moored in a protected yard, both men had grown accustomed to a constant state of vulnerability and kept their weapons close as they tucked in for the night.

Thomas scratched his beard as he looked to Jon with a grin. They had made it. They looked and felt like completely different men but they had made it out of that war.

"It's hard to believe I'll be looking in Beth's eyes tomorrow," Tom said while fluffing the sack of clothes he planned on using as a pillow.

216

He flipped onto his back and looked to the stars above. "I know she waited for me."

The soul crushing years Jon had spent at war had rid him of his propensity for inspiring prose. "Don't get your hopes up mate. She's probably married," he said before stretching out.

"So's Isabelle!" Tom quipped in spite.

"It doesn't matter. I made her a promise."

"She'll tell you to kick off, if she speaks to you at all."

The faint sound of a luffing sail suddenly caught Jon's attention.

"Quiet," he hushed. The hair on his arm stood straight up as he silently brought his finger to his lips — all the ships in the dockyard had their sails furled for the night.

There it was again.

Lifting his hand to the sword at his side, Jon sat up to glance around the dark river. With no moonlight or lanterns lit, he stared into the pitch black willing his eyes to find the taunting white sail.

When he looked back to Tom's widened eyes, Jon saw the reflection of a glowing flame come flying over the side of the ship before erupting onto the deck in a fiery blaze.

Taking a firm hold of Tom's shirt, Jon quickly rolled them away.

They were under attack! The Dutch hadn't surrendered — they had followed England's wounded fleet back to the dockyard and struck when they least expected.

Jumping to his feet, Jon pulled his sword just as he heard Tom's firearm go off. Dutch soldiers, dressed all in black, leapt onto the decks as every ship in the yard began erupting in flames.

The ship burned around him but Jon's feet were swift as he fought through the fire. His body pressed hard through his sword, thrusting it clean through his enemies before leaving them to burn in the blaze.

But it was the middle of the night, and he'd been caught off guard. Jon felt their swords slicing through his flesh — enemy blades, warmed by a raging fire.

The deep gash on his side was bleeding heavily, making it harder for him to raise his sword. Pausing just for a moment, he reached down to check the wound and felt his fingers slip inside his own flesh. Slowly, he raised his hand to find it completely covered in blood.

He glanced to Thomas who was reloading his firearm on the far side of the fiery ship.

With his focus broken, Jon failed to notice the sly soldier slinking up behind him. A curved blade flashed before his eyes just as the hot steel sliced back across his throat.

BANG!

A bullet whizzed past Jon's ear, exploding in the skull of the Dutch soldier at his side.

As the dead man slumped to the ground, Jon looked to his best mate whose firearm had a ribbon of grey smoke rising from the tip.

He smiled at Thomas, suddenly grateful for his decision to choose a firearm.

As the ship burned around them, Thomas returned Jon's grin.

In that brief moment, the kinship of their eternal brotherhood filled Tom with an unexpected sense of peace in this burning nightmare.

But a swaddled heart has no place in times of war. Thomas had let his guard down, and didn't seem to hear the soldier creeping up behind him.

He was still looking in Jon's eyes when the sword came thrusting straight through his chest!

Jon yelled, but found no air in his lungs.

Frozen amongst the flames, he watched a crimson stain seep through Tom's white cotton shirt as his wide eyes slowly rolled into his head.

The Dutch soldier turned his sword then pulled it back through the dead sailor, letting his body crumple to the ground as though it was nothing more than the corpse of a dead goat.

Jon began heaving like a wild beast. Tears of fury boiled his eyes. His quaking hand flipped his sword to a fresh edge.

Shouting out in primal rage, tears exploded from his eyes as he charged towards the fleeing assailant who quickly turned to block Jon's blow.

Crossing his sword with the soldier, Jon pressed down upon him as he watched Tom's blood spread to his blade.

Flames from the burning ship lapped Jon's flesh but he felt nothing.

He grabbed the Dutchmen's grip, spun the soldier around and thrust his double-edged sword straight through his back.

Barrels of gunpowder began erupting through the deck. Jon knew he needed to flee the burning ship but he stayed — he wanted to hear every last gurgling blood-filled breath of the man dying on his sword.

When silence finally settled upon his blade, Jon pulled his sword from the dead man and started for the gangplank.

His legs lagged beneath him. The tip of his sword dragged across the planks as the blood dripping from his wounds left a trail of defeat at his heels.

He was nearly at the gangway when the ship's entire powder magazine exploded beneath him!

Shattering what was left of the flaming vessel, the explosion sent Jon's lifeless body flying from the ship.

With the dockyards set ablaze and their mission complete, Dutch soldiers retreated to their ships and sailed back down the Medway, leaving what remained of England's Royal Navy to go up in flames.

Chapter 27

BURIED EARTH

For awhile, there was nothing but darkness.

Then the faint echo of agonizing screams began to grow louder.

Flames climbed through the deck Jon found himself standing upon. Ready to leap from the ship, he glanced over the railing to find the dock below completely engulfed in flames.

The entire world was burning — there was no escape.

Ready to surrender, Jon took one last look around the square and noticed a golden angel standing peacefully in the flaming inferno. Straining to focus, he realized he was staring straight into Isabelle's glowing amber eyes.

Glaring at him from within the fire, tears seeped from her stoic gaze. Jon watched her arm float up gently to point directly at him. Her mouth silently gaped open in a haunting sight as her skin began melting in the flames.

"Stay with me!" boomed through the blackened sky.

Gasping for air, Jon's eyes shot open.

It took a moment for him to realize he was wrapped safely in the sheet of a single bed.

"I was wondering when you were going to wake up."

Jon gathered his wits then looked over to find a skinny man with a long face, and even longer raven hair, holding a small notebook and a writing pen.

"You were found on the side of the Medway after the raid a few days ago. I've been interviewing soldiers here for two days but you've been out the entire time."

"Who are you?" Jon's raspy voice uttered.

"Oh, of course, how rude of me. My name is John Evelyn. I've been commissioned to take recordings from all the soldiers in this infirmary to ensure your recollections of the war are properly recorded for later reflection."

Jon looked to the ceiling as all the garish memories came flooding back; the cannon fire, the flames, the bloodshed...the never-ending bloodshed.

Tom's death.

He could still see his best friend's eyes — his wide fear-filled eyes as the blade came plunging through his heart.

Not ready to face it all, Jon shut his eyes again. "I don't wish to speak about that right now."

Mr. Evelyn watched a single tear slide from Jon's tightly shut eyes and realized this may not be the best time. "I'll let you rest," he said before gathering his things. "Oh...before I leave, you kept uttering one word over again. I couldn't quite make out what it was exactly. It sounded like, Lizzy, or Izzy. Was that the name of your ship?"

With her booming plea still fresh in his mind, the simple utterance of Isabelle's name made every scar on Jon's body wince in pain.

"Perhaps you'll tell me another time," the journalist said politely before excusing himself and leaving the wounded soldier to rest.

Jon's recovery was painful and lengthy. Having pushed his body beyond its limits for nearly two years, he welcomed the attentive care of the infirmary nurses, who sometimes fought over which one would get to change the handsome soldier's bandages.

Mr. Evelyn had returned on quite a few occasions but Jon turned him away every time. He still wasn't ready to speak the names of his fallen brothers, nor talk of the atrocious perils of war. Recounting the details of each swipe of his blade would only send him further into the empty pit slowly swallowing his life.

The lovely aids tried to cheer him up but Jon's heart was only focused on finding Isabelle. If there was anything left in this world that could soothe his broken soul, it was her smile. He knew she likely wouldn't live in Gillingham anymore but Bluefields would still be his first stop in hopes that the Tilly's would know where to find her.

One of the nurses brushed Jon's thick shoulder length curls for the last time, trimmed his beard then helped him into a dapper set of clothes donated by the church. "I hope you find her," she said with a heartbroken smile as she fixed Jon's collar.

Dressed like a gentleman, Jon stepped out of the infirmary and took his first steps towards Bluefields Manor, but his body was weak — he definitely didn't feel like the strapping young sailor who'd first stepped foot in Gillingham years ago.

When he finally reached the dirt road, his heart began to ache. He wished she was here now. He could feel her right next to him in her pale-yellow silk dress — her innocent honey eyes smiling back at him.

Jon's pace was slow. Nearly every step shot pain through his body but he persevered. He reached Bluefield's gates just after midday and was surprised to find them open and welcoming.

After making his way up the cobblestone laneway, he knocked on the front door for the first time, realizing only then that he was about to come face to face with Milly. Through Isabelle's many stories, he felt like he already knew this woman and half expected to meet an old friend.

When the squeaky lock turned and the door pulled open, a tall slender butler in white gloves looked Jon up and down. "May I help you?" he asked in a refined tone.

Confused by the elderly man, Jon was hesitant. "Yes," he finally answered, "I'm here to speak with Lady Isabelle."

"There is no one here by that name. You must have the wrong house. Good day, sir," he replied before closing the door.

"Just a moment please!" Jon pushed in, holding the door from being closed in his face. "She's the daughter of Lord Arlington. This is his estate. If she no longer lives here, perhaps you might know where I could find her."

The butler's face sunk. "Oh son, you haven't heard."

"Heard what?" Jon managed to utter.

The butler eased the door. "Please accept my apologies, but Lady Bennett perished when the plague swept Gillingham two years ago."

Jon's racing heart stopped instantly. Through all the injuries he'd sustained in the war, none had paralyzed him quite like the butler's simple words.

"They say Arlington was the only one to walk out of this house alive. The sickness took his entire household — his wife, the servants, everyone."

Jon didn't believe it. Of all the people he'd lost in the past two years, he never once thought Isabelle would be one of them. "Are you certain?"

"From my understanding, the plague struck late that summer. There was a party for some foreign princess. Everyone in attendance fell ill shortly thereafter. My master was at his Norfolk estate. We were safe there, but they were not so lucky here it seems."

A sudden ringing pierced Jon's ears. He tried to pay attention to the old man's words but they were barely audible.

"Arlington was one of the few who survived in this town but he soon sold this estate, and I'm not sure where he's moved on to."

The earth sunk beneath Jon's feet.

The butler noticed his guest's face begin to flush and offered his condolences. "I'm sorry for your loss. This woman was a friend of yours?"

"Yes," Jon answered meekly.

The elderly man looked into the house before stepping onto the landing and closing the door behind him. "Everyone who perished from this household was buried on the property in their family plot. It's quite a good walk up that hill."

"Yes," Jon swallowed hard, "I know it."

"My Lord is in the library on the other side of the manor. If you go quickly, I'd be happy to allow you some time on the grounds to say farewell to your friend."

Weak and broken, Jon's words were empty. "Thank you. That's very kind."

The butler respectfully bowed his head and returned inside.

After walking back down the steps, Jon paused on the cold cobblestones. For the first time in his life, he felt completely alone. He had no one to watch his back, no one to laugh with — no one to love.

It felt like he was trudging towards his own death as he crossed the grounds. His body suddenly ached. His boots grew heavier with each step up the hillside but he kept climbing, determined to say a final farewell to his beloved.

The moment Jon spotted the tombstones his eyes welled with tears. He realized right then, the dream that had kept him alive during the war — the thought of spending the rest of his life with Isabelle, having children and starting a life of their own, was nothing more than a fleeting fantasy now. Just like his mother, and father, just like Thomas and his brothers at sea — Isabelle was gone too.

Overcome with emotion, he fell to his knees mere feet from the graves. His fractured body was led only by the will of his strong heart, and now, that too was broken.

He cursed God as he wailed at the sky, and prayed for the earth to swallow him whole. His heart bled as he sobbed for everything and everyone he'd ever lost — for they were now nothing more than sea foam, ashes, and dust.

He wanted to be with them.

He was ready to leave this earth.

With a deep breath, he decided he would say his final goodbye to Isabelle, walk to the lagoon where they made love for the first time then draw his sword, and seal his own fate.

Still resting on his knees, a soothing breeze washed over him. His body suddenly felt light for the first time in as long as he could remember.

With a few more breaths, Jon's strength returned to his body. He pushed himself up and walked over to say his final goodbye to Isabelle.

The first two graves were older than the others — *George William Bennett 1585-1656*, and *Theresa Jane Bennett 1586-1654*. The next two were newer but quite small — *Bernard Harrison Tilly 1589-1665*, and *Moira Louise Tilly 1595-1665*.

Jon's heart sunk. He wondered if Isabelle was forced to watch her beloved servants grow ill and die or if she had been taken first.

The next grave was large and quite regal. The towering, white marble headstone read; *Here Lies Eternally, Countess Marguerite Francoise Bennett of Arlington 1625-1665*.

Jon respectfully bowed his head, drew a deep breath then turned to face Isabelle's grave.

It was then that he realized there were no gravestones left.

Confused, he retraced his steps and looked through the plot again but he didn't find Isabelle's name anywhere.

He brought both hands to his head in an attempt to contain his whirling thoughts. The butler said everyone in the household had perished. Arlington left on his own. He certainly wouldn't bury his wife at Bluefields but have Isabelle laid to rest someplace else.

Was she still alive?

In a haze of confusion, Jon intently searched the graves one more time before turning to look down at the manor in the distance.

A smile broke his grim face and Jon gazed to the sky. Laughing at God's twisted humour, his injured body could no longer withstand the flood of elation and he collapsed to the ground.

Still laughing, he rolled onto his back and looked up at the puffy clouds above.

With the sturdy ground beneath him, Jon began to breathe easy. Isabelle was still alive, and nothing upon this earth would stop him from finding her.

Chapter 28

SOLEMNLY SEEKING

Stepping onto the dirt road, Jon left Bluefields behind and walked back to the dockyard with purpose. He entered the treasury to collect his pay, standing silently as the clerk behind the desk flipped the chits looking for his name.

As the clean-cut overweight man leafed through his books, Jon watched the names of his fallen brothers flip by.

One after the other they were passed over.

Jon's nostrils flared as he took a deep breath. He knew those men would never step foot within these walls. They would never see their families again, or have children of their own. They had given their lives for a war that was lost and a pay they would never receive while this gentleman holding all the coin had enjoyed his nightly feasts and dry linens.

Jon's blood steamed when the clerk handed him a heavy purse and casually thanked him for his service without looking up from his books. This well-kept man had no idea how many times Jon had bled for this country — how many men he'd watched die — how many lives he'd taken.

An empty thank you and a coin-filled purse did little to fill Jon's hollowed heart. He left the office without another word and stepped back into Gillingham's rundown square.

Having pushed his body too far on his first day out of the infirmary, his legs were weak. He knew he'd have to find a room in town tonight, and with nearly two years of a King's salary burning a hole in his pocket, a broken smile slid to Jon's lips — he would be sleeping in Gillingham's finest room this evening.

Looking around the square, Jon spied the bench at the river's edge where he'd first met Isabelle — the air was much warmer that day. He pulled his collar up to stop the chilly April breeze from slipping down his neck as he made his way to the bench.

His legs sighed with relief the moment he sat down but every scar on his body suddenly began to throb. Wincing in pain, Jon looked to the sky and closed his eyes.

He took a few breaths to clear his head but couldn't sweep Isabelle's face from his mind. He needed to get to London. He knew Arlington had a home there and was a prominent courtier at Whitehall — surely his chances of finding her were better in the city.

He could purchase a small boat to see himself up the Thames, but in his weakened state, Jon knew his body could never withstand the voyage alone. He thought for a moment about renting a coach to take him into the city, but quickly quelled his thoughts of opulence. He had a new plan for his life — one that required saving as much money as possible.

When a sharp pain shot through his side, Jon let out a groan. He opened his cloak and pressed his hand down to stop the throbbing.

"You alright, son?"

Jon glanced up to find an elderly man in a blue cap seated on a horse at the top of the dirt road. In his free hand, he held the reins of a black Friesian stallion trailing behind him.

"I'm alright," Jon politely replied just as Isabelle's voice flit through his head — *"Even a dead man could ride a horse at this pace."*

Jon looked back to the sky with a smile, pushed himself from the bench, and went see a man about a horse.

.   .   .   .

Jon barely slept that night. Though his body lay upon exotic cotton sheets, his soul found no rest. Haunted by the screams of his dying brothers, he rolled in the expensive linens but there was no escape — the terror was a part of him now. The sight of Tom's heart draining to the planks didn't disappear when Jon shut his eyes to sleep.

Hoping to outrun his ghosts, he rose as the twilight began to bloom, packed up his new horse and left Gillingham behind at first light.

The journey to London was long but Jon was grateful for the sturdy four-legged companion who carried him the entire way and somehow made him feel like he wasn't entirely alone.

He entered the city to find it bustling and smoggy. It had been years since Jon had stepped foot in such a populated space and his body began to buzz. With his sword at his side, he kept his focus on finding Isabelle. The sooner he found her, the sooner he could get the hell out of this crawling city.

After unsurprisingly being denied entrance at Whitehall, Jon moved through London stopping in shops to ask about Lord Arlington and his daughter. Though he came across quite a few people who knew who they were, no one was able to say where either one had gone. It was as though they had both been lost to the passage of time — become folklore of London before the plague.

The sun had set long ago leaving the night air frigid and Jon still had no leads on his love. With his gloved hand on the door of a tavern, he decided this would be his last stop before turning his focus on finding lodging for the night.

He pulled the door open to a waft of perfume, but not the cheap kind the sea hags always reeked of. This scent reminded him of Isabelle — silky and expensive.

He looked around the sea of periwigs and satin gowns moving about the well-decorated room in a wave of chatter and clinking glasses. This was definitely one of the fancier places in town.

When he didn't spot Isabelle anywhere, Jon walked straight to the bar. "Pardon, sir."

The well-dressed tender, busy filling crystal glasses with wine, looked up from his duties. "Pull up a seat and I'll be right with you."

"I'm looking for a woman named Lady Isabelle Bennett. Her father is Lord Arlington. Do you have word on them?"

The man shook his head as a server slid the full tray off the counter then disappeared back into the crowd. He threw his cloth over his shoulder and picked up a bottle of brandy. "I've never heard anyone by that name in here before but if you buy a cup of ale, you're welcome to ask around."

Jon nodded and reached in his pocket for some coin.

"Excuse me, sir. Did I hear you inquire about Lord Arlington's daughter?"

Jon looked over to find a tiny unassuming dark-haired man with a kind smile and a very expensive suit.

"Yes!" Jon shouted in elation. "Do you know her?"

"No, I'm afraid not but my wife was a friend of hers some time ago. She may be of help to you."

Jon's eyes grew wide. "Is she here?"

"Yes, come this way."

While following the gentleman back to his table, Jon scoured the room for a familiar face but didn't seem to recognize anyone.

The man finally approached a table near the back window and leaned down to speak with a seated woman deep in conversation. "Excuse me my love, but this man was asking about an old friend of yours. I told him you may be able to help."

The plump woman with the thick cinnamon curls turned her head to meet her husband's gaze then glanced over his shoulder at the ruggedly handsome man with a full beard standing just behind him. "How may I help you?" she asked.

Suddenly breathless, Jon's raspy voice was soft. "Beth?"

"Do I know you?" she asked, not recognizing the best mate of her long-lost love.

"I'm Jon."

He watched Beth's eyes strain then widen in disbelief.

"Do you know this man, my love?" her husband asked.

Without a word, Beth rose from her seat, exposing her pregnant belly, then walked up to the stranger at the end of the table.

"Is it really you?" she asked quietly, still searching his eyes.

Unsure if she was witnessing a full-bodied apparition in the middle of her favourite restaurant, Beth's breath began to quicken. "We were told the Barrington had been destroyed — that all of you were dead."

"I likely ought to be," Jon replied. "Truthfully, I'm not sure how it is I'm still standing," he said with a charming smile — one that Beth recognized instantly.

"It is you!" she shouted, throwing her arms around him in an excited embrace. "I don't believe it." She pulled back to look in his eyes. "And Thomas?" she asked desperately.

Even though her womb held another man's child, Beth's eyes were suddenly hopeful.

Not wanting to upset her delicate state with stories of Tom's grisly demise only weeks ago, or perhaps not ready to speak of it himself, Jon softened and silently shook his head.

Though Beth had surrendered to his death long ago, she still thought of Thomas nearly every day. Her heart broke all over again when she spotted the agony in Jon's eyes. Watching him fight back tears quickly became too much for her to witness and she dropped her gaze.

Standing in a room filled with new friends who knew nothing of the red-haired sailor she fell in love with years ago, Beth only looked to Jon. "Do you have a place to stay tonight?"

Jon shook his head. "Not yet."

Beth turned to her attentive husband. "Please send Fredrick on ahead of us. Tell him to prepare the red suite." She glanced back to Jon with a grin. "We'll have a guest tonight."

The moment Jon stepped inside the stately brick home on the outskirts of the city, it quickly became evident that Beth was the head of this household.

A small crowd of awaiting servants removed the couple's outerwear as Beth gave her instructions. "Have Jon's horse brought into the stable for the evening then take his things to the red suite," she asserted while handing over her gloves. "And light the fire in the front sitting room — we have much to discuss." She glanced to Jon as a butler removed his cloak.

"Shall I join you?" her husband asked while being helped into his house-slippers."

"I wouldn't want to bore you with stories of people whom you've never met." She gave him a kiss goodnight and a reassuring smile.

Ripe with brandy, he was happy to see himself to bed. "As you wish. Try not to stay up too late, you need your rest." He looked to Jon. "Good evening, sir."

"Good evening," Jon replied with a polite dip of his head.

As Beth led him through her home filled with expensive furniture, tapestries and china, Jon came to realize she did much better for herself than any life Thomas could've provided.

She showed him to a cozy sitting room where an imposing stone fireplace contained a roaring fire, warming a pair of green velvet wingback chairs perched just in front.

Beth placed both hands on the armrests then lowered herself onto the seat.

"May I help you?" Jon lunged to offer his hand.

"Don't bother," she said, brushing him off. "I've been carrying this child around for eight months. I'm getting quite used it."

A servant placed two teacups on the circular table between them as Jon took his seat. "Would you prefer a brandy?" Beth asked as a servant began pouring tea.

Hoping to retain every word about to spill from Beth's lips, Jon politely refused. "Tea is fine, thank you," he replied, looking to the young servant who smiled sheepishly.

"I presume you've been to Gillingham." Beth rested her saucer on her protruding belly then took a sip.

"Yes. It certainly wasn't the same as I remembered."

Lowering her cup, Beth was slow to reply. "Everything changed after the masquerade." Her eyes shifted to the fire. "Your ship left, Izzy disappeared...everyone started getting sick. I still remember Anne telling me she wasn't feeling well during the bon voyage party. She retired to her room early that night...and I never saw her again."

"She died?"

Beth nodded but kept her eyes on the flames. "Anne was the first, followed closely by her mother then three sisters."

"Victoria?" Jon asked gently.

Beth looked to Jon. "When everyone started falling ill, Victoria and the Prince left immediately. They were not a full week into their journey when we received word that nearly their entire fleet had been consumed by plague. She and the Prince were kept in complete isolation and managed to make it safely to Calvaria...but Gillingham was devastated. It was even worse in London."

Jon's eyes dropped to his lap. The violence he'd experienced over the last two years had felt so isolating, as though England sat in perfect peace while brave men fought the evil at sea. But winning those battles didn't end suffering — it didn't quell fear. Innocent people were still forced to watch their loved ones die while they stood helpless to protect them. Whether on sea or solid earth, there would be no end to tragedy.

"What of Arlington?" Jon asked gently.

The smallest hint of a smirk appeared in Beth's eyes. "The King was convinced the Dutch were responsible for the explosion of the London and ordered an investigation...but it was discovered The Netherlands had no involvement whatsoever. It seems Arlington had procured faulty gunpowder from foreign sources in the Far East."

Jon's brow furrowed. He and his crew had retrieved that haul. He had rolled barrels of that very gunpowder into the London's storage before her departure.

"The King was furious," Beth continued. "He striped Arlington of his title and had him exiled from court for causing him such embarrassment. We have no word on where he went. He sold everything and vanished."

"Did he take Izzy with him? What did you mean when you said she disappeared? You don't know where she is?"

Beth shook her head. "We asked of her whereabouts but Arlington only said she had been sent away to be married. No one heard anything more until William saw Mr. Graham here in London. Apparently Arlington dismissed him the morning Isabelle was sent away and he was ready to spill his secrets. He said a carriage had come from Plymouth and she was to be married to some Baron down there." Beth's eyes dropped to her teacup. "William fell ill shortly afterwards. That was the last time I spoke to him."

"He's dead too?"

Beth nodded and looked to the fire. "The sickness took my mother as well. I inherited everything, but without Thomas here, I was completely devastated." She turned to the sailor at her side. "I waited for him, Jon. I never so much as looked at another man for months after the Barrington sank. The thought of losing him...it stopped my heart."

Jon pressed his head to the back of his chair, willing his own heart not to stop every time he heard Tom's name.

"But when I met Edward — his eyes were so kind," she said with a smile. "He was so worried for me. Before I noticed, he was by my side nearly every day trying to find ways to cheer me up or make me laugh. I am grateful for his loyalty but," Beth glanced back to the flames, "I know I'll never love him as much as I loved Thomas."

With a heartbroken grin, she looked to Jon. "There's something about the first time your heart fills with love. I fear I'll never feel anything like that again," Beth confessed before raising her teacup for another sip.

Jon swallowed the lump in his throat. "I need to find Izzy," he said hopelessly.

"Yes," Beth smiled before placing her teacup back on the table, "you do. I suggest you start in Plymouth. It wouldn't surprise me if her father sent her as far away from here as possible."

Beth pushed herself up from her seat. Jon sprung to help but she swatted him away. "That tea has suddenly gotten the better of me. I should see myself to bed."

She clasped Jon's hands and smiled. "I'll have some fine clothes delivered in the morning. You should look like a proper gentleman when you see our girl." She took a hold of his scruffy chin. "And I suggest shaving this beard off as well. She'll never recognize you."

"I like it," Jon replied with a smirk. "It hides me well."

A warm smile slid to Beth's cheeks. "You're beginning to sound like Isabelle."

Chapter 30

TRAVELLING SOLDIER

Beth's satin bedding slid easily beneath Jon's scarred body, finally providing a pleasant place for him to rest. A gentle stirring from the same butler who saw him to bed, woke Jon from the best night sleep he'd had in years.

After a warm bath and a quick trim, a servant helped him into the expensive clothing Beth gifted him while the butler packed two more outfits and a few other useful supplies into a new sack for Jon to take on his journey.

He enjoyed a full breakfast with the Lord and Lady of the manor then packed up his horse in preparation for his journey to Plymouth.

He turned to the couple who had welcomed him into their home. "Thank you for everything," he said with a grin as Beth clasped his hands. "Seeing your face again has brought me more happiness than I've felt in a long time."

"You are always welcome here," she said with a warm smile and a tight hug. "Travel well."

Jon thanked them both again then mounted his horse.

As her hopeful eyes watched him ride away, Beth said a silent prayer that Jon be given the blessing she was denied — that he would one day be reunited with his true love.

Jon found himself apprehensive of the trip ahead. By land or sea, he'd never travelled this far alone.

His body ached on the days he rode hard, but when he slowed his pace to recover, the gentle sway of his horse reminded him of his life upon the waves. Although grateful for the work of his ebony companion, Jon was already beginning to miss the soft lulls of the sea.

Driven by his promise to Isabelle, he was undeterred by long days and cold nights. He stopped at hostels along the way and found life on land much easier with a full purse on his hip. At every stop, he asked about a young noblewoman who may have stopped in years ago on her way to Plymouth but no one recalled anyone matching her description.

Climbing back onto the horse he'd named Koal somewhere along the way, Jon set out on the last leg of his journey. By midday, he would finally arrive in Plymouth.

The familiar scent of salty sea-air filled Jon's nose when he arrived in the bustling portside town. Koal's hooves clicked along the cobbles as they entered the busy marketplace.

Men brushed by hauling wagons stacked with caged chickens and barrels of wine, while ships filled with goods from the New Americas secured themselves to the docks after a long journey home. Stepping back onto dry land, the crews unloaded their worldly wares directly into the adjacent market; a labyrinth of stalls assembled right in the middle of the square.

Jon dismounted, secured Koal to a post then started weaving through the marketplace asking about a Baron who married a young woman with long golden hair, who rides horses, writes stories, and is perhaps a little feistier than the other women in town.

But his inquiries were only met with stares of confusion, or explanations of how women in this town would never behave in such a way. "I don't know where you're from, but noble ladies out here ride in carriages, not on horseback," a merchant laughed in Jon's face before turning to help another customer.

Jon's entire afternoon in the market had only led to his first stages of dismay — perhaps Isabelle had finally acquired the illusiveness she so desired.

Slightly discouraged, he mounted Koal then started towards the docks where he spotted a crew unloading furs from the New Americas. As he watched the sailor's hands transfer pelts down the line, Jon thought of his father and decided that ship would be his first stop.

Unsure of the wooden planks, Koal hesitated at the dock's edge. His ears turned back.

"You're alright," Jon assured him with a pat on his neck.

Heeding Jon's confidence, Koal slowly started towards the ship.

"Oye!" Jon shouted to the captain counting his latest purse.

The captain looked up to see a well-dressed man seeking his attention.

"Do you hold contracts with any noblemen in town? I'm looking for word on a young baroness."

"Nay," The captain tucked his purse away and walked to the gangplank. "This here's my ship, the Aurora Nova. I lead a hard workin' crew. We split what we earn runnin' furs from New York. We're headin' back there at first light."

Jon laughed silently. Isabelle was right — the King's brother had named the new colony after himself.

The burly captain studied Jon's face. "Hold on...I've seen you before."

Jon searched the man's eyes but didn't recognize him in the slightest.

"Our crew was commissioned to haul provisions to Lowestoft last year. We were unloadin' when a ship came in full of men blown half to bits. We ran aboard to help, but shite...it was a bloody mess."

He studied Jon's face. "I remember you. You had pieces of wood sticking out of your arm and a bad gash to your head." He looked Jon up and down. "It's good to see you again, soldier," the captain said with a respectful smile. "Name's Hammond."

"Jon," he replied with a grin.

"Pardon, sir," a raspy woman's voice called from Jon's heels.

He looked down from his horse to find a tiny peasant woman wrapped in a dark blue shall with a basket of flowers resting on her arm.

"You the one's been askin' bout a noblewoman who rides horses?" she asked with a cockney slur.

"Yes!" Jon exclaimed.

"Well, me sister works in an'household up in the hills. Her letters speak of a woman, the Baroness. Says she goes out every evenin' for a ride on horseback, gown and all," she said with a dry cackle.

"Yes!" Jon yelled with a smile. "Her name is Isabelle?"

"Oh now I don't know'er name, but me sister works for Lord Beaumont — up there." The woman pointed to a hill that started at the end of the market and climbed to the clouds. "They say she's so

244

beautiful, he keeps'er locked away so no man can look upon'er. Never allowed to leave the grounds, poor thing."

"Beaumont?" Hammond interjected. "He owns half the ships in this harbour. What is it you want with his young wife?" he asked with a chuckle.

"We're old friends," Jon casually replied while reaching into his pocket. "How do I get there?" he asked the woman as he handed her a coin.

"Go out the market that way. Where the forest starts, you'll see a road that'll take you all the way up."

"How many estates are up there?"

"One. Beaumont owns the entire hill." She tucked the coin away then scurried back into the market.

Jon turned back to Hammond. "You know Beaumont?"

"Not personally. No one's seen him in years but his fleet still sails in and out of this port. I heard the rest of his ships were sent to war with you mates."

Jon looked up the hill. A beautiful baroness who rides on horseback every evening. A fleet of ships sent to aid the King in his war. Could it really be her?

Jon's mind started working quickly. He looked back to Hammond. "Do you have a private cabin aboard? I'd like to book passage with you to New York. I'll help with the lines when I can." Jon reached into one of his saddlebags and pulled out a small purse. "I'll also need passage for this horse and another guest as well," he tossed the pouch to Hammond.

The heavy sack clinked hard against the captain's palm. He opened it to examine the contents.

"The more the merrier," he said with a grin.

Jon dismounted, walked over to meet Hammond at the gangplank and shook his hand. "Please bring my horse aboard now." He handed over Koal's reins. "I must speak with someone but I'll be back before you get underway."

"Aye, but we sail at dawn, with or without you." He jingled the bag in his possession.

"I understand," Jon assured him. "I'll be here."

Chapter 31

UNSTABLE GROUND

Jon left the market on foot. He knew an unexpected guest would likely not be permitted passed Beaumont's gates and planned a more sly approach. But the uphill walk proved more challenging than he anticipated. Having sat lazily upon a horse for days on end, Jon's legs weren't prepared for such a strenuous climb but he kept pushing.

His entire body ached by the time he finally spotted two towering pillars in the distance. Knowing those must be Beaumont's gates Jon ducked into the forest and started through the woods.

The spring's thaw had left a soft ground underfoot, but each time his boot cracked through a branch, Jon feared the sound may alert a guard, or worse — a hunting hound. Surviving the war only to die as an intruder in a nobleman's home was definitely not the legacy Jon had hoped to leave behind.

He suddenly realized how vulnerable he felt on land. Ships were confining but familiar. He knew the sound of every creak aboard the Barrington but here, animals stirred beneath the foliage, crows cawed in the branches, and a constant rustling in the trees deemed his senses nearly useless.

When the forest finally began to thin, Jon walked to the tree line and glanced over Beaumont's expansive grounds.

He found himself looking upon the palatial yet sterile mansion in the distance and realized he'd found himself on the backside of Beaumont's estate.

A toothy smile parted his lips when he noticed a large stable on the hill with a few horses grazing in the paddock. If Beaumont's Baroness really was Isabelle, she'd likely turn up at the stables before sunset.

He tucked back into the forest, walking only a short time before he noticed a dirt path in the distance. Upon closer inspection, he found fresh hoof prints and followed them right to the stable.

With his hand gripping his sword and his eyes on his surroundings, Jon quietly inched his way toward the stable's back door then peered through the small glass window.

He spotted a young stablehand mucking the stalls while the horses grazed outside. Jon watched the young lad cross into an adjacent room and climb a ladder into the hayloft. After tossing a few bales onto the floor below, he climbed back down, forked some hay onto the wagon then hauled it out to the awaiting horses.

With the stable completely empty, Jon snuck in, climbed the ladder to the loft then hid behind stacks of hay where he planned to wait patiently for the Baroness.

He stared through the small circular window looking for any sight of Isabelle but only spied Beaumont's many servants moving about the property.

He watched the young stablehand lead the horses back into their stalls below, and by the sounds rattling beneath him, Jon believed the boy to be tacking one of the horses.

The sound of leather stirrups being pulled through a belt tickled Jon's neck.

His heart started racing but he kept his eyes glued to that window.

When a door opened on the backside of the manor, Jon jolted up from his seat as he watched Isabelle step out into the setting sun.

He had found her.

She wore a golden bouffant satin gown with puffy sleeves that drooped off her shoulders. Her long hair was tied back in a fancy twist. As she walked up the hill towards the stable, Jon noticed a different air about her — she held herself with a maturity he had never seen.

As he watched her smile at the young stablehand who greeted her at the door, his lungs clutched every breath he had left.

"Good afternoon, Arthur."

Jon's eyes squeezed shut at the sound of Isabelle's voice below him.

"Everything looks well. You may take your leave for the evening."

Jon waited until he heard the barn door shut. He took a few breaths to pull himself together as he watched the young stablehand walk down the path. When the boy was far enough away, he took one more breath then moved towards the ladder.

Isabelle had led her horse to the backdoor and was just about to mount when she heard the floor boards creak in the hayloft.

The sound instantly froze her still.

George wasn't working today and Arthur had just left. Her pulse quickened when she heard the ladder begin to creak — each lumbered step bringing this intruder closer to the ground.

Isabelle sheepishly moved behind her horse when she remembered her dagger was no longer a part of her dress here, leaving her to the mercy of her small hands alone.

Sliding silently along the wall, her hand caught the edge of a wrought iron poker. She quickly slipped her fingers around it and pulled it to her chest.

Grasping it with both hands, she suddenly found her courage.

Her eyes grew stern as she quietly skulked into the room where she spotted a cloaked man climbing down from the loft. His foot was nearly on the ground when Isabelle snuck up behind him, wound up, then smashed the heavy iron rod down on his shoulder!

The intruder groaned at the unexpected blow and stumbled off the ladder, but Isabelle was ready and wound up again.

"Not today you bastard!" she yelled before smacking the rod against his knee.

Howling in pain, Jon looked up just as she wound up again.

"Izzy, STOP!" Using the force of her swing, he grabbed the weapon at her grip, spun her around and clasped her tightly to his chest, giving him time to catch his breath and gather his wits.

Facing away from the intruder, Isabelle began to tremble.

No one had called her that since the day she left Gillingham.

His voice was raspy, and deeper than she remembered.

But...Jon was dead...it couldn't be him.

Isabelle's limbs went completely numb. If he weren't holding her up, she would've crumpled to the floor.

With his body throbbing in pain, Jon gently loosened his grip.

Isabelle left his arms slowly, her hands still gripping the rod close to her chest as she stepped away.

When she turned to face him, her wide eyes were tear-filled and trembling.

He didn't look at all like he used to...but her body remembered being wrapped in those arms.

"You're dead," she whispered as a quivering tear slipped down her cheek.

Jon rubbed his aching shoulder. "If I were dead, I presume that would've hurt much less."

Spellbound and shell-shocked, Isabelle was speechless.

She wanted to run to him but she couldn't move.

She just stood there, shaking...staring back into those sea-blue eyes.

The clammy iron rod slowly slid from Isabelle's hand.

Clanking hard against the wooden floor, the sound ripped Isabelle from her ghostly trance and she leapt into his arms.

She wrapped her arms around his shoulders and kissed him as tears streamed down her face.

Jon's entire body went weak. He suddenly felt no pain. One hand slid into Isabelle's hair, the other around her waist.

She tasted exactly as he remembered.

Having not felt the touch of a man in nearly two years, Isabelle's morals were easily punctured by lustful desire. She undid Jon's cloak then tossed it on the mounds of unfurled hay.

Jon smiled when she pulled her lips away but he never took his eyes off her. His hands were still in her hair when he felt her undo his belt.

In that moment, there was no world outside their beating hearts. Everything else had simply disappeared.

Jon lifted his love off her feet then sat her down on a bale of fresh hay. His hand slid along her thigh as she pulled her skirt up. His other hand gently grasped the back of her neck.

When she finally released his trousers, Jon's heavy sword dropped to the floor.

Finding himself between the legs of a married woman should've felt different. It should've felt sneaky and sinful. But when Jon thrust himself into his lost love, he only felt deep, overwhelming pleasure.

Wrapping her legs around his waist, Isabelle pulled him close. With his fingers lost in her hair, Isabelle's golden tresses slipped from their pins. Each thrust of Jon hips freed another golden lock as his tender lips muzzled her moans.

Scooping her up beneath her hips, Jon carried her to his soft cloak and laid her down gently.

Hovering above her, his thick curls dropped into his eyes. She reached up to brush them from his face as he leaned down to kiss her lips again.

With their fingers and bodies intertwined, Jon lost control of himself when he felt Isabelle's tongue against his. Sliding his hand to her chest, he gripped the top of her bodice then exploded with a sensuous moan.

Isabelle wrapped her arms around the panting man collapsed on her chest and took a moment to catch her breath.

Jon kissed her neck gently then pushed himself up to look in the amber eyes of the woman smiling up at him.

That smile always knew something he didn't.

As the wave of lustful delusion began to lift, Jon realized Isabelle led an entirely different life now — she was a baroness who belonged to another man.

Isabelle raised her hand and twirled one of his locks in her fingers. "Chestnut curls," she said with a grin.

"What of it?" Jon chuckled.

"You always kept your hair so short. I never knew it was curly."

Jon shook them in her face with a playful smile then helped her to her feet.

"Are you staying for a visit?" she asked while plucking bits of straw from her hair.

Jon smiled. "I'm not leaving just yet."

"Good," she said while pulling some pins from her hair and handing them to Jon. "Tie your hair up. There's someone I'd like you to meet."

Chapter 32
LIFTING THE VEIL

Unsure of what he was walking into to, Jon followed Isabelle towards a flower-filled garden with slight trepidation.

As he looked over the elaborate gardens, Jon spotted a young babe in a hooded cape chasing an ivory butterfly through the flowers. The child looked like a drunken sailor stumbling around the stone path but the safe arms of his governess were close behind.

Likely a grandmother herself, the broad shouldered woman wore her grey hair in a poofy bun, and her stern face looked as though it had never cracked a smile.

"Magdala," Isabelle called, "please bring my son here."

Jon's knees went weak at the words.

Isabelle was a mother.

His plan of sweeping her off these grounds to sail into the New World together quickly shattered when he watched her smile at her young son.

He'd never seen that smile before — it was hopeful and proud.

"Your son?" he asked without taking a breath.

When Isabelle looked to Jon, her proud smile quickly turned cheeky. That mysterious grin reminded him of their first walk home together — back when he knew absolutely nothing about her.

The elderly governess swooped the wobbling child into her arms and carried him to his mother.

"Thank you," Isabelle said while taking her son. "Please tell chef that we will have a special guest for dinner tonight — a soldier with the Royal Navy," Isabelle asserted as she glanced to Jon.

The old governess looked Jon up and down with no change to her expression. "I was not aware we had a guest upon the property," she said, glancing back to Isabelle.

"He is an old friend. I had just begun my ride when I spied him walking on the road. He said he was coming for a visit so I brought him back with me." She raised her chin slightly. "Please have another setting laid at the table. We will be in shortly."

"Yes, Baroness," she replied with a dip of her head. She clasped her hands and walked back to the manor without another glance at Jon.

"She says very little, but I think I prefer it that way," Isabelle said quietly as she watched the governess walk back inside the house.

Isabelle knew they would still have eyes upon them, especially once word spread of the handsome stranger joining the Baroness for dinner, but for now, she knew they were at least out of earshot.

"Jon of the Sea," she grinned, "I'd like you meet the next Baron of Beaumont," Isabelle said proudly.

She pulled the child's hood down to reveal a mound of chestnut curls.

Jon gazed into the almond shaped eyes of the boy staring up at him; they were sapphire blue...like the deepest parts of the ocean.

When he noticed a tiny cleft in the child's chin, Jon slowly began to realize he was looking down at a tiny cherub version of himself.

From the safe arms of his mother, the child calmly stared back as though he too recognized a small part of himself in the bearded stranger looking down at him.

Not believing this moment would ever be possible, Isabelle was barely breathing. She didn't take her eyes off Jon for a moment.

Here they stood, on the edge of her English garden — the three of them — together for the first time.

"I...I don't understand," Jon chuckled.

Isabelle waited for Jon to look at her before revealing the truth. "I didn't end up running away that night in the storm," she admitted. "I collapsed on my bed and wept until I fell asleep. The next morning a carriage picked me up and I was sent here to become *Baroness Isabella of Beaumont*," she said mockingly. "I was wed the night I arrived here...and bedded," she added gently, awaiting his reaction.

Even though Isabelle was a married woman, Jon's muscles tensed at the thought of another man laying a lustful hand upon her. He suddenly couldn't look at her and shifted his gaze back to the child.

"I was ill the entire ride down here," she continued. "The coachmen had to stop many times for me to be sick. I thought it may be the lingering wine from the masquerade or the sway of a new coach, but even after I'd arrived, it persisted. I spent my first days here wailing in bed. I'd never cried so much in my entire life as I did those first few months."

She looked to Jon. "I hated you," she added bluntly. "My heart was broken. My chambermaids thought it was home sickness, but when it was discovered that I was with child, that I, Baroness Isabella had finally secured an heir to Beaumont's fortune, everyone was overjoyed. They were more than happy to let me start my laying in. I stayed shut up that room for months…wishing I'd never met you."

Her hurtful words pierced Jon's soul. He had spent every day longing to see her again while she sat here, cursing his very existence.

"I wished I'd never let you walk me home. I hated myself for running to meet you the next day."

Jon's eyes burned as Isabelle broke his heart word by word. He searched her face for any sign of regret for speaking so harshly but there was none. She meant every word.

"Then one morning during breakfast, we received word that England had lost nearly half her fleet in one battle. The list included many of my husband's ships. The Barrington was on it as well. We were told all the men aboard had died."

Jon said nothing. His eyes dropped to the ground. That battle had taken his brothers, his captain, the ship he'd called home — and nearly his own life. Still unable to face it all, Jon took a breath to banish his ghosts, then looked back to Isabelle.

"Any piece of my heart that still held hope for you shattered that morning," she snivelled. "I was full with him," she glanced to the babe in her arms, "but I ran straight for your mother's ring and held it as I sobbed. As much as I hated you," she looked to Jon, "in that moment…I wanted to be with you."

She sniffed back a tear. "I thought of throwing myself upon my dagger so we could be together," she admitted, embarrassed now by her selfish desires. "But no sooner than I finished the thought, did he squeeze me horribly from inside." She bobbed her son on her hip. "I screamed. I wailed for hours. My husband summoned the doctors and they pulled him from me. 'It's a boy' they cried! I was treated like a queen from that moment on. No one second-guessed me — no one spoke back. I had done it. I had given Beaumont exactly what he had paid for," she added proudly.

"But when they placed him in my arms, and I looked down...I only saw your face." She smiled through her budding tears. "The shape of his head, his eyes, his chin," she started to weep, "everything was you." A tear rolled from her eye as she glanced to her son. "That was the first time in my life...I cried because I was happy."

Jon felt helpless at the thought of missing that moment. He wished he could've been there with her as she brought their son into this world. For the first time since he set sail those years ago, he regretted his decision to leave her behind.

"I should've been there with you," he uttered with little breath.

As Isabelle stared hopelessly into Jon's welling eyes, the manor's backdoor swung open and out walked the staunch governess followed by a lanky, well-tailored butler. They stepped onto the pathway and started straight towards the whispering pair.

"Your governess is coming back," Jon said, wiping his eyes in an attempt to pull himself together.

Isabelle turned her back to the approaching attendants as she lightly dabbed away her tears. "Am I complete mess?" she asked, regaining her poise.

"You've never looked more beautiful," he said with all sincerity.

"Apologies for the interruption," the governess said as she approached with a stiff curtsey. "Dinner will be served at seven. An extra place will be set and a guest chamber is being prepared for your visitor to wash and change. A proper set of clothes has been laid out for dinner service." She glanced to Jon without turning her head. "Archibald will show your guest to his chambers."

The butler held his hand out to receive Jon's sword. "Guests are not permitted to carry weapons within this estate," he stated.

Isabelle watched Jon's eye grow stern and she quickly interjected. "This man is a soldier with the King's Royal Navy. I feel better protected with him here and I speak for him. He may keep his sword by his side if that is what he chooses."

The butler obediently bowed his head and lowered his hand.

"Lady Jane is awaiting you in your chambers," the governess said before looking to the child, "and the young master's meal is ready in the nursery." She extended her arms to receive the boy.

Isabelle quickly glanced to Jon, feeling for a moment as though she needed his permission before giving away the child.

"Of course," Isabelle replied, handing her son to the governess. "I will be in to kiss you goodnight," she said sweetly before the governess whisked him away.

As Jon watched the woman disappear into the house with the child, he wondered if that was the last time he'd ever lay eyes upon his son.

Chapter 33

SMOKE AND MIRRORS

Jon found Beaumont's home cold and overbearing. Constantly attended to, or perhaps surveilled from the moment he stepped inside, he was accompanied into an enormous guestroom where a chamberlain, butler and groomsman prepared their guest for dinner.

Skilful hands scrubbed Jon clean, trimmed his beard, and combed his thick curls into a neatly twisted bun. Having nearly worn through the lavish duds Beth had generously donated to his cause, they were left strewn on the bed while attendants dressed Jon in an outfit more adequately suited for dinner in a nobleman's household.

On his way downstairs, Jon noticed the many oversized portraits hanging throughout the halls. Most featured a dark-haired, robust man in various stages of life — and wives.

The Baron's dark eyes glared at Jon from the haunting frames, silently judging him as he passed.

Jon's personal butler showed him into the extravagantly decorated dining room where he was surprised to find the lengthy table set for only two. Wondering if the servants had ignored Isabelle's request to add a place for him, Jon's confusion grew slightly worrisome when a steward pulled out the chair next to the head of the table.

Taking his seat, Jon looked down at the ornamental place setting; a set of gold utensils flanked a gold-rimmed plate, matching the solid gold candelabras and the shiny gold pitcher resting in the hands of the stoic steward standing next to the empty chair at the head of the table.

Jon's knee bobbed nervously as he feared he might be dining with the man whose wife he'd just made love to mere hours ago.

The sound of footsteps approaching spiked Jon's apprehension, but the moment Isabelle appeared on the arm of her escort, any looming fears evaporated and he respectfully rose with an enchanted smile.

The Baroness held her back straight and her chin level as she sauntered towards her handsome dinner guest.

Her silver gown shimmered. The diamonds dripping from her ears and neck mirrored the glinting candlelight as she strolled past him to take her place at the head of the table.

Mesmerized by the sight of her all over again, Jon waited for her to take her seat. "You still take my breath away," he said quietly as he sat back down.

Expecting a playful grin in return, Jon was shocked to see a slight fear in her eyes before they shifted to the many servants lining the room, one of whom stepped forward to fill her glass from the golden pitcher.

"You've taken to wine with your dinner?" Jon asked in surprise, knowing Isabelle used to detest her mother's indulgence.

"Would you like some?" she offered politely, ignoring his intrusive comment.

Feeling the entire household's eyes upon him since the moment he entered Beaumont's home, Jon wanted to keep a clear head in the unfamiliar space. "No, thank you." He covered his glass before the steward began pouring. Jon's shoulder ached as he lowered his arm. He reached up to massage it.

The butler standing behind him quietly leaned in. "Are you alright sir? I could call upon the Baron's physician," he offered.

"No, I'm well. I just..." he glanced over and caught Isabelle's glare. "I fell from my horse earlier today."

In a room full of onlookers, Isabelle's face went unchanged but Jon still found her smile — locked within her tawny eyes, he saw it there — he'd always been one of her secrets.

"He's just upstairs should you change your mind," he said with a bow before returning to his place along the wall.

Jon looked to Isabelle and raised his eyebrow. "Why is there a physician upstairs?"

Isabelle swallowed a sip of wine. "My husband has not been well for quite some time. I feel better knowing we have a physician here at all times. For my son's sake as well," she added as two servants placed a steaming plate of food before each of them.

Isabelle was served a simple selection of beets and asparagus upon a swipe of potato mash, but Jon's plate contained the juiciest slab of beef he'd ever laid eyes on. The smell of perfectly blended seasonings seared into the cooked meat had Jon salivating, but Isabelle's comment left him uneasy. "Is the boy not well?"

Isabelle smiled as she swallowed a bite of food. "He's absolutely perfect," she said, placing her gold fork at the edge of her plate, "but it seems he took my husband's good health the day he was born. I simply feel safer having a doctor on the grounds at all times, for all of us," she said, reaching for her wine again.

"He stays upstairs and you dine alone? They set this all up just for you...every night?"

Isabelle nodded as she took a sip. "Every night," she replied while lowering her glass.

The shiny rubies glinting on her finger caught Jon's eye. She was wearing his mother's ring. The polished silver sparkled and the missing stone had been replaced. "That's a beautiful ring you're wearing," he said with a sly smile.

"Thank you," she calmly replied. "It's the only piece I brought with me from Gillingham. I haven't worn it in a very long time."

Realizing their entire dinner conversation would be riddled in code, Jon decided a more generic tone may better suit this room.

As though reading his mind, Isabelle changed the subject. "Tell me solider, what are your plans now that the war is over?" she asked while slicing a spear of asparagus.

Jon cut another piece of meat. "I found a ship on Porter's dock leaving for New York in the morning. I booked passage with them. We leave at dawn." He casually popped the bite in his mouth then leaned back to catch her reaction.

"Leave? But you've just..." Isabelle swallowed hard as she looked around the room. Straightening her posture, she began again. "You've just arrived in Plymouth," she said confidently.

Pleased that Isabelle seemed slightly upset at the idea of his departure, Jon continued. "They say the fur trade has put quite a bit of money in men's pockets. Perhaps I'll try my hand at trapping."

Losing her appetite, Isabelle placed her cutlery on her plate and took another sip of wine while her mind searched for ways to keep him in her life.

"My husband's fleet brings goods from New York. Perhaps we can find you a post aboard one of his ships."

"Thank you but once I step foot in the New World, I'm never coming back here." Jon held her glare hoping to make his point very clear, but his pertness left her insulted.

"Has England been so terrible to you?" she asked curtly.

Staring into her piercing eyes, the screams of Jon's ghostly brothers wailed through his mind. They had all fought for the country they loved — yet her seas had swallowed them all.

"I need a new life, Iz," he finally uttered.

Her eyes softened at the sound of her old life slipping from his lips.

"England isn't the same for me now. War, death, disease...I have to leave it all behind," he said quietly, almost ashamed of his words.

Showing her maturity, Isabelle held her poise. "Leave it all behind," she repeated while raising the wine to her lips. "How predictable," she added callously before taking a sip.

Jon's jaw clenched. He kept his stern eyes on Isabelle as he popped another piece of meat in his mouth to give his grinding teeth something to chew on.

His frustration was beginning to turn spiteful. With his sword confidently at his side, he needed to know if there was any truth to the rumours of her being held here against her will.

"Tell me, Baroness," he said before swallowing, "do you ever leave this place?"

Isabelle didn't lash out. She didn't even flinch. "Why would I need to leave this place? I'm perfectly happy here," she added with a slight lift of her chin.

"Are you saying you haven't been outside these gates since the day you arrived?"

"Word of the plague chased us the entire way from Gillingham. By the time I was with child, the sickness was everywhere. We shut in here, the servants, the doctors — everyone. They say it is safe again but my husband prefers that we stay here," she said with a broken smile.

Isabelle swallowed the last of her wine. "We stay here, and the world goes on without us."

Jon's brow furrowed at her answer. "Are you saying that boy has never been beyond the gates?"

"The world is not ready for him yet — nor he for it. He is safe here," she said confidently as though she truly found some comfort in this arrangement. "Besides, there is no need for us to leave this place. We have everything we need right here." She raised her empty glass to the side where it was immediately refilled by the golden pitcher in her awaiting steward's hand.

Weary of this new Baroness, Jon studied her face. She was speaking in a tone he'd never heard. This certainly wasn't the passionate, fiery young woman he fell in love with years ago but he pressed on, determined to find her again.

"You haven't been off the grounds to see Beth, or visit your father?"

"I haven't seen my father since the day I left Gillingham. I heard he hasn't been the same since the plague hit. He sold Bluefields," she added casually.

Surprised by the coolness in her voice, Jon replied without mentioning his recent sorrow-filled visit. "I'm sorry. I know you loved it there. That place was special to me as well," he said, catching her gaze.

266

For a moment he saw it glinting in candlelight — the truth in her eyes. The memories of their time together; the love he knew she still held for him.

"Well," Isabelle took a deep breath, "that was a long time ago. It feels like someone else's life now." She glanced at her wine glass, refusing to look up and face him.

Jon watched her cheeks begin to flush. He wanted to reach out for her, but he knew laying a hand on the Baroness of the estate while her sickly husband lay upstairs would certainly create more problems than it would solve. "Is there a place where we could take in some air? I'm finding this room a little...stuffy," he said, glancing to the servants awaiting her every command.

Unwilling to let him sail to the other side of the world without telling him everything she'd been holding inside for nearly two years, Isabelle decided it was time for some privacy. "The east gardens are lit every night. Perhaps you'd fancy a stroll?"

Chapter 34

THE GILDED CAGE

With a full moon above there was no need for a lantern's light. Having dismissed most of her household for the evening, Isabelle led Jon down one of the many candlelit paths in the east garden.

"Must be hard to skulk through the night with these paths so brightly lit," he teased.

"I have no need to skulk around here. Besides, I prefer they always know where I am, should my son need me or my husband. But I still do prefer the night." She glanced to the sky. "There's something so magical about moonlight."

Following a path that wound its way far from the manor, Isabelle led him into one of her favourite places on the grounds — a green arbour tunnel covered with spiralling vines of starry white Moonflowers already in full bloom under the silvery light. Glass lanterns hung from the armature, and lit candles lined the entire tunnel.

Knowing they were far enough away from curious ears, Isabelle pulled the ruby ring from her finger. "Here's your ring back," she said, stopping them both as she held it out in front of her. "I presume that's why you've come all this way."

Jon chuckled at her unexpected gesture. "I didn't come here to collect a ring, Iz," He realized she must have led him to a place where they could speak honestly. "I came here to find you — and now I find I have a son as well."

"*I* have a son," she corrected him, "and I have secured him a promising future. He will not be the son of some merchant sailor who leaves his loved ones behind at the behest of a King. He will be raised an heir and a nobleman and h—"

"And he'll suffer the same upbringing that you despised," Jon said sternly. "Where is my comfort in that?"

Isabelle's brow slowly furrowed. "Your comfort? Is that why you came here? Is this some attempt to make yourself more comfortable with your decision?" Isabelle felt herself growing frustrated. "Take this," she commanded, tucking the heirloom in his breast pocket.

As she closed the flap, Jon gently clasped her wrist. "I came here because I promised I would come back for you," he said, peering into her eyes. "I want you to leave with me, Iz — for both of you to leave with me," he corrected himself. "I've booked us passage on that ship departing at dawn. Come with me," he pleaded. "We can spend the rest of our lives together in a land where no one knows who you are, just as you've always wanted."

Isabelle laughed but didn't pull herself from his grasp. "Have you gone mad?"

"I know I won't be able to give either of you as much as this, but I earned a King's salary for nearly two years. I have enough to buy land and build us a home. It won't come with titles or servants but I don't believe you'd mind that," he added with a grin. "We could have a stable and horses. You could teach our son to ride, just as you taught me." Jon saw a smile behind those guarded eyes. "Come with me, Iz. I want..." his hands slid to her shoulders, gripping them gently, "I need you to come with me. I have nothing left in my entire life but my love for you...and my son."

She felt herself slipping but Isabelle had learned the consequence of his potent charm years ago and sturdily held her ground. "He may be yours by blood, but he is not yours by law."

Jon's brow grew stern and he let her go. "Your husband is old and unwell. When he dies, what becomes of you both then?"

"Then my son will become the Baron of this estate and everything carries on just as it is now."

"Your son...*our* son, is an infant. Your husband's partners will come for their share of his business just as they did to Beth's mother — as will his competitors. Both of you could be left with nothing. Who will protect you then? Even the untouchable Earl of Arlington has been disgraced. No manor, striped of his title—"

"Keep your voice down," Isabelle interjected with a hush.

Jon took a breath to regain himself. "Life is so fragile, Iz. Come with me so I can make sure you're both safe, everyday."

Isabelle looked to his sea-blue eyes with a guarded heart. "I'm sorry, we won't be going with you," she said firmly. "Not today."

Jon's nostrils flared. "It's always not today with you Iz! It's never now!"

Isabelle's eyes narrowed with a piercing fury while nearly two years of resentment surged through her body. "It was now the night of the storm," she replied calmly. "You chose your family over me then, and now, I'm choosing mine."

Jon raised his chin in an attempt to summon his courage.

"If you wish to be in that boy's life, then stay here with us," she suggested.

"As what, one of your stablehands? And watch my son be lied to everyday of his life by the woman he will grow to trust more than anyone in world? I couldn't bear it. That's your hell to choose, Iz — not mine."

Isabelle felt her fury smouldering as he scolded her. She had nearly fallen for his spellbinding fantasy all over again, yet here he stood, insulting the very life she'd built for her son, *their* son, without any help from the man who'd chosen to abandon them both.

Two years of disdain and a lifetime of abandonment boiled within her, but this time she was not about to run back to the safety of her manor.

"Fine!" she shouted. "So leave me again. If you can't bear to see the life I've given our son then go on!" She shoved him with both hands. "Leave us again!"

Caught off guard by the explosive force of her tiny frame, Jon stepped back but stood firm as he waited for her to calm down.

"I asked you not to leave with them! I begged you to stay...but you left me — you left us!" she yelled, gesturing to the house where their tiny son lay sleeping. "He was already in my womb when you sailed away."

Realizing he had abandoned her in such a precious state, the words regretfully rattled from his lips. "I did not know about him then."

Isabelle took a long breath and shook her head. "It doesn't matter now. The only thing that matters is that boy's safety and happiness. I have nothing left within me for you," her voice trembled as she lied. "I've released everything I ever felt for you."

Stepping closer, she glared into his eyes. "I've even grieved your death," she added coldly.

Her scornful words slashed Jon's chest, ripping through his scars, old and new. Silently staring down at her, he watched her quivering eyes well with tears.

"You are nothing but a ghost to my heart," she continued. "An apparition that will fade with the light of dawn as you always did."

Searching her eyes for the truth, Jon didn't believe a word of it and decided to test her. "If what you say is true, then I will leave on that ship come sunrise, and I'll settle into a new life on the other side of the world. Perhaps I will even fall in love again, and it could grow into a love as true as ours...then one day, without me noticing, you will become a ghost to my heart as well."

He leaned down to meet her stern glare. "But it will be I who haunts you, Izzy," he added confidently. "Every time you look into that boy's eyes, you will see me staring back at you. You'll know that I'm still out there, walking this earth...not really a ghost at all."

Crippled by his truth, Isabelle lost her guard. "I cannot take him from his home," she mewled. "My husband will send an entire fleet to look for us. That boy, his heir, is the only reason I was brought here in the first place."

"We may have only had one summer together, Iz, but I know your convictions," he persisted. "I heard every word you spoke of your hatred for this lifestyle. How empty and fruitless it felt to be kept, people constantly watching you — yet here you are about to condemn our son to that very life. Do you choose this for him, or do you wish to see him raised in a world where he is free to follow his heart? Free to run through the untouched forests with no eyes upon him but our own."

Jon clasped her hands. "You would be free to do as you wish. We could have as many horses as you'd like. You could ride them all like a man," he said with a smile, one that instantly spread to Isabelle's lips. "We could make love every night," he interlaced their fingers, "in a bed...we've never done that before," he said with a chuckle.

Isabelle dropped her gaze. His ocean eyes were luring her in.

She wanted to kiss him.

She could feel herself slipping.

"We could have more children," he continued, softy sliding his hand up her neck then into her hair.

Scared she was about to fall completely, Isabelle looked up to the heavens for strength, but found her view blocked by the starry Moonflowers her husband had planted — just for her.

The reality of her life came rushing back. This was her child's home. He played beneath the shade of this arbour.

Clasping Jon's wrist, she lowered his hand. "I'm sorry Jon. We will be staying here." She looked into his sea-blue eyes as her deepest fear seeped from her lips. "I could never put him on that ship."

"The ship? Is that your worry? The crossing shouldn't take more than a few weeks with a strong breeze. Living upon the shore doesn't keep anyone safe, Isabelle. Look what happened right here in England. Civil war, plague...deaths in the thousands—"

"Precisely! That is why we live safely behind these gates," she huffed. "Oh, you won't understand until you have a child."

Jon's eyes grew stern at her unintentional slight. "I do have a child."

His sharp glare pierced her, ripping into the wounds she'd worked so hard to heal. But the seething rage in Isabelle's chest reminded her why they were all here in the first place and she finally lost her wits.

"You left us! You chose that Jon! You chose your brothers over us!" she shouted. "My son is the Lord of this manor, the heir to this estate, and he will remain in his home!"

"You are going to condemn our son to the exact life you despised all because you're afraid?"

"Yes," she conceded, "perhaps you're right...perhaps I am afraid. I'm afraid of being abandoned by you for something your heart desires more than I. You left me once already. How can I be sure you won't do it again? If I'm on the other side of the world all alone, what shall I do then? How could you ever expect me to trust your loyalty?"

"My loyalty?" Jon couldn't believe what he was hearing.

He stepped back in astonishment. "I swore my loyalties — my life — to those men long before I ever met you," he explained. "The fact that I didn't abandon them for the safe haven of your arms should prove the loyalty of my word above all else!" he yelled, frustrated that she was pulling his demons to the surface yet again. "It would have been much easier to ride into the darkness with you that night, to not watch my brothers die before my eyes, but I made a promise to them."

He took a deep breath. "Before we signed with Arlington, we sat in the mess and swore to each other," Jon's tone grew grim, "whatever horrors we may face, we'd be in it together."

Lost in a distant memory with his dead brothers, Jon raised his arm in a ghostly cheers to his fallen mates as he recited their oath again. "Till the end of it all," he hauntingly proclaimed.

Lowering his arm, his gaze shifted back to Isabelle. "That is why I could not stay with you then." A long breath left him. It had taken nearly two years, but he was finally able to properly explain himself.

Isabelle reined her empathy and drew her shoulders back. "Well, I too have made promises," she calmly replied, "to a young boy who sleeps just over there. I've promised him a life of safety and happiness and—"

"And what of honesty? Did you promise him that?" Jon interjected, knowing she'd been lying to the child, her husband, and everyone within that household for the entirety of her son's young life. "You say that boy's happiness is the most important, yet you can look in his eyes everyday and lie to him?" he shouted. "His own mother?"

Beaumont's Baroness was not about to quiver over the judgmental scorn of a lonely sailor. She held her chin steady. "It must be so easy for a man who has nothing to criticize someone who has everything," she sneered.

"Everything? It seems there are quite a few things you're missing *Isabella*," he mocked. "Courage, integrity...any sort of moral compass whatsoever—"

"Enough!" she blurted. "I would never expect someone like you to understand the magnitude of responsibility that comes along with a life like this."

"Life is the same for everyone, Iz," he calmly replied. "The difference lies in the decisions we make."

"Yes — it certainly does," she replied coldly, knowing they were all in this situation because of his fateful decision.

Ignoring her passive accusation, Jon pressed on. "So then, you'll choose to remain here, a liar *and* a coward? What a brilliant role model for our son," he said, partially in jest but his words slashed her still. "Pardon me, for the Baron of Beaumont," he said with a deep bow.

He was poking her — she knew it. His mocking tone reminded her of the day they first met, when he teased her just the same.

She stepped right into him, pressing her pulsating rage into his chest. "He *is* the next Baron of Beaumont, and you are nothing but a wayward seaman."

"I am a soldier with the Royal Navy."

"I want you to leave," she said firmly before turning to storm back to the manor.

"I don't think you do," Jon said slyly. "I'm not walking away without you again," he yelled after her. "You'll have to kill me here in this garden, Izzy!"

Stopping in her tracks, she slowly turned to face him. "My name is Isabella Dubois, Baroness of Beaumont and you are now trespassing on our property. If you do not remove yourself immediately, I will alert the guards."

"*Isabella*...you wouldn't," he teased while flashing that dashing smile.

No longer the naive young woman so easily charmed by handsome sailors, Isabelle placed her hands on her hips and marched back towards him.

Stopping mere inches from his face, she glared into his eyes. "I've grieved the loss of you twice already. I'm getting quite good at believing you're dead."

Her chilling tone sent shivers down his spine as he peered into the angry eyes glaring up at him.

Who was this person? He came looking for the free-spirited, adventurous young woman he fell in love with — not this cold baroness who feared everything outside her gates and wished him dead.

Flabbergasted by her anger, he stepped back. "I spent nearly two years fighting that war." Suddenly aware of every wound on his body, Jon's painful confession came slowly. "Men were killed right before my eyes."

He glanced to the ground as his soul finally caved. "My mates…" his breath grew heavy. "I still hear the cannons."

In a hellish daze, he looked to Isabelle. "I took so many lives after that day, but it never brought one of my brothers back…not one. It only made their screams louder."

His shoulders slumped as sorrow seeped through his scars. "And Thomas," he continued, "we were ambushed at our own base in the middle of the fucking night." Jon turned away as he started to weep. "My best friend…my brother…sliced clean through right in front of me. Every day of that war was a living hell!"

Tears streamed down his face. No longer able to conceal his haunting collection of torment, Jon threw his head back and wailed at the sky.

Isabelle wanted to run to him, to console him, but she couldn't move. She just stood there…trembling.

With his plaguing demons finally released to God above, Jon took a few breaths to summon his strength.

"I was nearly killed that night," he said softly before turning to face the woman he loved. "I should've died so many times."

Watching his pain weep from Isabelle's tear-filled eyes, Jon stepped closer. "Every night before I fell asleep…I'd see your face," he said calmly. "We would be lost together in some timeless dream. I could see you but...I couldn't feel you," he said, grazing her cheek. "But then I would wake...and you'd be gone."

He heard Isabelle's breath flutter from her chest. "You may have lost me twice — but I lost you every time I opened my eyes."

Isabelle gazed at him through blurry tears, wishing she could take all his pain away. Looking into his mournful eyes, she felt the wounds of every battle he fought; the loss of his brothers — the weight of an entire country on his shoulders.

Slipping his hands around her hips, Jon pulled her to his chest and wrapped his arms around her, but Isabelle's breath soon quickened and she burst from his arms.

"Oh! This is all a consequence of your decision!" she cried. "You sold yourself to my father — to that war! You chose to be there when Thomas died...to be present when your entire crew fell to the bottom of the sea! Then I was sent here, away from everyone I've ever known, forced to live a life that no one will ever know the truth of —"

"Yet through it all...here we are again," he said, gently taking a hold of her arms. "We're together now."

When Isabelle grabbed his waist to stabilize herself, Jon wrapped his arms around her and pulled her close.

He closed his eyes as Isabelle gently wept against his chest. With tears rolling down his cheeks, he surrendered himself to all pain he may have caused her — to all the lies she was forced to tell — to all the suffering they'd both survived.

Jon slid one hand onto her heaving chest, letting it rest upon her heart. Pressing his forehead to hers, he took a few deep breaths to help calm them both.

Isabelle had spent so many nights dreaming of being back in his arms. She never thought it would be possible, yet here she was, wrapped safely in his embrace while she faced the biggest decision of her life, or more importantly — her son's.

Her son.

Taking a deep breath, Isabelle grounded herself back to reality, however false it may be.

She slowly pushed herself from his embrace and stepped back.

Jon watched as she bent down to lift the hem of her gown. For a moment, he thought she may pull her dagger and grant his wish of dying here in her garden, but instead, she revealed a small leather-bound book strapped to her calf where the metal blade once lay.

"I finished my story." She sniffed before shoving the book to his chest with more force than was certainly necessary. "I don't mean to spoil the ending for you, but when she asked him not leave..." she glared into his eyes, "he stayed."

As Jon watched tears quiver in her eyes, he reached up to receive the book but clasped her hands and stepped closer.

"I still love you, Isabelle."

"It's not enough now," she whimpered.

Leaving the book in his hands, she pulled herself from his grip and stepped back. "I am mother to an heir. I—"

"An heir to a lie! That man is not his father!" Jon shouted, pointing towards the manor.

"Keep your voice down!" she said, grabbing his arm to lower it. "Are you trying to see me killed?"

"Of course not. I'm trying to see us together — the three of us, as a true family. This is our fate."

Isabelle huffed a sigh of disbelief. "Our fate was never each other, Jon." Her tone was hopeless. "Perhaps there is no such thing as fate. There is only what we do, and what we don't do. Every one of your decisions led you here. They created everything you feel — every memory you conceal. You choose to keep your secrets hidden, and so do I."

"Well at least I know what my truth is, and you know yours, but our son will never know his."

"Truth?" Isabelle asked with a wrinkled brow. "What is truth, Jon? Where do we find it? Is it what has already happened? Is it what others believe?"

Isabelle's words started strong but her breath began to tremble. "Does it lay in our desires? Is it what I feel in my heart?"

"You want to know where to find the truth, Iz." Jon's eyes were confidently strong. "In blood. Those men aboard the Barrington, Thomas, they were my brothers yes, but I never felt for them what I felt when I looked into my son's eyes."

Isabelle had nothing left. She summoned any remaining strength with a single breath and raised her chin. "The truth is — what you feel is no longer my concern."

"If your words are true, then why can't you walk away?" he asked, staring deep into her eyes. "You say you've cursed me...that you hate me. Then why are you still here?" he asked sternly, quickly growing frustrated again.

Staring back at him in silence, Isabelle offered nothing.

Jon's tense glare suddenly softened, as though he'd found a secret hidden in her eyes. "You can't leave can you? I am no longer a ghost in your world, am I?" he said confidently. "Your truth is different now...even if it is full of lies."

A tear dripped silently down Isabelle's cheek as Jon stepped in one last time. "Go get our son, Iz," he pleaded softly, wiping the tear from her face. "Please. I beg you to live the truth of your heart. I beg you not to raise my boy, our son, this way. You may raise him as a noble lad but his soul was not meant for this life. You know the truth, and I know it...and God knows it."

Isabelle was empty. This day had tried every last one of her emotions. "I'm sorry Jon," she said finally, "we are staying here. You may do as you wish. Stay or go...the choice yet again is yours."

Jon studied her glowing eyes as she stared back at him, and he finally saw it.

Her truth.

He was defeated. Nothing he could say or offer would convince her to leave her son's lifestyle of power and luxury.

Exhaling his surrender, Jon let his hope slither to the earth. "Aye...you stay here and raise our son as a nobleman," he said calmly, "but one day you will catch him staring into the open sea, gazing far into the distance. It will seem as though he's searching for something amongst the waves — and you will be the only person in his life who will know what it is that he's looking for."

Jon watched her eyes soften but his resentful heart persisted. "And you...you will have an ear out for any sailor named Jon who returns to this harbour for the rest of your life. You will know that I'm still out there, holding on to that piece of you that lifted out of your body all those years ago. That was true love, Iz — I know it was. I've travelled half way around this world...but I've never felt anything like that."

Isabelle kept her chin level as she blinked back budding tears. "It's time for you to leave," she commanded softly before shifting her eyes away from the soul she could no longer bare to look into.

Her chilling tone flushed the blood from Jon's body.

This wasn't a game of lies — she meant what she said.

Standing tall, Jon slowly began to nod. He took a long breath, looked down his nose at her and calmly uttered two words.

"Goodbye Isabelle."

He turned and started walking towards the end of the leafy tunnel.

"I will have a messenger deliver your clothes to the dock before dawn," she shouted after him.

"Keep them!" he yelled over his shoulder. "They're Beth's. Perhaps you can return them if you're ever allowed out of this gilded cage!"

The unrelenting pieces of his heart finally shattered at the thought of never being able to lay eyes upon his son again. Bits of it were sure to remain under this arbour for years to come, lapping at his son's heels as he flit through the garden — unknowingly walking the faded footsteps of his true father.

As Jon made his way off Beaumont's property, he listened for her to call out for him, but the only sounds he heard were the twigs cracking beneath his feet as every crestfallen footstep carried him farther from Isabelle, and the young son he never got the chance to love.

Chapter 35

RISING DAWN

Out of the blackened sea, a thick fog prowled across the harbour, erasing the earth as it enveloped Plymouth's port. The bow of the Aurora Nova slowly disappeared beneath Jon's feet as he stared blankly into the gloomy morning twilight.

With his payment still in Hammond's hand, Jon was not required to man this voyage but he hoped some hard work might take his mind off the two pieces of his heart he had reluctantly left upon the hill mere hours ago.

Alone in the darkness with lines in hand, lost somewhere in the heartbreak of his shattered life, Jon closed his eyes and let the fog swallow him whole. No longer plagued by visions of Tom's gruesome death, he only saw the eyes of his young son staring up at him from Isabelle's arms. That brief moment would live in the remaining pieces of his broken heart until his last day on this earth.

He focused on moving the damp air in and out of his lungs as he willed himself to stay put on that ship.

The only part of Isabelle he carried with him now was the small storybook tucked away in his pocket.

He stayed.

Isabelle's words rattled through his mind as Jon prayed to hear Hammond's command to cast off, starting the journey that would take him as far away from here as he could possibly go.

"Jon!" Hammond shouted.

Shaken from his gloomy trance, Jon peered through the thinning fog at his captain shouting from the bridge.

"There's a messenger for ya! Hurry up, we're pullin' lines!"

Jon dropped his rope and started for the gangplank, embarrassed that their departure was now being held up by a sack of clothes he didn't even want.

Peering through the fog, he spied a pudgy messenger waiting on the dock with a large sack of Beth's clothing.

As Jon crossed the gangplank, he noticed the bag seemed much fuller than it needed to be and wondered if Isabelle, racked with guilt, had decided to include a care package in an attempt to apologise for robbing him of their happy ending.

"I'm Jon," he announced, approaching the hooded messenger.

The caped servant stayed silent as she raised her head to look up at him.

Jon's body seized as he stared into the amber eyes peering at him from beneath the shrouding fabric.

Engulfed by the fog, Isabelle said nothing as she slowly lifted the seam of her cape to reveal a sleeping curly-haired babe wrapped safely to her chest.

Still unsure of her decision, but finally willing to listen to the tiny whispers of her heart, Isabelle's voice quivered. "He'll send an army to look for us."

In complete shock, Jon could barely speak. "I...how did you get out?"

Isabelle's eyes softly surrendered. "I've spent a lifetime hiding in the shadows." She looked to her sleeping child. "I don't want our son to live in the same darkness."

Diluted by sheer disbelief, Jon choked back tears of happiness as he wrapped his arms around her.

With Isabelle pressed safely against his chest, he took a few breaths before looking into her fearfully brave eyes. "My loyalty will lie with you until my last breath," he vowed.

Staring deep into his eyes, Isabelle found his truth and nodded softly. With her fate in God's hands, she managed half a grin. "If this ship doesn't start moving, that day may be today."

Overjoyed by her courage, Jon kissed her with a smile. He knew how difficult that decision was — how scared she must have been to leave on her own. With his lips pressed against hers, he fell in love all over again and knew he would belong to her forever.

"Let's get you aboard," he said as he picked up the sack.

Taking her hand, he brought them safely across the gangplank and informed Hammond that his second passenger had arrived.

Jon passed his line to a young shipmate, one with bushy red hair, likely not a day over fifteen. As he handed the line over, he lightly smacked the young sailor's back and shot him a hopeful smile.

Turning back to Isabelle, Jon took her by the hand and led her to the aft deck as the captain sounded his call to cast off from Plymouth.

In anticipation of his first sail, their young son had awoken and was enjoying his first sights of a world outside the gates through the slit of Isabelle's cape.

Knowing the safest place on this ship would be in Jon's arms, Isabelle handed the boy to his father who tucked him warmly in his cloak.

Jon wrapped his other arm around Isabelle and pressed her gently to his chest, letting his chin come to rest upon her head. He didn't notice, but Isabelle's eyes were locked on the steep road she'd just descended, waiting for an eruption to come ploughing down the hill at the discovery of Beaumont's most precious assets gone missing.

But for now, the road was still.

As Isabelle watched England slowly disappear in the distance, she felt a part of herself slipping away with it. She had left behind a path not chosen; a fearful girl, one who still stood on land, ghostly watching Isabelle sail away in the arms of her lover...a girl who was too afraid to answer her heart when it whispered — *what would love do?*

Wrapped against Jon's beating heart, Isabelle sighed. She didn't know what the future held, but for now, they were safe in each other's arms.

As both land and sky surrendered to the light of a new dawn, they watched the sun rise from the earth, together, for the very first time.

Look for the sequel,

Only Now

coming soon.

Instagram: nevernowstory

LZDpublishing.com/nevernow

If you enjoyed this book,
please consider leaving a review on Amazon.

About the Author

Never Now is the first novel by new author, Lindsay Dee who lives outside Toronto, Canada.

Made in the USA
Monee, IL
01 October 2021

Thank you
Sara!
Enjoy the story!
XO - Lindsay
Dee